REACHING BACK

REACHING BACK

Nea Anna Simone

sepia

BOOKS

BET Publications, LLC
http://www.bet.com

SEPIA BOOKS are published by

BET Publications, LLC
c/o BET BOOKS
One BET Plaza
1900 W Place NE
Washington, DC 20018-1211

All Kensington Titles, Imprints, and Distributed Lines are available at special quantity discounts for bulk purchases for sales promotions, premiums, fund-raising, and educational or institutional use. Special book excerpts or customized printings can also be created to fit specific needs. For details, write or phone the office of the Kensington special sales manager: Kensington Publishing Corp., 850 Third Avenue, New York, NY 10022, attn: Special Sales Department, Phone: 1-800-221-2647.

ISBN: 1-58314-317-3

First Printing: August 2002
10 9 8 7 6 5 4 3 2 1

Printed in the United States of America

*This book is in loving memory of my Dad,
Captain Robert L. Varner USMC. ret.*

ACKNOWLEDGMENTS

As in all things, I acknowledge Him for the gifts he has given. If not for His grace and mercy, where would I be?

A few years ago, I received a midday telephone call from my long-time friend and prayer partner, Dana Nelson. At first the call did not strike me as unusual, until I realized that Dana was hesitant to end the conversation. Finally, I asked her if anything was wrong. Assuring me that all was well in her life, she added, "But I have something to tell you and I just don't know how you'll take it." It was my turn to become hesitant, and then I suggested that she just tell me what was on her mind. I rationalized that whatever was burdening her, we had been friends long enough to be able to work through it.

To my surprise, Dana began by telling me that when she prayed that morning, the Holy Spirit had spoken to her with a message for me. She then stated that she felt stupid saying this to me, but since her prayer she had an urging in her spirit to speak with me, and that was the real reason for her call. Surprised, I told her to go ahead and tell me—if I didn't agree, then she had done her part.

"God wants you to write," she said. For moments you could have cut the tension in the air with a knife; then I responded by asking her what type of writing she meant. I had only written correspondence that was either personal or related to business. Having recently gone through some personal trials and loss, I asked if I should have recorded it in some way. Immediately she responded, "No . . . I'm not certain exactly what you're supposed to write. The Spirit tells me that you should write, and everything else will take care of itself. Don't worry about the order of things—it will take care of itself."

Dana had no way of knowing that she had spoken aloud what I had only dreamed of doing, but always lacked the confidence—more than the self-discipline—to do. To write was a commitment; it was like singing in public: either you could . . . or you couldn't.

I hesitated again and then confided to Dana that in fact I had wanted to write creatively for years, but I had always found an excuse not to start. I was completely blown away and knew that only God could have sent that message to me. So that evening after walking past my computer a hundred times, I put my children to sleep and began the prologue to this book. I have since learned how to hear Him. I may not always listen, but I'm getting better.

I thank my mother, Annie Varner, for giving me life and teaching me how to be strong and soft, how to endure and overcome—shoulders back, chest out, stomach in. Mom, I still hear your words as I make my stride . . . Without thinking, I demand that my daughters proceed in the same fashion.

To my sister, Renee Smith. Although not by birth, God gave me the sister I longed for and could depend upon to encourage me along the way. To Amy and Traci . . . Thank you for being my friends and allies. Amy, thanks for tirelessly reading the rewrites and scrutinizing the plot. Bravo! To my editor, Glenda Howard . . . You are awesome. Thank you to my publisher, Linda Gill-Carter, for sharing my vision and enthusiasm, but most of all for helping me to realize my dream. To my brothers, D and Rob . . . Love you, for being you. To Robert Murphy, who spoke life into the project. To my pastor, "Chip" Murray . . . Thank you for walking with me through the valleys and shadows. To my Joe . . . Thank you for the sunsets on your porch, the reflection of the tin roof from the boathouse on your lake, the smile in your eyes . . . and all the times in between. And last but not least, I would like to thank my daughters—Endia, Aja, and Caramia—for allowing Mommy to realize her dream, for lifting me up each night during family prayer . . . It is your prayer and God's hands that keep pushing me along . . . I know He hears you. And to Dad . . . I will finish as you began: The Lord is my shepherd, I shall not want.

PART ONE

Leaving . . .

PROLOGUE

As she stood at the end and the beginning of her life, Mignon gazed out from the balcony onto the terrace at the beautifully landscaped gardens. Turning her attention to Miss Thompson, the nanny, she absorbed the tranquillity. Then she lovingly monitored the children while their swim instructor gave them their swimming lessons. As she watched her children playfully splashing water on each other and Miss Thompson, she envied them their carefree and innocent bliss. Mignon knew if she could just feel their joy for a period as brief as a few hours or as long as an entire day, maybe—just maybe— she'd change her mind and stay. Lost in thought, she reflected on the events that surrounded her desire to leave the home she had built with her husband and return to a time when her life was far less complicated. She was certain that although her heart mourned the decision that she was finally forced to make and the effect she knew it would have on her children, it was the best thing for all involved. To anyone on the outside looking in, Mignon had it all: Gerald, her handsome, light-skinned, rich husband; beautiful children; fabulous clothes; beautiful homes; exotic vacations; fancy cars; and expensive jewelry. Who in their right mind could—or, for that matter, would— leave all of this? This question had periodically haunted her for many years. But instead of making a decision, she made excuses, and when excuses didn't work, she made babies.

Not this time, she thought, as she turned away from the balcony and walked through the French doors. Entering her sitting room, she went straight to the antique carved mirror that hung above the fireplace and came face-to-face with her own reflection in the glass. Examining the weariness in her face, she recalled how she had always been described as an exotic beauty. But now, instead of beauty, she saw pain etched into every pore. As a young girl the term *exotic* had been a constant source of humiliation and aggravation when it was used to describe her, because her tan complexion and waist-length hair were uncommon traits among her peers. As a consequence, she was often ostracized because she did not have the stereotypical attributes of either of the distinct groups of African-American girls: Mignon was not dark enough to be accepted by the darker-skinned black girls and not quite light enough to be accepted by the light-skinned black girls. As a result she walked a tightrope that she had eventually transformed into a runway.

In college her goal had been to seek and find a light-skinned, rich husband. In one fell swoop during her final year in graduate school, she had attained the desires of her heart and the admiration of her family, who sought both wealth and complexion, although they generally settled for one or the other. However, without her realizing it, the pressure of maintaining the charade of a happy marriage had caused her to step from the runway back onto the hated tightrope again. She constantly felt at odds with herself, trying to maintain her balance and fit in, always fighting to be accepted. Finally reaching her breaking point, she refused to continue the charade by creating excuses to stay in a hopeless situation.

"Not this time—no more excuses, and definitely no more babies!" she stated out loud to the empty room as she sat down heavily, reclining on the chaise longue. With an odd sense of detachment she inspected the exquisite furnishings, recalling how she had worked ceaselessly for over a year to complete this room, seeking to create the perfect haven for them . . . for him. Hoping against hope he would take his refuge here with her . . . praying he would understand it was all done to please him. Maybe if he was pleased he would leave the others for her. Even now she could not believe her self-esteem had been reduced to the point of being that insecure. But now was not the time for remorse; it was time to regain the woman she had lost. As she continued to survey the room, her eyes were drawn to the ornate table that had been used to cover the slight discoloration in the white carpet. Although it had been four months, the chill still crept over her whenever she was reminded of the night she had almost died on that spot. However, this was not the reason for Mignon's leaving him. No, this was just one incident in a chapter that spanned the many years of their tumultuous marriage.

Who could leave all of this? She could—and she would! Now that the decision was made, she concentrated all of her energy on putting her plan into action. Gerald was in the Caribbean golfing for a few days—at least that was the version she was given. But his relaxation time was her release. She would need Miss Thompson's cooperation, and knew that she would be able to count on her. Miss Thompson had been with Mignon since the birth of her first child.

Now that the decision to leave her husband had been made, she had to take another difficult step—breaking the news to her parents—especially her mother, who feared the possibility of Mignon's becoming another single black mother. Reluctantly she picked up the phone and dialed the number with no regard for the difference in time. But instead of hearing her mother's familiar greeting, as she expected, she heard her father's sleep-filled voice as he mumbled a groggy "Hello?"

"Dad, were you asleep?"

"No, baby. How's my moving star?" It was a term he had used to refer to her since she had decided that she wanted to live the life of a bohemian out of college and began to travel the world, living only a short time at each destination. She smiled at the shared joke between them, and his referral to her: "Baby, you're not a movie star . . . but you are Dad's moving star."

"I'm ready to move on, Dad," she said, feeling her confidence waning.

Stunned, he asked hesitantly, "Are you sure that this is what you want?"

"Yes," she responded in resignation.

"When do you want me there, baby?" He asked the question that he knew she never would.

Mignon felt the tension easing away as her father soothed her fear of making the cross-country journey alone with small children. She never would have asked him to get involved; it was the nature of their relationship. But in her heart she knew asking was unnecessary; he was always there when she needed him.

"I'll have everything ready to leave by Friday. Gerald is returning Saturday, and I want plenty of road between us."

"You hang tough! I'll take care of things on this end and call you when I arrive," he replied, easily taking command.

"All right." She sighed, and let her voice trail off softly, trying not to let the tears she had so carefully held in check fall and betray her lack of composure.

Now that she had taken the first step, the rest fell easily into place. Before she knew it, the three days had flown by in a flurry of packing, shipping, and tying up loose ends. To her surprise Gerald had written a check from their personal account to pay for his trip; he had also made a cash withdrawal and had taken close to ten thousand dollars in cash. This left her with considerably less cash than she had originally planned. But even this would not hinder her plot to flee. Nothing short of the will of God would stop her from leaving.

On Friday morning her father arrived, true to his word. Calling her from the airport, he instructed her to finish her last-minute packing, assuring her a cab would bring him in. As she finished and awaited his arrival, she took a final nostalgic stroll through the house that she had tried to make into a home.

Mignon thought back to when they had finished building the house. She remembered standing in the grand entrance hall and imagining all the parties they would have. A house filled with friends, family, warmth, love. None of those dreams ever came true; instead it was a house filled with objects and artwork, nothing but possessions. No friends, no family. On occasion Gerald would generously invite a few friends over. Many times these were people she had never met before. He would preen, sticking his chest out, reminding her of a cross between a high-strutting rooster and a boastful peacock. She was always repulsed as she watched him take these so-called friends on the grand tour. Once they were obviously humbled and dutifully impressed by his storybook-perfect wife, children, and home, he normally excused himself and left her to entertain these strangers until it became apparent to all that he had no intention of returning.

This role in her marriage was not a part she remembered reading about in any of the fables that had been read to her as a child; nor was it in any of her storybooks or romance novels she had devoured as a lovestruck teen. She remembered only the maiden and the prince living happily ever after. Unfortunately, the books never wrote about the "ever after." The writer cruelly crafted a tale that caused a youthful mind to crave it, to spend her youth seeking the source of such passion and bliss. As a little girl, Mignon dreamed of growing up to live in a palace with her handsome prince. When she became a woman, she learned that palaces could be pretty prisons. And a handsome prince to the world could be a festering, oozing sore of immorality and cruelty that even a handsome countenance couldn't camouflage for long.

When Mignon thought she had finally found her prince she discovered the fairy tale was really a carefully disguised horror story. Life with Gerald was not a life at all; it was Beauty finding out the Beast really preferred being a beast, and no matter how much he was loved he never could be a prince. Now, whenever she read fairy tales to her children, she didn't give the prince much importance, and she never, ever used the words *happily ever after,* because she knew it never was. Visibly shaking her head as if it took motion to clear her mind of this notion, she thought, *God has something better for me. He didn't put me on this earth to live in an "un" state: unhappy, unfulfilled, unaccepted, and unwelcome.* This alone had been the single motivating thought that caused Mignon to flee her gilded prison.

Completely engrossed in a bittersweet moment of reflection, Mignon was startled by the insistent ringing of the doorbell, abruptly bringing her back to the present. She hurried to open the door, not realizing how stressed she was until she felt her body relax when she saw her father's strong brown face and loving, reassuring smile. Immediately she was put at ease. Returning his smile, she ran to him for the comfort only a father could give. She was transported back to a time when she was much younger and he was there to give her comfort in her pain.

The new Range Rover was packed and ready for the cross-country drive. She explained to her father that it would be the best choice for a trip this long. After securing the children in their seats, Mignon embraced Miss Thompson in a tearful farewell.

"If things work out and you want to come, I'll send for you," she assured the older woman, who held her in a motherly embrace.

"They are like my babies, too. I will come when it's time. I'll miss my babies." The two women embraced again, both wondering if it would be the last time they would see each other.

Mignon refused to be caught in the numbing whirlwind of emotions that threatened to overwhelm her, and turned the nanny's attention toward the children. Miss Thompson kissed each of them, promising to visit as soon as they were settled. As Mignon moved away, turning to get into the driver's seat, her father blocked her way.

"I came to take you home, and that's what I'm going to do!"

At first she started to protest, but then realized the futility of arguing with her father. As a retired officer in the marines, he believed in a strict code of chivalry that would not allow him to accept anything less than being the knight in shining armor. Once he had made his mind up, there was no chance of changing it. Acquiescing, she followed him to the passenger side, waiting as he chivalrously opened the door for her. After she was seated he handed her a beautiful leather-bound journal. "Your mother asked me to give this to you. She thought now was as good a time as any to read up on your family history."

Slightly bewildered, she hesitantly accepted the journal. "Thanks, Dad."

"Thank me after you read it. I told your mother I don't agree on the timing. She is certain that the time is right. I guess you will let us both know after you've finished."

"That sounds a little ominous, don't you think?"

"As I said, kiddo, you'll let us know."

Taking the timeworn journal, she turned it slowly, caressing the soft leather as she sat and contemplated its contents.

As they pulled away from the house and turned down the circular drive, Mignon never turned to look back—not even a glance. No looking back, like Lot's wife as they'd fled Sodom and Gomorrah. She was afraid if she looked back she would give in and stay in the hated loneliness of safety; it would be the same as turning into a pillar of salt.

As she began carefully flipping through the pages of the journal, she felt her father quietly studying her. She could almost feel his unspoken question, wondering why she was hesitating. So she turned to the first page and began to skim the page, noting the painstakingly neat penmanship. Immediately she recognized the handwriting of her grandmother, Carrie Devereaux. She felt transported to her childhood, remembering the echoes of whispered conversations between her mother and grandmother. Without being told, she knew this journal contained the stories of the women who paved the way before she was born. Again she hesitated, but this time from the uncertainty of youth that stumbles upon and uncovers a treasure it may be too immature to justly comprehend. She did not feel that she could possibly live up to the women that came before her, nor have any point of comparison to the trials they endured or the lessons they had learned through their lives. Clutching the journal in her hands she imagined the strength and determination of these women. In a moment of stunning clarity, she was aware of the flow of life that passed through her body and understood that the same strength and determination of the women before her now existed within her. This vision and her recollections made her certain her only option was . . . leaving.

1

"**L**eaving for good! Hallelujah!" Carrie exclaimed loudly as she stood under her favorite tree at the edge of the farm where she had spent her entire life. Spreading her arms out, she basked in the warmth of the sun as it gently caressed her skin, wiggling her toes in the soft, fresh grass beneath her bare feet and enjoying the warm Louisiana breeze that blew through her long, wavy, waist-length hair. She was completely unaware of her natural beauty, or the effect it had on those who first laid eyes on her. Her auburn hair, the color of a warm fire, and almond-shaped eyes that perfectly matched her hair were accented by her naturally tanned skin. It was the latter that caused her beauty to be overlooked. She was too dark by Louisiana standards to be considered beautiful. Brown as a paper bag was too brown. However, this simple fact of inbred racism made her determined to marry a high-yella, educated man, not one of the black field hands or common laborers whom she was supposed to marry by virtue of her complexion.

Carrie, Mignon's maternal grandmother, had grown up on a farm on the outskirts of Devereaux, a small Louisiana town so named for the largest plantation and landowners, Robert and William Devereaux, who were cousins. She was the eldest sibling and the only one still at home. Her parents, Jesse and Megan Devereaux, were born to second-generation freedmen who were once house slaves owned by the Devereaux family.

As children, Jesse and Megan played together when the Devereaux cousins visited each other's plantation. Each child was an offspring of one of the cousins. Robert was Megan's father, and William was Jesse's father. As teenagers Megan and Jesse fell in love; they planned to marry when Jesse turned eighteen. But fate delayed their plans; Megan became very ill and was sent away for nearly a year. When she returned to the Devereaux plantation, the Devereaux cousins gave Megan and Jesse permission to marry; however, Megan withdrew from Jesse, refusing his offer of marriage. Stunned by her withdrawal and refusal, Jesse refused to take no for an answer. He courted Megan tirelessly and over time won her hand in marriage. By this time Megan was nineteen and considered a spinster. After Megan and Jesse wed, Robert Devereaux made a bargain with Jesse to oversee the planting and harvesting of crops in exchange for allowing them to live in the overseer's house. Megan continued her job working as the laundry girl in the Devereaux home. At first Jesse was proud to be able to provide a nice home surrounded by ten acres of land to plant and harvest to feed them. By colored standards they lived high on the hog: the overseer's house had a full porch that ran around the entire front half of the house, as well as a parlor and one separate bedroom. The lean-to was less than forty feet from the back door.

"No, sir, Megan . . . my wife is too good for the woods," he remarked jokingly as they moved into their home the few pieces of furniture that he had lovingly made. However, Jesse's jovial mood would not last long. Shortly after the end of his first year as overseer, Robert Devereaux upped the stakes of the agreement in a wager that he made with Jesse. He offered to give Jesse and Megan the house and the ten acres of surrounding land if Jesse doubled the amount of crops that would be harvested in the coming season. In return, should Jesse lose the wager, he would become no more than an indentured servant until he turned fifty years old. Ignoring the probability of defeat, Jesse instead grasped for the opportunity to own land, and work to support his own family. After Jesse accepted the wager, he worked tirelessly to win. However, no amount of hard work could compensate for the drought that plagued Louisiana: the lack of rain that year made it the worst crop year that Jesse ever remembered. But instead of accepting defeat, Jesse devised a plan to escape with Megan.

Coming into the house one evening, he held Megan closely, whispering in her ear, "We have to leave this place real soon. . . . As soon as I say it's time to go, you got to be ready."

Megan jerked away as if Jesse had slapped her. "You in some kind of trouble, Jesse?" Unconsciously her eyes began to search the horizon for night riders.

"No, m'lady, I just can't stand being a slave for no man . . . not even your father. We can leave here one night and move into New Orleans. Once we get there we can pass—you'll see—we'll have a fine home there, Megan, and no one will ever know we's colored 'cept us."

"Okay, Jesse." She smiled, relief flooding her eyes as she released the breath she had held at the thought of the night riders coming for Jesse.

Just as the time arrived to leave Devereaux, Megan noticed tenderness in her breasts and swelling in her waist. She tried in vain to disguise her condition from Jesse, knowing he would never agree to the journey if he discovered she was pregnant. One afternoon as she was heading for home, Jesse intercepted her on the dusty, tree-lined road to their home. Momentarily disconcerted, she exclaimed angrily, "Jess, you and that raggedy mule near about scared the life from me!"

"Well, it's for sure I'm not trying to do that!" he replied watchfully. "I met up with you to ride you home—you're in no condition to make this hike every day, especially in this heat."

Walking around the clapboard buggy, he lifted Megan onto the splintered bench he had thoughtfully covered with an old blanket. Releasing a deep sigh, she turned and watched her husband thoughtfully. Most menfolk never knew when their women were expecting until they were bulging like overripe fruit or until they denied them their bedroom rights.

Then she remembered the conversation she had had just a few days ago with her mother, Belle, the madame of Robert Devereaux's plantation. Megan's mother, still a stunning dusky-skinned, green-eyed beauty just fifteen years her daughter's senior, had confronted her about her condition as she completed her chores in the main house. Although Carrie adamantly denied it, she could look in her mother's eyes and know that she already knew the truth. Throughout

Carrie's childhood it had been rumored among the sharecroppers that Maman—as Belle was referred to—had special powers. As usual, instead of arguing with Megan she simply made a demand: "Hold out your wrist to me!"

Megan complied with her request, watching silently as Maman pulled a needle from the apron of her skirts, holding it by the thread. Megan began to feel queasy as the needle swung like a pendulum across her wrist, dangerously close, but never touching her skin. When the needle appeared to be slowing to a stop, it changed directions and then began to swing in a circle. Abruptly breaking the hypnotic effect, Maman returned the needle to her skirts and pronounced, "You'll have a daughter come spring. You and Jesse might want to reconsider leaving these parts—I think this one will look like me." She smiled knowingly at her daughter.

"You may be able to pass for white . . . this one won't." With that she turned her attention away from Megan, silently dismissing her. Stunned by her mother's cruelty, Megan wondered, *How could she know about our plans to leave?* Megan became rigid with indignation; she looked at her mother with loathing. "Did you forget, *Belle,* I can only have white children? Me 'n' Jesse are almost white—we can't have no other." Furious, she turned to leave, even more convinced that she had to hide the pregnancy from Jesse long enough to leave Devereaux and make their home far away from her mother and Robert Devereaux.

Now she had to deal with the fact that Jesse knew they were having a child.

"Yes, sir, we're gonna have us a babe come spring, so if you ask me, we better get a move on and get down to New Orleans, so we can be settled in by the time this child comes." Looking at him earnestly, she hoped he would agree that they should move right away.

"Well, now, I don't think that's such a good idea, Meg. What if something goes wrong? All we have is this here buggy, an old mule, and a few pieces of clothes and furniture. It will take almost two weeks to get to New Orleans—that is, if all goes well. Then what if I can't find work right away? You're in no condition to find work. Now I know you are upset, but we have no choice but to wait until the babe is born. By that time we will be able to save a little more; until then we will make the best of being here." Smiling at his wife, he gently took her hand and placed it on his arm.

"Giddup." He clucked to the mule as they rode along the bumpy, dusty rode back to their home.

Six months later, on a rainy afternoon in March, Jesse sent for the sharecropper's midwife. Megan labored for hours before she gave birth to a daughter. When the midwife handed the infant to her, Megan's heart sank. Maman had been right—this child had reached back. The infant girl was beautiful, except she was too dark. Her skin and eyes were the light brown color of caramel; even the little wisps of hair were the same color. Megan broke down and cried because she knew freedom was now beyond their reach. "Poor little thing, life will be hard for you because of this color you carry."

Four days after the birth of her daughter, Megan had still not named her child. She was distracted and fearful that Jesse would reject them and leave her alone to raise their child. She constantly imagined him leaving to move to New Orleans alone. The knowledge that she could never move to New Orleans and pass for white because her child betrayed her heritage caused Megan's depression to sprout and grow. Megan had fully expected to have a child that had white skin like them; she had even chosen a fine white name to match. Now that her daughter was here, she was at a loss for a name. As Megan sat on the porch, staring at the infant in the basket next to her, she looked up, surprised to see Jesse smiling at them.

"You surprised me. I guess I've been woolgathering and didn't hear you." Standing up slowly, she turned to get the water bowl for Jesse to wash his face and hands.

"Be still, Meg, I got it! I just came home a little early to see my family! I just couldn't take being away no longer—this young'un already looks like she growed since this morning." As he spoke Jesse took the infant from the basket and held her tenderly, studying her face intently. Silently Megan returned and sat beside Jesse.

"She's a bit of me and a bit of you, and some that reached back to people we don't even recall. But God recalls, Meg—yes, sir, He knows."

As she looked into his eyes and saw the unchecked tears slip down his face, she knew everything would be all right—her Jess wasn't going anywhere.

"Jess, I thought of a name for her today . . . what do you think of Carrie?"

"I think it's a mighty fine name, Meg, but why Carrie? I thought you had another name picked out."

"Yes, I had thought about Anna, but I think Carrie is better. We can make Anna her middle name, but her first name should say who she is! This child carries a burden of being born the wrong color, at the wrong time, and in the wrong place. She will always be reminded, so we will remind her first."

Staring at his wife intently, Jesse could not believe her words, but he also realized that what she spoke was a reflection of the loss she felt at having to spend the rest of her life in Devereaux. "Okay, Meg. That's a mighty fine name . . . a mighty fine name. Now we just have to make sure we have a mighty fine life right here in Devereaux, my girls and me." Smiling, he stood up with Carrie. "I think I'm going to take our daughter for her first stroll and tell her how to raise crops. Would you care to join us, Mother?"

"Yes, I would enjoy a stroll; after all, I've been cooped up in this house for nearly two weeks!"

Megan took Jesse by the arm, and the new family began a nightly tradition.

2

After Jesse and Megan decided to stay in Devereaux and accept Robert Devereaux's conditions, they settled into their old and familiar routines, with one exception—Carrie.

Carrie was a lovely and peaceful baby. She rarely cried and had a ready smile for all. Whenever Jesse came into the room she would light up, smiling and gurgling to get his attention. Father and daughter had had a special bond since he'd first held her at birth. Megan loved Carrie in her own way: she was an attentive mother, but not very affectionate. She could not help feeling betrayed by Carrie's dark complexion. This simple fact of skin color had changed the course of Megan's life, and made it hard for her to display maternal affection, a struggle that she waged daily.

Megan was accustomed to the special treatment she had always received from colored folk, due to her white skin and the fact that she was the accepted daughter of Robert Devereaux. As a result, she was completely unprepared for the ridicule she had to endure when Carrie was born.

As Carrie grew to adulthood her strongest desire was longing to be accepted by the lighter-skinned coloreds. Megan, who feared any further tainting of their almost-white bloodline, even further instilled this thought into her. She taught Carrie how to act like a fine lady, hoping that this and Carrie's undeniable beauty would help her get a good catch.

As time passed the colored folk continued to spread rumors about Carrie's birth, it was their chance to mock the uppity Megan Devereaux. They were so intent on causing her discomfort that no one ever considered that Carrie suffered the most from the rumors. It was said that Belle had switched her at birth and that the real Devereaux baby lived in a shanty on the edge of the Devereaux plantation. When Carrie was five, one of her playmates told her of the story. Afterward, she lived in constant fear of her grandmother Belle and that her parents would take and exchange her for the little white-skinned child. So she tried very hard to be a good girl and do exactly what her parents asked. Carrie was always quiet, attentive, and eager to please. As a result of the cruel rumors, she had nightmares many years of being taken and given to the "dark" strangers that lived in the shanty in exchange for the better white-skinned child.

For five years Carrie remained an only child. Whenever she asked Megan for a brother or sister, her mother would look sadly at her and say, "I can't take no more of you, Carrie, you'll be the only one." Even as a small child Carrie knew that because of the color of her skin, she was considered an unfortunate mistake, a burden to her parents. Then the unexpected happened and changed the course of Carrie's lonely existence.

Megan delivered a baby boy named William and was ecstatic with his arrival. She would take him on daily walks into town, telling anyone that would listen how William was the spitting image of Jesse's father. Carrie's parents basked in the acceptance they received after the birth of their son. Megan thought a curse had been broken and had four more children, in as many years.

Being the eldest, Carrie's siblings never accepted the fact that she was their blood sister. They loved her as you would a distant cousin, all except Carrie's favorite sister, Stella. The rest seemed to believe Megan and Jesse had taken her in and christened her as their daughter out of the goodness of their hearts. Carrie grew up repeatedly being told, she had "reached back." However, neither parent would acknowledge the "reach" coming from their side. It became clear by insinuation that "reaching back" was not a desirable outcome.

Carrie took no real pleasure in the company of her siblings, so she sought out the children of other neighboring families to befriend.

Carrie became best friends with a boy named John and his sister Mary. They were the children of the colored blacksmith and his wife, who was the Devereaux cook. Carrie would seek them out whenever she could, to run and play in the vast fields. Many times they would just sit, hold hands, and tell make-believe stories. Carrie especially liked those days, but they were short-lived. As soon as they were ten years old, they had to start work.

Carrie and Mary both worked in the Devereaux house washing and pressing laundry. John worked with his father as a smithy. As they grew up, they also grew apart because of the division caused by color and inbred racism. John and Mary were much too dark to be accepted in Carrie's household. However, from time to time Carrie would sneak away to meet her two loyal friends. Sometimes they would sneak away to the fields, lie in the wheat grass, and share their dreams. It became their habit to meet each other at the creek in the summer to swim and then lie on the bank letting the sun dry and bake their bodies.

During the summer of her fifteenth and his seventeenth year Carrie and John met by the creek to swim as usual. Mary did not join them because she had gotten married to one of the sharecropper's sons after he got her pregnant during the winter season. As the two friends treaded the water in their makeshift swimsuits, Carrie became uncomfortably aware of the handsome brown teen swaying on the edge of manhood. It was as if John had changed overnight from a gangly boy to a lean, well-muscled teen. She admired his chocolate skin as the sun and water seemed to battle for its attention. John was also aware of the beauty she had become. Instead of splashing water in her face or challenging her to a race as he had done in summers past, John tried to impress Carrie with a dive he had been practicing in anticipation of this day. As they climbed from the water onto the shore, Carrie blushed as she imagined what it would feel like to be kissed by John. She couldn't suppress the butterflies that danced in her stomach. Pretending at nonchalance she lay on the rock slab watching him through half-closed eyes as he climbed from the water and lay on the warm rock next to her. Closing her eyes, she enjoyed the heat of the sun on her face and the close proximity of John next to her.

The silence between them was comforting, not strained as it had been at first. Feeling a shadow cover her, Carrie opened her eyes expecting to see the sun going behind the clouds. Instead, she looked into John's liquid brown eyes as he lowered his lips to her in a gentle kiss. Slowly, his tongue entered her mouth gently prodding, searching. It was her introduction to passion, a first step in their exploration of each other. Their hearts seemed to beat in accord rapidly keeping pace. For several minutes Carrie lay contented in John's embrace, until she thought of how her friend and his sister Mary had been caught with Marcus one of the field hands. Now Mary was expecting her child by the winter. *How could I be so stupid?* she thought. *What if I get pregnant?* Abruptly getting to her feet Carrie jumped unceremoniously into the tepid water trying to put some distance between them. Startled, John watched Carrie plunge into the water and quickly followed. Swimming to her, he followed her to the opposite bank. Tenderly he held her again in his embrace, bending slightly until their lips met, he explored the sweetness of her mouth. Carrie's stomach filled with butterflies as she enjoyed the feel of his firm lips and the sensuous exploration of his tongue. Leaning against him she felt her knees weaken under her as he guided her gently onto her back. At the feel of her back in the cool mud on the bank she drew away breathlessly trying desperately to regain her composure. Fumbling, she pushed him away. "I gotta go!" She propelled her body away from him, panicked by the thought that she could give in to him so easily. John stepped back and lightly touched her elbow as if assisting her departure. As he released her, he leaned toward her and whispered, "You'll be mine one day Carrie, my wife." Before he could say anything else, Carrie turned and ran for home. Each time they met after that day was strained. She was never able to meet his eyes and only able to mumble a greeting. For years she daydreamed about John and that day by the creek. From time to time she even imagined what it would be like to be his wife, but as she grew older, she pushed those thoughts away. Carrie would never marry a man that dark. She could care less how handsome he had become or the fact that they had been best friends. She wanted better, she wanted a light-skinned husband and children in order to be accepted into proper colored society.

As all the children grew into adults, Carrie's parents planned acceptable marriages with other light-skinned families for all of her siblings who remained in Devereaux, except Carrie. Her brother William had moved to New Orleans and was passing for white, as was

Stella, Carrie's favorite sister. She moved to Houston, Texas, and was rarely heard from. One afternoon after the announcement of her younger sister's engagement was made, Megan took Carrie aside. "Carrie, I hope you do understand we're not playing favorites; we want the best match for you and we will just have to wait until the right one comes along." Megan tried to sound encouraging, but the truth of it was, none of the good families wanted darker-skinned wives for their sons. Carrie's parents didn't realize that they had unwittingly made their values, her values. Her desire to please her parents by not tainting the Devereaux bloodline with darker blood was stronger than their desire to see her married to a good man. Carrie would accept nothing less than a high-yella, educated man.

3

The Louisiana sun was setting, and the warm glow of orange and red hues rested on the fresh grass. Carrie sighed and reclined in her favorite spot, beside the fig tree at the border of her parents' land. Gazing at the setting sun, she recalled the matchmaking catastrophe her father had devised. He had all but demanded she marry John Browning—her John, kind, considerate, handsome, but too dark for her to marry. Her father was so pleased with himself when he announced his plans to her. She could still recall her father sitting stiffly on the stool in her room, saying, "He's the only qualified blacksmith in the county, and he's a respectable man. He'll be able to appreciate a gal like you, Carrie, and you've known him since you were children playing in the fields."

Carrie mentally replayed the scene, recalling how livid she had been. She exploded at the last remark. "A gal like me? You mean I'm as bright as he could ever hope for? I will not marry him or any other man that you and Mama choose! What about love, Daddy? Shouldn't I love him? Or is that too much for me to want? I want what you want; I want love and to be happy, not downtrodden with some common laborer!" she yelled in exasperation.

Megan overheard Carrie raise her voice at Jesse. Surprised, she stopped what she was doing to find out why Carrie was so upset. As she entered the room, Carrie whirled around, angrily pointing her finger at Megan. "You have raised me to act like the light-skinned coloreds. I have their ways; I want to fit in with them. Then you say, 'No, Carrie, you're not light enough to fit; you shouldn't want the same things—take what you can get.' And I say *no!*" She stared defiantly at her parents. "I know I'm not like the other ones, but I won't let you ruin my life." For the first time in her life she stood up to her parents. Carrie's unwavering glare and tear-filled eyes caused her parents' hearts to break for her.

As she reflected on that emotional day, she reclined, enjoying the feel of the fresh grass beneath her. *All of this is behind me now; I'm leaving Devereaux and maybe even Louisiana, all because of Logan.* She thought God had answered her prayers . . . He had sent her Logan Daniels.

Logan, with his lean, muscular build, his white skin, and wavy black hair. It was just his nose that gave him away as being colored. But that was all right—her nose was straight and narrow; their babies would come out just fine! Carrie held that thought to her, babies, a home, and the high life, maybe even New York. Logan told her that after they were married, he would take her back home to New York to meet his family. If she liked it there, he would ask the church to reassign him and they would settle in New York and build their life together. Opportunities were good for colored folks in the North.

She thought back on the day they had met, almost two months ago. Carrie had gone to church with her parents, sitting in their usual seat in the front pew. They had fussed at her the entire way to church, going on about how she would end up as an old maid. Still angry with them and troubled by the truths they'd spoken, she failed to hear Reverend Douglas announce that the message would be delivered by a visiting minister. When the choir finished its selection, she finally turned to give the service her full attention. As her gaze fell upon the visiting minister standing at the pulpit, she was so entranced she forgot to breathe for a few seconds. In the pulpit, preparing to deliver the message, was Rev. Logan Daniels, visiting from Houston, Texas.

Carrie was mesmerized by his poise and commanding presence. When he spoke, shivers ran down her spine at the sound of his rich, baritone voice. Tears sprang to her eyes when he finished the sermon by singing her favorite hymn, "Amazing Grace." She was not the only person he made that impression on: every woman in the congregation sat stock-still, as if unable to believe their eyes. *How fine this man is! I wonder if he's single? Lord, if you'd replace Reverend Douglas with this man, I'd make every Bible study, prayer meeting, and bake sale,* Carrie thought, smiling to herself. When she glanced at the pulpit, to her surprise and unease, Logan was looking—no, staring—right at her. He seemed to know what she had been thinking. She felt a slow flush rising to her face, and for the first time in her entire life she thanked God for making her too dark to show a blush.

After the service was over, the ministers stood at the church doors to receive the members of the congregation. Reverend Douglas was not a bit surprised by the line of inquisitive single young women and their mothers waiting to make the acquaintance of this visiting minister. As they made their approach, Carrie let her parents walk in front, hoping to slip past without the mandatory greeting of the ministers at the door. However, much to her chagrin, as they approached the point of her escape, Jesse grabbed Carrie's, elbow preventing her escape.

"Good sermon, Reverend Daniels; we always welcome good preaching."

"I'm mighty glad I had the opportunity to deliver the Word to this fine congregation," Logan replied easily.

"Well, we won't take up any more of your time. I'm Jesse Devereaux; this is my wife, Megan, and our daughter, Carrie." Logan reached past Jesse and caught Carrie's hand in both of his. In that moment, she felt the heat of his touch course through her entire being. Logan looked her straight in the eyes with an expression of mutual surprise, as if he, too, had felt it. Holding her hand firmly, he turned to her parents and asked, " Mr. Devereaux, would it be improper for a visiting man of the cloth to stop over for supper?"

Amused, Jesse looked at Logan, after registering the surprise in Carrie's eyes. "Why certainly, Reverend, there is always a seat open at our table for a man who spreads the Word of the Almighty. Dinner is ready at three, but you're welcome to come sit and visit around two." Jesse surreptitiously eyed Carrie, amused at her discomfiture over the plans that had been arranged.

"I'll be there at two o'clock, sir." Logan nodded to Carrie, releasing her hand from his. "I look forward to seeing you this afternoon, Miss Carrie." Turning his back, he continued greeting the parishioners in the line that awaited his attention. Carrie strode in agitation to the buggy, her mind racing as she tried to decide what to prepare for din-

ner. She always cooked Sunday dinners, but she was completely unprepared to cook for a man who unnerved her as much as Reverend
Daniels did. She rode home in silence; Megan and Jesse smiled knowingly at each other. Maybe their prayers would be answered in more
ways than one.

At two o'clock sharp, Logan rode up the path in Reverend Douglas's buggy. Seated on the porch, Jesse greeted him: "You're just in
time, Reverend."

Logan smiled, confused, "You mean *on* time."

"No, I said what I meant," replied Jesse thoughtfully. "Come sit on
the porch and enjoy the breeze, while my womenfolk finish with the
preparations."

"Blast! He's here already!" Carrie exclaimed nervously, checking
every pot and pan to make sure nothing burned or overcooked. She
had never met a man who had this type of effect on her.

"You know I don't take to no cussing in my house, Carrie!
Especially one of my own young'uns . . . you getting a little to sassy for
my liking!" Megan chastised her daughter, watching her in silent
amusement.

At three o'clock Megan went to the front door and called Jesse and
Logan in from the front porch for dinner. Carrie was nervously fussing with the flowers she had hurriedly picked to place on the table.
Being an honored guest, Logan sat at the head of the table opposite
Jesse; Megan and Carrie sat on either side. After they were seated and
the food placed on the table, Logan blessed the food and their home.
He ate heartily, profusely complimenting Carrie on her cooking,
telling her it was the best meal he'd ever had, second only to his
mother's cooking. Several times she looked up to find him openly admiring her as a slow smile played across his lips. Again she felt a slow
flush rising to her face, and for the second time in her life, she
thanked God for her complexion. Carrie was secretly delighted that
none of her sisters were there. Surely a man of his complexion and
position would immediately dismiss her for someone with lighter
skin.

After dinner Carrie walked beside Logan in nervous silence, waiting for him to speak. Sensing her distress, he quickly eased the ten-

sion by making small talk. Slowly he began to draw her out as he
asked her what it was like growing up in Devereaux. Carrie became
animated in her description of the town and its people. She became
especially enthusiastic when she described some of the antics of her
siblings. Logan noticed that she spoke only of others and never about
herself. As they strolled down the path, he reached out and took her
hand gently in his. Neither one spoke for a while; they just walked in
companionable silence. As they neared the pond, he began to tell her
about himself, his childhood, who he was and how he came to be
called to preach the Word.

His ease and self-assurance quickly dispelled her nervousness.
They sat on the sun-bleached rocks by the pond and talked for hours.
When she spoke, he listened closely, watching her as if memorizing
her every move. She finally told him about being raised in Devereaux
and her desire to live somewhere else. Although she never spoke of
the pain and humiliation she had faced growing up, Logan sensed
sadness. It tugged at his spirit, making him want to protect her from
all of her pain, and give her all that she dreamed of. They talked until
the sun began its long journey to darkness. "I'd better get you back
home now," he said as he gazed into her brown eyes, memorizing the
way the setting sun kissed her caramel-colored skin. Now that he had
found her, he didn't want to leave her for a moment. Leaving the
pond, they walked back up the path to her house, hand in hand, each
deep in their own thoughts. "I'll be here tomorrow and every day
after that, if it's all right with you, Miss Carrie?" Logan asked hopefully.

"I'd like that very much, Reverend Daniels," she said, a slow smile
playing at the corners of her mouth.

True to his word, Logan was at the Devereaux house each afternoon, spending time with Carrie and her parents. Each evening after
dinner, Logan and Carrie would either sit on the porch or take a
walk, both looking forward to the next day, when they would be together again. After a month of courting, Logan asked to speak to
Jesse privately one evening. Nervously he asked permission for
Carrie's hand in marriage. Jesse gladly gave his approval and called
Megan and Carrie in to share the good news. Megan was pleased; it
was obvious Logan came from a good family—and he was as white as
Jesse. Who would have thought their Carrie would have done so well?

Logan was not only white-skinned, he was educated and a minister! Megan's mind raced as she thought of all the families to invite to the wedding.

Carrie was so deep in thought, reminiscing about recent events, that she hadn't noticed the sun had set and it was almost pitch-dark. The wedding was only two weeks away, and here she was daydreaming again. Carrie had waited all of her life for Logan, and now that he was here, she couldn't help daydreaming about their future. Getting up, she dusted the grass from her hair and clothes, and walked hurriedly down the path to the house. Seeing the lights on, she knew her father was standing just inside the door, worried. She quickened her pace and began walking faster, so she never saw the man in the shadows, even at the last moment as he grabbed her from behind. Before she knew what was happening, his hands were over her mouth and she could not scream out.

"Uppity nigga bitch," she heard his ragged whisper in her ear. Carrie could not make out his face, but his voice was somehow familiar. She felt her clothes being torn from her body as she fought futilely for release, until she was overpowered. Though she struggled against this invasion of her body she was overcome when her face was pushed into the grass, suffocating her until she passed out.

Carrie later awoke to find her father standing over her, tears in his eyes, and her mother wiping her brow with a cool cloth. Looking around slowly, she realized she was in her room, in her bed. *I must have had a horrible nightmare; maybe I came down with a high fever,* she thought. Then she felt the sticky soreness between her thighs and knew it was not a dream. She could not bear to look in her father's tortured eyes. "Who did this to you?" he asked, trying to suppress the murderous rage that threatened to consume him.

"I didn't see his face, Daddy," she whispered, her throat burning from the pressure of her tormentor's hands. "Where's Logan? Does he know?" She felt her tears threatening to spill over.

"No, baby, your ma and I got worried after you didn't come home. We went looking for you and found you in that patch of wheat grass. I carried you home. We told Logan you had wedding jitters." Sighing heavily, he said, "You'll be all right; we'll see to it."

As Jesse tried soothing Carrie, Megan stood back, staring at her.

"What did he say to you?" Megan bit out each word, attempting to keep her rage under control.

"I didn't see him, Mama!"

"I know you didn't see him. I asked you what he said to you. I need to know!"

Carrie looked meaningfully at her father. Feeling helpless and confused, Jesse stared down at his weathered hands as though wishing for a strength he didn't possess. "I'll be outside if you need me," he said wearily. She had never seen him look as old or defeated as he did at that moment. Waiting a moment until the door had completely closed, Carrie could not meet her mother's eyes. "He called me an uppity nigga bitch!" Barely choking the painful words out, Carrie felt the dam finally burst. Sobbing heavily, she relived all the pain and humiliation that she had endured, culminating in this final act of suffering. Megan held her child, trying to rock the pain from her, and take it herself.

When the storm of tears passed and Carrie was spent, Megan spoke to her eldest daughter as if she were just a small child, very slowly and very softly: "You'll be jus' fine, child; he won't come after you no more. He took me the same way two years before I came to your father, same way he took my mother, except I was born from it. I tried to do for you what she wouldn't do for me—I tried to protect you. I never wanted him to know you were born. My Maman be my mama and my sister. After he got to me it took a while for me to get right again. But he's a wily old devil; he knew you were here, so he jus' lay in wait, jus' lay in wait. One of these days, chile, I'll be waiting for him. I be of his blood, his fruit, but as sure as I'm your mama I promise you, I'm gonna see that devil return to dust." Megan held on to Carrie as her words of repressed hatred spewed forth, surprising them both for different reasons. Megan was trying not to drown; she was fighting to stay afloat on the sea of sanity and not fall into the undertow that threatened to pull her in.

Carrie was bone of her bone, flesh of her flesh, good and clean from Jesse. *Good and clean, good and clean.* Silently she chanted this mantra.

Carrie now held Megan. Somehow she instinctively knew their roles had been reversed and she was now her mother's protector. She became the anchor.

Carrie longed to be away from Devereaux and forever free of its name. Two weeks from now she would be at the church to marry Logan. She would no longer be Carrie Devereaux—that Carrie had died in the field near the path last night. She would start a new life, a new beginning, as she married Logan and became Carrie Daniels— without a past, only a future . . .

4

Studewood Heights, Texas, in August of 1917, was not quite what Carrie had in mind. But she had been determined to leave Devereaux, Louisiana. Shortly after they were married, Logan told her his request to be released from his assignment in Devereaux had been granted, and she was overjoyed. They were both eager for him to accept the reassignment to Houston, for different reasons. Logan was elated to return to Houston with aspirations of being offered the opportunity to build his own church. He knew he had been selected because Rev. Thomas Norton, the president of the Church Alliance Council, held him in high esteem. Carrie, on the other hand, often daydreamed of the beautiful home they'd have in one of the nicer areas, like the Fifth Ward or Sugar Hill, where the other light-skinned, educated colored folk lived.

But to Carrie's frustration, Logan had been assigned to build a church and congregation in Studewood Heights. Studewood Heights consisted of approximately four square miles of dirt roads and shotgun homes. It was not colored high society, as she had hoped. Instead its population was comprised of dark-skinned colored folks who were either domestics, fieldhands, or common laborers. Carrie was living in the midst of what she had tried so hard to detach herself from. However, she found she could not maintain her indifference for long. The people were kind and generous toward Logan and Carrie. Her neighbors frequently stopped by to see if she needed anything, and many times would just come to make small talk. Everyone knew she had left her family behind in Louisiana, so they went out of their way to befriend her.

Soon Carrie started to pay visits to her neighbors. She loved to bake and would often bake peach cobbler or lemon pies as gifts for birthdays and anniversaries. After a while, Carrie knew most of the people in the Heights and grew fond of them. Logan understood that Carrie dreamed of a different life; he constantly assured her that once the building was complete and the congregation established, they would move to the Third Ward, where many of the affluent colored folk lived. With that in mind Carrie fully took on the varied responsibilities of a minister's wife.

She visited the sick and shut-in with fresh fruit that she would pick from the trees in their yard. She held a children's Bible-study class each Wednesday at the schoolhouse. Logan was proud of his wife and impressed with her many attributes for ministry. He knew they would have a loyal and dedicated congregation as a result of Carrie's loving ways and generosity toward people.

Sitting on the front porch, fanning herself, Carrie tried to stay cool in the summer heat. It was almost a hundred degrees, and the dark clouds spoke of a threatening storm. She hoped the homes in her area could withstand the torrent of rain during this storm season. Most of the families could ill afford to rebuild, and many of the houses were held together now by a song and a prayer. She was relieved that she didn't have to be concerned about their house. It was a nice white two-bedroom house with black shutters. the Church Alliance Council ensured that the church-owned homes were the nicest and always well maintained. This house had luxuries Carrie had never experienced, such as running water and an indoor bathtub. Although the home was furnished, Logan gave her a small allowance to decorate and give it a woman's touch. All in all, it was a very warm and comfortable home.

Early evening was Carrie's favorite time of the day. It was her routine to sit on the porch watching the sun began its slow descent and wait for Logan's buggy to turn the corner. Shifting her body slightly, she tried to prevent the weight of her swollen belly from numbing her legs and feet. She had never been this hot or this uncomfortable in her entire life. Fanning herself futilely, she paused and began to worry her thumbnail until she had chewed it almost to the quick. The baby was due any day now, and she had never been so fearful in her entire life. Not of childbirth—she had seen enough to know what to expect. No, she was worried about the child itself. Would it be normal and healthy? She prayed daily that the baby would look like Logan. After the rape, Megan had given her a concoction prepared by Maman. She told her it would kill any seed Robert Devereaux left. After drinking the thick, sickly-smelling liquid, Carrie became violently ill and had to stay in bed for a week. Although she felt much better, less than one month after she and Logan were married Carrie discovered she was pregnant. Feeling confident that she was pregnant by her husband, she told Logan that they were going to have a child. Carrie was both excited and fearful at the same time of his response. She knew he wanted children; it was just that they had never discussed how soon they would start a family. Carrie sensed he would have preferred completing the church and establishing the congregation first.

Strolling hand in hand with Carrie toward home one evening, Logan remarked, "Carrie, you seem to be barely able to make it through the day. You would tell me if you weren't feeling well, wouldn't you?"

"Logan—" she began hesitantly.

"I mean, I know I'm busy and all with the church," he interrupted, "but I never want you to think I'm too busy for you."

"No, honey, I know you're never too busy for me."

Slowing her pace, she gazed tenderly into his eyes. "I am not ill, my love; I am carrying our child. I just hope that you're not too upset that it happened so soon."

"Upset! Why, I'm elated! The Lord doesn't make mistakes, and so now has to be the right time."

"Good, because there is not a lot I could do about it now." She stood slightly on her toes, gently kissing his lips.

"When are we expecting this blessing?"

"I will have to see Dr. Washington to know for sure, but by my count, this summer."

Placing his arm firmly around her still-small waistline, Logan whispered in a conspiratorial tone, "Well, wife, we'd better make good use of the time we have until you won't want my touch."

Slapping his hand away playfully, she quickened her pace to return to their home and the comforts of each other's arms.

Carrie was pleased with Logan's response and settled into the new experiences her body held in store for her. However, as the pregnancy progressed, she became increasingly anxious and restless in anticipation of the birth of their baby. Many times she still felt unsure whether the concoction had worked; then she would begin to doubt the child's paternity. Today she tried to shake these thoughts as she awaited Logan's arrival. Instead, she let her mind wander to the baby shower being held in her honor tomorrow. Louise, her best friend and mentor, had stopped by earlier to deliver the gown she had had designed by her dressmaker as a gift for Carrie. Considering that they had been friends just a few months, Louise's friendship had considerably changed Carrie's life.

It all began when she had received an invitation to the monthly luncheon held at Louise's home, comprised of ministers' wives. For the occasion Logan surprised her with a new outfit. It was an emerald-green wool suit with a matching hat. Carrie was so proud of her suit. It was the first store-bought outfit she had ever owned. However, much to her agitation, the suit was too tight and had to be let out in the waist due to her condition. After the waistline was loosened to accommodate her slightly swollen belly, she preened in front of the full-length mirror. Seeking Logan out, she twirled, openly admiring herself in her new outfit. Nothing could spoil the moment.

When Carrie arrived at the Norton home, she couldn't believe her eyes. This house was as big as the Devereaux house, but grander in many ways. Astonished that colored folk lived in such splendor, she was further impressed when the door was answered by a colored maid, who greeted her and took her coat. As Carrie stepped from the vestibule, she was amazed at the size of the main hall and the beautiful marble floors; she marveled at the winding staircase and longed to touch the lifelike oil painting of Reverend and Mrs. Norton. At that moment Carrie knew this was exactly the lifestyle she desired—acceptance by colored society, a home like this, and, of course, Logan and their children. Now that she had seen this home, she wouldn't rest until she attained her heart's desire.

When the maid announced the arrival of Mrs. Carrie Daniels, a hush came over the room as faces filled with curiosity turned to inspect the new arrival. Standing self-consciously in the archway of the dining room, she endured their curious stares and wondered, *Should I just stand here and stare back, or find an open seat?* Just as she'd decided on the latter, Carrie noticed an elegant woman who seemed to glide, walking toward her.

Louise Norton made her way to Carrie, exclaiming, "Why, Carrie, you are more beautiful than any of us could have imagined! Come, I've seated you next to me." Carrie followed in her wake as Louise confided, "We have all been dying of curiosity to meet the woman who captured the attention and obviously the heart of Logan Daniels. Every unmarried woman—and even a few of the married ones— sought after him. We even made a bet that with such a selection of women he'd never be able to choose just one and would remain a bachelor. Then he returns to Houston, claiming you as his new bride!" Louise surreptitiously glanced at the small bulge in Carrie's stomach and said knowingly, "I see he wasted no time in getting you with child. Can't say I blame him; he's staking his claim so there's no question of his dedication to you." Carrie frowned at the last remark. *What does she mean, he's staking his claim?* she wondered. Before she could ponder this thought, Louise directed her to take the seat beside her.

As she took her seat she glanced at the guests seated around the dining table. She noted that most eyes were still fixed appraisingly on her. All of the unexpected attention made Carrie feel uneasy with their perusal. She decided to busy herself by preparing her tea, but she was so nervous that her hands had a slight tremble when she held her cup. Louise, who appeared to be listening intently to an elderly woman seated opposite her, leaned over and whispered, "Relax and let them stare; your composure will unnerve them."

Carrie smiled her thanks and did as instructed, calling on every bit of her inner strength to appear unmoved by the obvious inspection of these women.

As she relaxed, so did they, and eventually they began to lose interest. Most of the women returned to their conversations, with the exception of the woman seated directly opposite Carrie. In an attempt to distract her from her intense inspection, Carrie smiled at the woman in the hope of initiating conversation. Instead of returning her smile, the woman fixed her with a glare that was filled with pure and unadulterated hatred. Flinching from the hostility that emanated from this woman, Carrie quickly averted her eyes, stalling for a moment to regain her composure.

Carrie's posture unconsciously changed to an almost regal position. This time she looked directly at the woman who had stared so rudely. Again she was met with the same hate-filled, unwavering glare. However, she did not turn away this time. Instead she returned the stare and deliberately appraised her adversary. She had never run from confrontation in her life, and wouldn't start now. The woman seated opposite Carrie was a few years older, with skin that looked like fresh cream, icy blue eyes, and brown hair. She was the colored person's description of a rare beauty. Her clothes were expensive. She wore a dark blue velvet suit, to enhance her eyes, and red lipstick—which was unheard of for a minister's wife. Then Carrie noticed that this woman did not wear a wedding band. In turn, the woman continued her scrutiny of Carrie, as if trying to etch every feature permanently into her memory. When her gaze fell on Carrie's protruding stomach, the blood seemed to drain from her pale face. She turned as if trying to dismiss the obvious and initiated a conversation with the woman seated next to her.

Carrie was stunned. She was sure she had never seen this woman before. She was also positive that she could not have offended her in any way. Carrie later found out the woman's name was Ruthelen Pruitt. Ruth, as she preferred to be called, had had her sights set on Logan—until now.

The exchange between the two women did not go unnoticed by Louise, although she decided not to interfere. *Let it run its course,* she thought. *Sooner or later they had to meet. It may as well be sooner and gotten over with.*

Turning her attention to the matters at hand, she began the luncheon. "Ladies, may I have your attention? I'd like to begin this month's meeting by introducing you to the newest member of our group, the lovely and, I might add, gracious Mrs. Carrie Daniels."

Louise paused momentarily for effect before continuing: "For those of you who don't know, Carrie is the new bride of our very own Reverend Logan Daniels."

Pausing momentarily, Louise locked eyes with the woman seated across from Carrie, enjoying every minute of her discomfort. She continued: "They have just returned to Houston from Devereaux,

Louisiana, and the council has assigned Logan and Carrie to build a church in Studewood Heights, where they currently reside." Louise finished, smiling brightly.

Carrie also smiled, confidently this time, as she again became the object of interest. Once more she felt the hate-filled glare of the woman seated opposite her. Instead of turning away or avoiding her stare, Carrie turned to face her, smiling brilliantly, and nodded in her direction. This time the woman recoiled as if she had been struck. Chuckling to herself, Carrie knew that every woman seated at the table saw the exchange and knew she had the victory.

Unexpectedly, Louise interrupted. "Ladies, pardon my oversight. I failed to mention that Logan and Carrie will be parents soon . . . so ladies, you know what that means! We'll have a godbaby to spoil. . . . Lord knows we're all too old to start having babies." Again Louise smiled meaningfully at the woman seated across from Carrie, enjoying every moment of her obvious humiliation.

Enjoying herself for the first time that day, Carrie turned her attention away from the hateful woman and studied Louise Norton, her hostess. Louise was the epitome of elegance. She was fashionable and sophisticated. Her mauve velvet and brocade suit was simple in cut and accented Louise's unfashionably brown skin and slim build. Like Carrie, she was tall for a woman. She wore her hair in a tight roll pinned at the nape of her neck. In her thirties, like Logan, she was neither plain nor beautiful, merely elegant. But Carrie was not as fascinated with Louise's appearance as she was with her self-assurance. She was refined, but without airs. *This is who I want to be like,* she thought. Carrie continued to observe how Louise gestured and smiled. She watched as she gave orders to the maid and directed the luncheon and conversation effortlessly.

The women's fellowship luncheons were held monthly. This occasion was the highlight of the month for many of the women in the group. They would wear their finery, strutting like peacocks, each trying to outdo the other. The luncheons provided an opportunity for these women to discuss the pressures of being the "first lady" of the church. Eventually they would get to the subject that interested them most: the hussies who pretended to want salvation, when what they really wanted was the preacher. This subject was discussed longer than any others, because it was always followed by the tearful confession of an unsuspecting wife who had caught her husband in a number of compromising situations. The faces changed but the story was almost always the same, with the occasional exception of the hussy being a he instead of a she. This was the glue that held this group together: they had all endured the pain and humiliation of marital infidelity. All it seemed, except Louise.

The subject of infidelity always made Carrie uneasy, especially as her pregnancy advanced. She would leave the meetings wondering if Logan was prone to this behavior, and if she had to worry that he would betray her. Whenever the subject arose, Ruth would always make a comment about how a man had needs that a pregnant wife couldn't fulfill. She would always look boldly at Carrie, as if challenging her to take the bait. Instead, Carrie pretended not to hear the comment or would look at the other woman as if Ruth couldn't possibly be referring to her and Logan. Regardless of how she responded, Carrie always left feeling depressed and inadequate.

Ruth had many friends in the group, and if they spoke to Carrie, it was always very condescendingly. On one occasion, Louise leaned over and whispered to her, "Pay them no mind, honey. Jealousy is a serpent, and you're standing in a snake pit. Look at them: they are all bitter, hurt, and confused women, but most of all they're afraid. They stay and tolerate the ceaseless betrayals and deception. They all proclaim to be Christian women, but they have no faith. You must always remember Hebrews Eleven and wear it as your armor. It says, 'Faith is the substance of things hoped for and the evidence of things not seen.' These women have no hope; don't let them suck you dry and make you like them."

Carrie smiled, tears filling the corners of her eyes. She thanked Louise, and from that day on, Louise became Carrie's best friend and mentor.

5

One afternoon, during one of Louise's visits to Carrie's home—which were frequent due to their blossoming friendship and Carrie's delicate condition—Louise was planning for the upcoming luncheon when Carrie exclaimed, "I'm so tired of those uppity women looking down their high-yella noses at me! Especially that Ruth Pruitt! You would think she and I were best friends and I had stolen Logan right from under her nose! One day I'm going to show them all! Once our church is completed we'll have the second-largest congregation in Houston." Smiling slyly at Louise, she continued enjoying her wishful thinking. "We'll let you and Thomas keep the title of being the largest church. Then Logan will move us out of Studewood into the Fifth Ward—or better yet, I'll be your neighbor and move into the Third Ward."

"I'd like that!" Louise exclaimed, sharing Carrie's excitement. "I can see the faces of all my high-yella neighbors as they think, 'Oh, no! Not another darkie!'" They both burst out giggling until they were near tears. This was their first acknowledgment of the bond of color that existed between them. They were too dark for the light-skinned coloreds, and too light for the dark-skinned coloreds.

Sitting on the deep-rose sofa in the parlor, Louise asked Carrie, "Did I ever tell you how those so-called first ladies treated me when Thomas and I moved to Houston?" Carrie looked at Louise, her eyes

filled with curiosity. "No, I guess I've never mentioned it." She continued: "I had even decided to forgive them for their unconscionable
treatment of me, but now that they're doing the same thing to you. I
won't stand for it." Louise proceeded to tell Carrie how the wives had
not wanted her to be a part of their group. "When we first arrived in
Houston and were introduced at a council reception, the wives
looked stricken when it was suggested that I receive an invitation to
their luncheons. That was until they found out Thomas was the Reverend Thomas Norton. They were forced to reconsider, and suddenly
I began receiving invitations. At first I decided not to attend, but
Thomas, with his forgiving heart, persuaded me to forgive and forget.
Well, I did forgive, but I haven't forgotten. Now these same women
can't get enough of me."

Louise told Carrie that after she had lived in New York, where she
found the women to be interesting and of some substance, she found
these women tedious, and she had absolutely no interest in befriend-
ing them. They now vied for her friendship as a result of her husband's prominence. Although gracious, she had always remained
aloof until she met Carrie. Louise admired her spirit and vitality, and
her refusal to be intimidated or put down. She knew Carrie's struggle
for acceptance would be an uphill climb, so Louise decided to help
her ascend the mountain. Carrie had violated an unspoken rule: she
had dishonored these high-yella women by taking what they considered rightfully theirs. By virtue of the color of their skin, they were
supposed to have the pick of the litter. The darker you were, the more
willingly you were supposed to gladly accept the leftovers.

Logan Daniels was considered the pick of the litter. Most colored
men preferred women who were as close to white as they could get.
This was considered a sign of an accomplished man, and elevated his
stature among other coloreds. If the man was dark-skinned and had a
high-yella wife, it was automatically assumed he was a successful man
by virtue of his wife's skin color.

Louise knew she was lucky to have her Thomas, and she also knew
that he had eyes for only her. They had married in 1896. The only regret they had was they were unable to have children due to an incident with the landowner's brutal son. After he brutally raped Louise,
he beat her unmercifully and left her for dead in the field. Thomas
discovered her and nursed her back from the brink of death. Since
then they had been inseparable, fleeing the cotton fields of Missis-

sippi to triumph and success in New York after Thomas followed his calling to the ministry. And now it seemed they had settled for good in Houston.

Louise ended by telling Carrie how Ruth had set her sights on Thomas. "Honey, she thought with her high-yella tail waving in front of black Thomas, it would make him leave me for her in a snap. But Ruth didn't know my Thomas. She tried every way she knew to get his attention. And when that approach didn't work, she tried to befriend me to get to him! Next she began following his schedule, trying to find out when he would visit a neighboring town. She intended to surprise him. Well, you should have seen the surprise on her face when she came knocking at the door to Thomas's room and I answered it! For a moment I thought she was going to pass out in the middle of the hall! Instead she cleared her throat and asked to speak to Thomas. I told her he couldn't come to the door just then. Well, she began to stammer and turn red, saying the council had some important papers they had instructed her to deliver to Reverend Norton. Well, I looked the hussy dead in the eyes until she squirmed like a cornered rat. I told her, 'Give them to me; I'll see he gets the papers if they're that important.' Well, Ruth started fumbling around and couldn't seem to locate these important papers. I just stood there with my arms folded, watching as she turned red as a beet. I told her she could quit looking; what she wanted she couldn't find in this room."

Louise continued her story as she tried uselessly to suppress her bubbling, contagious laughter. "Well, Carrie, her mouth flew wide open and she started trying to explain to me that I had the wrong idea. 'There is nothing going on between me and Thomas.'" Louise mimicked Ruth. "At that remark I looked at her like she had two heads. At first I started to really let her have it. Then I got so tickled that I burst out laughing in her face, like it was the funniest thing I'd ever heard. Girl, I laughed so hard, people started looking out their doors to see what all the commotion was about. Then Thomas came from the back, tickled at my laughter, asking what was so funny. Well, I told him with Ruth standing right there. She almost busted a vein, she was so furious. The best part is, she turned to stomp away, trying to look insulted, when she tripped on her skirts and stumbled a few steps. I hollered, laughing out loud, enjoying every moment of her embarrassment. Since then, Miss Pruitt and I have had very little to do with each other. We see each other at the luncheons, and I had the unpleasant duty of introducing her to Logan." Louise finished her story remorsefully. Glancing at Carrie sympathetically, she explained, "I sat them next to each other at a dinner held at our home. They were the only unmarried people at the dinner; it seemed logical at the time." Louise sighed regretfully.

Carrie smiled and said, "There's no way you could foresee the future, Louise. I know you probably could not have stopped that woman from getting to Logan."

Louise nodded in agreement and said, "You're absolutely right, whether you know it or not. She'd had her eye on him a long while."

After that day, Louise took Carrie under her wing. She would insure her a place in Houston colored society. Carrie was the daughter Louise would never have. The first item on her agenda was planning the most extravagant baby shower a colored woman ever had. She paid close attention to every detail, ensuring that Carrie's shower was spectacular and talked about for many years to come. At the shower she intended to ask Carrie and Logan, in the presence of their guests, to allow her and Thomas to be the godparents. This was quite an honor for Logan and Carrie, considering the Nortons' position in colored society.

6

Carrie stood up and had just decided to leave the front porch for the coolness of the parlor when she saw Logan turn the corner. As usual, she felt her stomach flip when she first caught sight of him. He was so handsome in his dark suit. She smiled brightly and waved to him, remaining on the porch until he made it up the steps. As he approached, she realized how tired he looked. Now that Ebenezer Church, their church, was almost complete, Logan's work was just beginning, and Carrie knew instinctively that she would have to be patient. He was so involved in the final stages and in making plans for his first sermon that often she felt neglected. Louise assured her that once the congregation was established, he'd return to being the man she'd met and married. Now that the baby shower in her honor was only a day away, she was looking forward to the celebration, and having Logan by her side.

The day of the baby shower there was a gentle breeze that offered some relief from the extreme heat and humidity. Carrie was thankful for the breeze; she hated the humidity—it drained what little strength she had, and she didn't want to ruin her lovely dress. As planned she wore the beautiful pale peach chiffon and georgette dress that had been a present from Thomas and Louise. Louise had taken Carrie to have the waves pressed out of her hair and hot curls put in earlier that morning. The effect was gorgeous; her hair hung down her back in soft curls. The front was pinned and held back with baby's breath. Carrie was breathtaking; she couldn't believe her own eyes. Instead of her thick, long mane, her hair was controlled and beautiful.

At two o'clock the eager guests began arriving. They exclaimed over the beauty of the decor. There were pale peach flower garlands lining the railing of the staircase and the chandeliers. Fresh flowers in shades of peach adorned the tables and mantels. A soft green was used as the accent color. It was also the color that Louise wore. She had decided early on that she would not use the anticipated pink and blue. In the formal parlor, Louise had a chair and footstool just for Carrie. It was also covered in the same pale peach chiffon as her dress. After most of the guests had arrived, Logan, bursting with pride, escorted Carrie into the parlor to take her seat. You could hear a sigh when she entered. She looked like a princess seated upon her throne.

Louise stood back, observing her guests' reaction to Carrie and the decor. She knew this would be an affair that would be remembered. It would be retold for months and Sundays to come. She could not help feeling elated over the desolate look of pain and envy on Ruth's face. *This will give her something to think about,* Louise thought. She continued surveying the room , making sure her guests were being attended to. The wives from the women's luncheons were all present and obviously impressed—and a little envious. As Louise had planned, the shower was a huge success. Socially, it would put another feather in her hat and proclaim Carrie's place in colored society.

For the first time in months, Carrie felt beautiful. She knew that Louise had taken great pains to ensure that everything would be just right for the shower. But she had no idea it would be so elaborate and elegant. It was like a dream come true; she couldn't believe how her life had changed since she'd met Logan. She felt like a princess, and he was her knight in shining armor. "This is the happiest time of my life," she murmured. In that instant, she felt a warm gush of water began to flow down her legs. Stunned, for a moment she thought someone had spilled tea on her beautiful dress. Belatedly she realized that her water had broken as she was blinded by a painful contraction. Crying out for Logan, she startled the women sitting nearby. Just as she spotted Logan and Louise making their way through the crowded room toward her, she was wrenched from her seat by a painful spasm so violent it caused her to scream out. Carrie was in the throes of full labor.

The room cleared around her as Logan knelt by Carrie, concern and fear etched on his face. "This should not be happening here!" he yelled fearfully.

Louise was immediately by his side. "Babies come when the Lord tells 'em, not when we ask. Now, make yourself useful—tell Thomas we need plenty of towels." Taking charge, Louise barked out orders: "Missy, get Samuel! Tell him we need hot water, and call Dr. Washington—tell him we need him now!" Pausing to quickly survey the room, she commanded, "Ladies, please retire to the dining room for dinner. After dinner we will all have a new baby to welcome." Clearly surprised by their hostess, the guests went along as directed.

Carrie was in more pain than she believed humanly possible. She felt the pressure on her pelvic bones as they were being forced to open for the entrance of this child into the world. Just when she thought it couldn't get any worse, she heard relief in Louise's voice as she moved aside so Dr. Washington could take over. He immediately told her to push hard because the head was almost out. She felt tugging as she pushed with all of her might; then she felt a pop and great relief. "The head's out!" he exclaimed. "One more push and you're all done, Carrie." Louise and Logan held her hands as Dr. Washington gave instructions. Pushing one last time, she felt the slithering exit from her body of her baby entering the world. "It's a boy!" Dr. Washington exclaimed. "He's big and healthy, too! I'd say about eight pounds. Carrie, you did mighty fine," said Dr. Washington, smiling as he finished with her. He handed the baby to Louise, and watched as she used the towels and dabbed them in the warm water to gently clean the baby off. Carrie motioned to Louise, holding out her arms for him.

"He's beautiful," Louise admitted, sighing softly as she surrendered the newborn to his mother's waiting arms.

As she grabbed the baby possessively, Logan gave Carrie a confused look as he watched her take their son in her arms. He studied Carrie as she scrutinized the baby, closely inspecting him from head to toe. When she had finished counting his fingers and toes, she looked at his face. There was a fleeting look of fear as she said in a whimper, "His eyes are blue, just like—" Then she shook her head as if dispelling a bad thought. As if an unseen storm had passed, she smiled and said, "Yes, he is a normal boy."

Logan felt an irrational rage at her remark. Was it just the inspection of a new mother who was fearful of having a less-than-perfect child? Or was there a deeper reason for the inspection and remark? Touching his son's brow, he thought, *He looks like a child I would have had with Ruth.* Studying his son's keen features, white skin, and blue eyes, a shiver passed through him as if he'd caught a chill.

Louise watched the exchange between Carrie and Logan. She was thankful there were no other observers. *This is not good,* she thought. Louise remarked to Logan, "Your son made a grand entrance; he gave a new meaning to a baby shower."

Logan visibly relaxed at Louise's words. Smiling to himself, he silently agreed.

Carrie had been so engrossed in her inspection of the baby, she had forgotten about the others. Looking up with a startled expression, she said, "Come, hold your son," and beckoned to Logan, smiling proudly. "What are we going to name him, husband?"

Logan replied without hesitation. "His name is Edward Jesse Daniels, named for both of our fathers." Carrie smiled her approval at his choice of names for their firstborn.

After observing the exchange between Logan and Carrie, Louise prayed that this child was Logan's. Turning, she went to look for Dr. Washington, who had gone to the bathroom to wash, to ask if it was okay to move Carrie to the guest room. Louise was irritated when instead she saw Ruth standing in the doorway. She knew from the smirk on her face that she also had seen the exchange.

Louise turned back to Thomas and Logan, reaching for the baby. "You two will have to carry Carrie to the blue guest room, so she can be washed and rest comfortably in bed."

Logan gently lifted his wife up. "I don't need help to move my Carrie, Thomas. I just need you to lead the way to this blue room. Whoever heard tell of colored folks naming a room after the color it's painted? You getting too uppity, Miss Louise," Logan said playfully, feeling his tension slip away and the joy from the birth returning.

"Humph!" said Louise, turning on her heel to properly wash Edward and dress him in his layette, a gift from her. He had more than fifty people awaiting his introduction in her dining room.

As Logan took Carrie to the blue room, Ruth slowly trailed behind.

He placed Carrie gingerly on the bed and allowed Missy to attend to
her. After kissing her softly on her lips and eyelids, he left her to get
some rest. On his way to the main dining room to be with his new son,
Ruth stood blocking the entrance. "Logan, I would congratulate you,
but the babe looks as though it was fathered by another!" she said,
smirking, cruelly enjoying the pain that momentarily filled his eyes
before he could recover.

Feeling his anger rise as never before, he glared with disgust at
Ruth and said, "I have never been happier. Carrie is not like you—
she's clean, decent. Yes, that is my son—I see myself in him."

Ruth cowered from the verbal assault as though Logan had dealt
her a near-fatal blow with his words. He pushed past her and entered
the dining room and gently took his son from Louise, holding him
tenderly as the guests cooed and exclaimed on his son's beauty and
birth, offering their congratulations. Louise chuckled under her
breath when she saw Ruth hurriedly leave with tear-filled eyes. As
usual, she had chosen the wrong time for her insinuations.

After the last guest left, an exhausted Louise, Thomas, and Logan
bade each other good-night. Logan returned to the guest room adjoining Carrie's room. Louise had taken the liberty of putting Edward
in a bassinet next to Carrie. Instead of sleeping in the adjoining
room, Logan felt an aching loneliness. He needed the closeness of his
wife. Gingerly he crawled into the bed and lay next to her, holding
her gently as he fell into a deep sleep. Edward awoke them in the middle of the night, hungrily crying for his feeding. Logan groaned. This
would take some getting used to, he thought as he groggily picked up
his crying son to pass him to Carrie's waiting arms. He watched
Edward suckle hungrily until he was full. Then he returned his sleeping son to the bassinet. Carrie stayed at Louise's home for five days to
recuperate from the birth of Edward before returning home.

7

During the time that Carrie recuperated at the Nortons', Logan, with the help of Louise, readied their home for Carrie's and Edward's arrival. After Carrie returned home, it took a while for her to become adjusted to being a new mother. At first it seemed it took forever to complete the smallest task. She thanked God for Louise, who was always around to help, with the assistance of Missy, who was in her employ. She was sore from the stitches and very uncomfortable when she sat for long periods or walked too much. She couldn't wait to be completely healed.

Unfortunately, the summer heat didn't make her recovery any easier. But by the time Edward was three months old, Carrie had her routine with him firmly established. He was the light of both Logan's and Carrie's life. They doted on every smile and gurgle.

After Thanksgiving, Carrie began to make preparations for Edward's first Christmas. Logan's and Carrie's parents were planning to visit them during the holidays. This would be the first time that Logan's family had met Carrie and her parents. It would also be their first time seeing their grandson. Megan and Jesse had written confirming that they also were looking forward to meeting their new grandson and in-laws at the same time. As usual, Louise pitched in to help Carrie with her plans. It was decided that both sets of parents would stay with the Nortons. They had much more room, and Carrie and Logan could rest knowing their parents would be comfortable.

The day their parents arrived in Houston, it was lightly flurrying. Carrie was so excited; she couldn't wait to finally see everyone. She especially missed her parents, whom she hadn't seen since leaving Devereaux over a year ago. Walking over to the front window, she nervously looked out again for the approach of the cars carrying Logan's family and the Nortons with her parents.

"It's nearing dusk, and they should have been here a half hour ago!" she said aloud as she checked on Edward. He was still asleep; she stood next to the crib, unable to suppress the smile that crept onto her face. Carrie loved watching him as he slept; it always amused her to watch the way he slept on his stomach with his knees curled beneath him and his hands holding either side of his face. *He looks like he's expecting a picture to be made of him,* she thought.

The ringing of the doorbell startled her out of her reverie, and she hurriedly left the nursery, running for the front door. Excitedly opening it, she was smothered by Megan and Jesse as they rushed in and embraced Carrie. Catching her breath, she was again smothered in the embrace of Edward Daniels, Logan's father. He reminded her of a huge teddy bear. Carrie was so overwhelmed by the size of this man that she didn't notice the reticence in Thelma Daniels as she hung back, quietly assessing their home and Carrie. Logan stood by the door, an amused expression on his face as he and the Nortons watched the frenzy of greetings and introductions. He didn't seem to notice his mother's reluctance; he was also enjoying the friendly exchange between his in-laws.

"Thelma, come greet our new daughter!" beckoned Edward, as he held his hand out for Thelma to grasp. Interrupted from her thoughts, Thelma conceded and went over to meet her daughter-in-law. She had to admit that, despite her caramel-colored complexion, Carrie was beautiful; no wonder Logan was so smitten.

Megan watched the exchange between Thelma and Carrie carefully. Carrie had not been aware of Thelma's hesitation. She had some misgivings when Logan and Carrie had first met about this very thing, but Carrie assured her mother that she had no reason, telling her, "Logan said I will fit right in with his family." After seeing Thelma's response to Carrie, Megan wasn't so sure. She glanced over at Louise, who was watching her reaction, and she knew they were thinking the same thing. As if by unspoken agreement Louise turned and left the room, returning moments later with Edward in her arms.

Both Thelma and Megan ran with arms extended toward their new grandson. Instead of choosing either grandparent, Louise handed Edward to Carrie. But instead of Carrie's having to make a choice, it was now Megan's turn to hang back. Thelma took Edward in her arms, beaming proudly.

"He's just perfect." She turned and spoke to her son. "He looks like you, Logan, but I wonder who he got these blue eyes from. Megan, do blue eyes run in your family?"

Megan froze at the question. Before she could respond, Jesse chimed in: "Both of our fathers had blue eyes, Thelma." Megan looked at Jesse, relieved at his response. Taking a seat, she tried unsuccessfully to regain her composure, realizing that both Carrie and Louise were watching her closely.

Megan politely refused to take Edward when Thelma finally relinquished her hold on him. Blaming her arthritis, she explained that the long trip had caused it to flare up and she would need to rest. Carrie was hurt and confused by what she perceived as rejection from her mother. Hadn't she given them just what they wanted—a nearwhite grandchild?

Over the next few days tensions eased and Carrie was finally able to relax. Between Thelma's measuring gaze and her mother's reluctance to be near Edward, Carrie's nerves were on edge. Logan sensed her unease, but he was not sure what to do. Completely enjoying this visit, he entertained them with his stories of building the new church, and of the various personal dramas of some of the Studewood Heights residents. Attempting to ease the mounting tensions, Louise suggested a shopping trip to her dress- and hatmaker. To her pleasure the group returned later in the day, laughing and gossiping. Even Megan seemed to be more at ease; she surprised Carrie by sitting next to the bassinet as Edward slept and gently rocking him. For the remainder of their visit, Carrie and Logan enjoyed their parents. After the Christmas holidays were over, the Danielses and Devereauxs said their teary farewell to their new grandson, thanked the Nortons for their hospitality, and made plans to visit during the summer. Although saddened by their departure, Carrie and Logan were exhausted from the visit and happy for things to return to normal.

8

Logan finished building the church in January, and the first Sunday in February the church was packed to the rafters. Because of the many acts of kindness of both Carrie and Logan over the last year, word had spread, and folks from Studewood and neighboring areas flocked to hear Rev. Logan Daniels preach. And preach he did! Carrie sat on the front pew, beaming with pride as she held Edward and listened to her husband's sermon. Logan and his message transported her back to Devereaux, when she had first met him and sat enthralled. She looked around at the full pews in wonderment. Their dreams were coming true.

As Carrie glanced around at the crowded pews, she felt a sinking feeling in the pit of her stomach, like a premonition. Looking down the pew, also seated in the front row on the opposite end, was none other than Ruth Pruitt. Carrie was infuriated. *How dare she show up at our church, especially today!* Edward felt the sudden tension in his mother and began to cry noisily. Trying her best to quiet him, but to no avail, she looked helplessly at Logan. He seemed to implore her to quiet him. Frustrated and angry, she got up and hurried out of the church through the side door. Standing outside in the cold air she tried to quiet her raging thoughts and Edward. After a few minutes Edward finally calmed down and she went back inside to wait in Logan's office, hoping Edward had not caught a chill. Reflecting on how she had reacted to Ruth's presence, Carrie made the decision to ignore Ruth Pruitt on future occasions. Louise had already warned her of Ruth's habit of tracking men down by following them from church to church. Ruth knew Carrie could not stop her from visiting the church and listening to Logan's sermons. It was just that Edward was only six months old, and Carrie was more than three months pregnant with their second child. She had not had a chance to return to her old shape before she was back in her maternity clothes again. To make things even more frustrating, Logan wouldn't touch her in an intimate way when she was pregnant because he feared hurting the baby. However, she couldn't help but feel that he was not attracted to her because of her misshapen body. Logan would never admit it, but in her heart she knew it was the truth. Now of all times Ruth was boldly hanging around.

Carrie decided to be more observant of Logan's behavior. After attending all of the women's council luncheons over the past year, she had learned a great deal about the nature of men from their scorned wives.

The days turned into months of Carrie's and Logan's lives being filled with church obligations. It seemed that almost overnight they had attracted one of the largest congregations in their area; as predicted, it was second in size only to the Nortons'. Carrie had no idea that she would be called upon so often to fulfill church-related obligations. Because of this she had to hire a full-time nanny to help her with Edward, especially as she advanced to the last stages of her pregnancy. Often feeling both tired and overwhelmed, Carrie became depressed because she rarely saw Logan except for a few minutes in the morning at breakfast. He worked incessantly, from morning until late in the evening. He also seemed stretched to his limits. When he finally came home in the evenings, Edward was already asleep, and Logan usually fell asleep in exhaustion on the sofa.

Carrie was disappointed and confused at the way their life was turning out. This was not the life that she expected after the church was complete and the congregation established. She decided to voice her concerns to Logan; surely he would agree that they had to have some time alone. To her surprise, he didn't find anything wrong with their lives. He explained that although the congregation was established, it still needed nurturing so it wouldn't slowly slip away. Unhappy with his response, but unable to find an appropriate retort, she let the subject rest for the time being.

So the pattern of their lives continued, with Logan growing more distant as time passed. That summer a daughter, Odele, was born to Logan and Carrie. She was beautiful; she had Logan's complexion with green eyes and softly curling blond hair and features like his mother Thelma.

Twelve months later a second daughter, Sofia, was born, also light-skinned with doelike brown eyes and brown hair. After Sofia's birth, Logan surprised Carrie with a home in the Third Ward section of Houston. She and Louise were finally neighbors. Carrie decided that Sofia would be the last child she would have for a while. It was time to return to her old self and get her husband back. She was aware of the rumors that he and Ruth were having an affair. Carrie had purposely turned a blind eye to the whole thing, hoping it was a stage he was going through and would work itself out. Apparently it was not going to be that easy; now *she* would have to work it out.

She should have stopped it at the onset. Now she was caught in a web of lies and deceit from Logan, so she lost herself in motherhood. Carrie spent all of her time with the children. She totally withdrew from all church organizations and lay groups. She even stopped attending the women's council luncheons. As time passed, the rumors were no longer spread; it was a whispered fact, hinted at whenever she was present. Carrie could not stand the humiliation. She even stopped going to church, and her vacant seat in the front pew caused more rumors to be spread. Some of the parishioners became angry at Logan's blatant infidelity and started leaving the church.

His trustees became alarmed at what they perceived could be an increasing trend. Calling a meeting, they demanded that Logan rectify the situation in his home.

That evening after dinner, Logan asked to speak to Carrie, but instead of apologizing for his indiscretions he accused her of trying to destroy and divide the congregation. Carrie turned on him furiously.

"How dare you insinuate that I have done anything against you when I can't walk down the block without someone snickering or whispering! You are the pastor and you have the nerve to confront me, when you're the one sneaking around like a snake in the grass!"

"Don't you speak to me in that tone, Carrie," Logan responded, angrily clenching and unclenching his fists.

"What are you going to do, Pastor?" she demanded, unafraid in her anger. "Is this what I deserve for loving you? For standing by you, bearing your children and the burden of your mistress? What surprise do you have in store for me next? Will you beat me until I submit? Even that could be no worse than the pain I already feel!" Without re-alizing it, she was screaming at Logan as a flood of tears fell unchecked down her face. She seemed to almost plead her case.

Unprepared for her accusations or the tide of emotions, Logan was drawn in. Moving woodenly, he embraced his wife and asked her for-giveness. Until this moment he had not realized the pain his indiscre-tions had caused his wife and family.

9

The summer of Edward's fourth birthday, Carrie planned a big celebration. She was happier than she had been in a long time. Logan was back to his old self, and she felt secure in her life. Carrie was pleased that they had finally attained their dreams; she enjoyed the pampered lifestyle and social acceptance that having the second largest congregation in Houston afforded them. All of their children were treated well, but especially Edward, who everyone had already determined would grow up to be just like Logan. For his birthday celebration, they were holding the party on the church grounds so they could invite everyone.

On the day before his party Edward became violently ill. Carrie had been at the church working with the women's auxiliary when she received the call from the nanny to come home because Edward was very sick. Leaving the church immediately, she rushed home and found him listless and flushed from a high fever. The nanny told her that he refused to eat or drink. Carrie immediately called Dr. Washington, who came over right away. After checking Edward, he gave him an elixir to help break the fever. The doctor wasn't sure exactly what had caused the high fever, but he told her that if the elixir didn't reduce the fever within an hour she should take him to the hospital.

After Dr. Washington left, Carrie monitored Edward closely, look-

ing for signs of improvement. Changing her clothes, she called Logan
to tell him to come home because Edward was very ill. To her dismay,
he wasn't at the council, where he told her he would be until later in
the evening. She shrugged it off—maybe the meeting had been canceled. She attended to Edward with the intention of trying Logan
later at the church. He would certainly return to the church or home;
there was nowhere else for him to go. As Dr. Washington had all but
predicted, Edward's fever returned and worsened; he was delirious.
Carrie tried to calm herself so she could think clearly. It had been
over an hour and Logan still did not answer at the church. She tried
Dr. Washington, but his wife said he had gone out on a call to deliver
a baby and she didn't know when to expect him back. Finally, at her
wits' end, she called the Nortons and asked them to meet her at the
hospital.

Carrie took Edward to the colored-only entrance at Hermann
Hospital. She was relieved to see Louise and Thomas waiting for her
inside. Thomas ran out to help her carry Edward. She immediately
went to inform the nurse that her son was very sick with a high fever
and pleaded nearly hysterically for a doctor to look at him right away.
In a reproachful tone, the nurse advised Carrie to lower her voice and
sign in. She directed her to be seated until she was called.

"Can't you see he needs help now!" Carrie screamed, forgetting
protocol or repercussions. "My son, my baby, needs help now!" She
forgot this was the South and she was colored. The only thing that
Carrie knew was that her baby was sick and could die if she didn't get
him help. The nurse warned the Nortons to keep Carrie quiet or she
and her son would have to leave. Thomas apologized for her irrational behavior, assuring the nurse that she would calm down until
Edward could be seen. The nurse explained that the colored doctor
had called in sick, which meant Edward would have to wait until all of
the white patients had been seen and treated. Upon hearing this,
Carrie broke down sobbing, pitifully pleading, "Won't someone help
my baby? Can't you see he'll die without help?"

Moving next to her friend, Louise tried to calm Carrie. "I'll go ask
the nurse for a cool towel; that will help with the fever."

Carrie nodded helplessly, feeling defeated.

Thomas and Louise did their best to calm Carrie and assure her
that Edward would be okay. But as they looked at the ashen child they
prayed that it would be so. Finally Carrie regained her composure

and held Edward as though her life depended on it. Thomas was not able to contain himself any longer. "Where is Logan?" he asked.

Shrugging her shoulders in reply, Carrie continued to stare at her beloved son, humming gently to soothe both of them.

Louise began feeling edgy and unsure. She whispered to Thomas, "You go find him; tell him his wife and son need him now!" Thomas got up, knowing immediately where he would find Logan, even though he hoped he wouldn't be there. Carrie continued to rock Edward gently, singing softly to him, completely oblivious of her surroundings. As she smoothed his hair down, she noticed his cheeks were no longer bright red and his eyelids had turned a bluish color. Carrie saw his mouth relax and open slightly; he was not breathing. Putting her lips to his forehead, she prepared herself for the heat from the fever; instead she felt a chill pervade him as the heat of life left his small body. She held him to her as if trying to hold the last ounce of life in. Feeling a moan rise from her throat, she began screaming hysterically. Louise and the nurses rushed over to see what was the matter.

At the same time Thomas and Logan were walking into the waiting area. *Who is that screaming?* Logan wondered. "Oh, no! Nooooo!" he wailed, as at that instant he saw Carrie doubled over on her knees while the nurse and a young white doctor struggled to take Edward from her. Louise held her from behind as she clung to him, gasping for air like a drowning woman. Logan watched, immobilized by fear, until her tortured eyes caught his. For a long moment their eyes met and locked, but he realized she didn't see him. It was that look of blind despair that finally broke the fear's grip on him, and he ran to comfort her. Instead of coming into his embrace, she retreated from him as if his touch burned. Louise motioned to Thomas for help.

Touching Logan on the arm, he instructed, "We better see about Edward. Louise will take care of Carrie for now. Your work will come later." He looked pointedly at Logan to make sure he understood. Thomas felt sorry for him as he watched the man's shoulders stoop. He looked confused and defeated. He had lost so much so quickly, only God knew if he could ever get it back.

Thomas and Louise took over the preparations for Edward's funeral. Logan was overcome with guilt and fear about Carrie's condition. She had been under heavy sedation since Edward's death, refusing to see or speak to anyone. The members of Ebenezer came daily to express sympathy and offer assistance, but Carrie wanted no part of it. She would not even allow Logan in the same room with her.

The funeral was held at Ebenezer Church on a hot Saturday morning. The church was filled to overflowing with people waiting to offer their sympathies for the family's loss. Megan convinced Carrie to attend the funeral; she knew that it was necessary for Carrie to see this through to completion. She would have to grieve in order to get on with her life. It was clear to her that something was very wrong between Carrie and Logan; she assumed it was the sudden and tragic loss of their only son. Megan was certain that after the funeral was over and Edward's death was behind them, they could repair or mend whatever had broken down in their marriage. After the Devereaux and Daniels families took their seats in the front pew by the tiny casket, the funeral began. Standing in the pulpit, intently surveying the bulging congregation, Rev. Thomas Norton cleared his throat that burned with unshed tears as he began Edward's eulogy.

"What comfort can be offered when a child passes on? What can I say to silence the loss of the womb? That it was a blessing? It was God's time? His mercy? The answer to it all is yes. Simply yes. I speak not just to Carrie and Logan, but to all present. The blessing is here in our midst." Pausing, he looked at Logan. "The blessing is that a soul, a spirit, whether its time with us is for a few days, months, or years, that season is as etched into our consciousness as the spirit that is allowed many years. It is not the time that we lived; it is how we lived in that time. In Edward's time, he filled our lives with beauty. Whether it was a hard-won smile, the recipient was always grateful once he bestowed it; or if it was a hug, he seemed to wrap his small arms around your shoulders and embrace your soul. This was evident to every single one of us in this church today." Despite his attempt to hold his emotions in, tears rolled freely from Thomas's eyes. "I am not here to mourn an unanswerable loss, a tragedy. I stand here to praise God and rejoice that He saw fit to bless us for a season with such a sweet, sweet spirit. As we stand here, lift up your hands, palms up, to praise Him. Lift up your hands in supplication that He gives us the strength to go on, knowing that we will see Edward again. God gave Edward parents whose love he feels even as his spirit soars above." In his rich, melodic voice Thomas began to sing: "There's a sweet spirit in this place. There's a sweet spirit in this place, and I can tell that it's the spirit of the Lord." The choir and entire congregation joined in. They stood holding hands across the aisle.

As the service proceeded Carrie sat motionless, her eyes focused on some distant point, wishing to be with Edward, in the safe place that she knew he was in. She hardly listened to the speeches or the songs. She just wished it to be over, feeling violated to have to share this last brief moment with all of these people. Carrie would have preferred to be alone with her son.

She sat woodenly waiting for the assemblage to view the tiny body in the small casket, and prayed for them to stop offering her their mindless sympathies. She focused her eyes straight ahead, preparing herself for her last look at her baby, her last touch of his soft skin. As the procession was close to the end, she noticed a slim figure in a violet suit bend over to kiss her son. *Who would wear that color to my son's funeral?* Carrie wondered angrily. She focused on the woman's face, blindly overcome by a savage rage that encompassed all her years of pain. Before anyone could stop her she was on Ruth Pruitt, tearing at her hair and face with her nails, screaming like a mother bear defending her cub. Momentarily stunned, no one could react as Ruth screamed miserably for help. In that instant Megan, Louise, Thelma, Logan, Thomas, and several others ran to pull Carrie off of Ruth. By the time they were able to pull Ruth free she was bleeding profusely from her mouth and nose and her clothes were torn and hanging loosely.

Megan, not understanding what had caused Carrie to react so violently, returned to check on Ruth once Carrie had been moved to the anteroom and sedated. When she looked at the woman and saw the icy blue eyes, she began to shake uncontrollably. When she sat down on watery legs, Louise noticed her reaction and came over to comfort Megan.

"That's the hussy that took up with Logan. He was with her when Edward died," Louise explained.

"What is her name?" Megan asked numbly, already knowing the answer.

"Her name's Ruth Pruitt. I can't believe she'd come here to the funeral!"

Megan sat in stunned silence, her mind racing. Ruth Pruitt! Logan with her! Her poor Carrie; her burden was heavy. This was all too much to absorb—no wonder Carrie had completely withdrawn. Megan knew she couldn't leave her daughter until she was strong enough to fight back.

Several weeks after the funeral, things still had not returned to normal, as Megan had hoped. Carrie became more reclusive, and continued to alienate Logan. She refused to look at her daughters, as if the very sight of them were unbearable. It was obvious to Megan her daughter was willing herself to die; she had seen the signs before. When Robert Devereaux was found dead by the creek, Maman, her mother, died five days later. Now her Carrie was trying to do the same to be with Edward. But Megan was not about to stand by and see that happen.

Megan had not moved from Carrie's room for hours. She stood vigil, watching and waiting for the sedative to wear off and Carrie to awaken. When she saw a slight movement of Carrie's head and her eyelids tremble, fighting to open and then finally losing the battle, her stomach dropped. She had seen this very same response from her own mother just hours before she slipped away to heaven. She did not intend to let the same thing happen to Carrie. Without thinking she shouted, "God gave him to you, and He took him back! He was never yours, Carrie!"

Carrie's eyes flew open, trying to focus on whoever was saying these dreadful things to her.

Megan continued battering her with words: "You're not the only one to lose. Logan lost, and Odele and Sofia lost. We all lost. And now we're losing you. How much death should there be before enough is enough? Did you ever stop to think maybe God had a reason for taking him? Maybe this one slipped by and shouldn't have been born! It's not natural having a child by your own granddaddy." Megan's voice was filled with fury; she would not let Carrie die like this.

"You're a liar!" Carrie screamed in a bloodcurdling tone, tears running freely down her face as she fought to sit upright to face her accuser.

Megan shook her head. "I'm not lying, Carrie. You've known it all along, but you've denied it. He never looked like Logan—you knew that. The thin nose, the icy blue eyes—that child be the spitting image of his granddaddy. The seed was sick, Carrie, and what looks like a punishment was mercy and grace. If the seed is sick, it's better off dead. I told you it all happened to me, child."

Inhaling deeply, Megan continued: "You were not my first child. I had one before you—my papa's baby . . . she was my daughter and my sister. She also had those same icy blue eyes. Maman sent me to live with a family in Evergreen, Texas. They were childless. I didn't want no baby for Devereaux, so I gave it to them. I never cared if she lived or died, 'cause I knew the seed was sick, poisoned. These people were named Pruitt; they named the baby girl Ruth. I came back to my Jesse and after years of trying we finally had you. At first I thought God had cursed me, because you were so dark, I thought Jesse would leave me. Turned out, of all my children, you were my blessing. Let God figure out your future, baby. Don't hold this against Him. You have a lot to live for. I don't know what's gonna happen with you and Logan. I do know you can't fight lying down. You have two children who love you, and Logan loves you too, but he's tasted from a jaded apple. I don't intend to leave until you can fend for yourself. This Ruthelen Pruitt be your half sister by birth, but I can't feel no love for her; she should have never been born!" Megan made this last statement with an unbending finality.

Carrie stared at her mother, allowing the words to penetrate. When the truth hit home, she doubled over in pain. There was just too much agony, too many wounds. She wanted to be free of it all, the lies and the suffering. She had pursued happiness and never found it. She had felt it near, but never close enough to touch. Closing her eyes tightly, she tried to clear her mind of all the disappointment. If she had to live, she could not—would not—continue to live as she had.

Swinging her legs off the bed and standing up shakily, on watery knees, Carrie hoarsely whispered, "I want a bath, I need to get dressed, and I want to see my children."

Megan got up, placing her hands on each side of her daughter's face. "Baby, you have to find your own peace; then before you know it you're filled with joy and happiness. I'm not saying there won't be any more walks in the valley or mountains to climb. I'm just saying that once you put all of your faith in God, you'll be better rested and fit for the journey. Sit down, baby; Mama will run your bathwater for you." Megan left the room to tend to Carrie's bath. Kneeling beside the tub to run the water, she wept in a prayer of gratitude.

10

The news of Edward's death had traveled back to Devereaux, Louisiana, by way of her parents, Megan and Jesse. When Carrie's childhood friend John Browning heard about the unfortunate tragedy, he became obsessed with concern about her well-being. He decided to travel to Houston to see her for himself. In the years after Carrie left for Houston, John had become one of the richest colored men in Louisiana. He started as a blacksmith and, in his spare time, created a handheld machine that picked and processed cotton in the fields. The machine caught on so well because it not only increased the speed with which the cotton was picked, but it was also much safer to use by the field hands. The machine became so popular that he patented his idea and opened a manufacturing plant. He was so busy developing his businesses that he had not found the time to settle down or get married. He also had never found anyone who could replace the woman he had fallen in love with as a girl, Carrie. When he learned of the death of her son, he waited a few months, then scheduled a trip to Texas. It would give him an opportunity to make new contacts and see Carrie.

One week after his secretary called her, Carrie met John for lunch near the campus of Prairie View A&M, a colored university outside of

Houston. She recommended this location because she didn't care to be seen by any of the local gossips. When the cab drove up to the restaurant, Carrie's stomach was filled with butterflies of excitement. John was waiting in front of the restaurant for her. He was even more handsome than she remembered. Success had indeed agreed with him. After seeing John again, Carrie was glad that she had taken such care in choosing an outfit for this occasion. She had worn an auburn dress with a matching coat trimmed in fox. The fox hat completed the dramatic effect of her attire; she wore her hair pulled in a chignon, a hairstyle that was popular for white women at the time.

When the door of the cab opened, John was mesmerized as Carrie swung her long, shapely legs out of the cab and stood up. He was transported to being the shy nine-year-old who would pull her long braids or tease her until she cried. He had not been certain of what to expect, especially since her parents had informed him that she was a mother of three young children. But nothing could have prepared him for her poise and beauty. They were both momentarily flooded with memories and full of emotions. When John flashed his brilliant smile, she knew what had been missing in her life—him. Escorting her into the restaurant, John beamed with pride as people stared admiringly at them.

After they were seated, he heedlessly reached for her hand across the table. Instead of pulling away, she relaxed at his touch. "I can't believe you're here," he began. "I kept checking with my secretary, expecting you to cancel."

"Why would you think that, John? If anyone was surprised it was me . . . that you even remembered me."

"How could I forget? Do you remember the last day that you spoke to me?"

Hardly tasting the food, Carrie looked slightly uneasy as she recalled that day. "Yes, I do remember that day . . . how could I forget? It was my first kiss."

"Then you recall what I said to you before you ran away?" he persisted.

"That one day I would be your wife . . . yes, but now that is not possible. I'm sure you know that I am married."

"Are you, Carrie? Is that door really closed? Or do the same standards apply?"

"I'm not sure what standards you're speaking of. . . ."

"All right then, I suppose I'll have to see for myself. Consider this a first step; I've been keeping my eyes and ears open, and somehow I don't believe you've found what you already had, or should I say have? Just know that I mean you no harm, but I have never forgotten my vow. You should have been mine."

Caressing each other's fingers, they talked for hours, as if their future depended on being caught up in the past. When they had nothing left to say, they tried to satisfy themselves in the simple pleasure of the touch of a hand.

Carrie knew it was late and that she should call a cab for the return to Houston, but she wanted to delay the inevitable departure. John reasoned that he should be satisfied with the time they had spent over lunch and let her go back to her life, but he couldn't—not this time. Not without a fight. That preacher had taken what was his all those years ago, when he wasn't equipped to fight. But time had brought about a welcome change. Now he had the leverage of both wealth and power. He would use both if he had to, in order to get what he wanted. And he wanted nothing more than Carrie. Furthermore, he knew she was not happy. When she looked at him, he felt euphoric, as he had when he was a child in Devereaux, many, many years ago. He was not a gambling man, but he would take a chance and bet that he'd win her this time.

John sensed that Carrie was not ready to leave for home either, but he knew that she must go, so as not to raise suspicion. "I'll call a cab for you. I know you have a long ride back," he said, gently touching the tips of her fingers.

"Thank you." She smiled and sighed, feeling torn; she wished it were only possible not to have to return to Houston. John ignited something deep within her that she hadn't felt in years. She had spent so much time trying to be accepted and approved of by so many, that she had missed what was always before her. She had wanted Logan for all the wrong reasons, and she had paid dearly for it.

"Carrie? Are you okay?" John asked softly, interrupting her musings.

"I'm fine," she replied, trying to record his face in her memory. "It's just . . . I was thinking how much I've missed you, and I hope that with your busy schedule you'll keep in touch with me."

"Of course I will. I've bought a home not far from you." His comment surprised himself; he had done no such thing, at least not yet. Now it was Carrie's turn to look surprised and a little uneasy. John, realizing he might have overstepped his boundaries and was perhaps moving too fast, explained further.

"I'm looking in Texas, primarily Houston, for new business opportunities. It is easier to move about and conduct business if I have a permanent residence here. It is my fourth home; I have one in each state where I presently own businesses."

"Oh, I see." Carrie's mind was racing. She was delighted that he would be so close, but fearful of her own self-control.

As they left the restaurant John escorted her to the waiting cab. Seating her in the back, he bent over and brushed her lips gently with his. Again the butterflies returned full force as she let out a deep sigh.

"I will be in touch, Carrie, and soon."

"Good-bye, John."

Closing the door, he stepped back and waved good-bye, watching as the cab pulled away from the curb and made its way back toward Houston. He had much to think on. First things first; he had to find a home in the Third Ward, and fast.

II

Carrie settled back into her routine of being a dutiful wife and mother. There continued to be an air of sadness that surrounded her, which most attributed to the loss of Edward. Only she knew that what she felt was not only the loss of her child, but also of what might have been. John had not contacted her since their lunch almost three months ago. She knew that he was very busy, but somehow she thought she would have heard from him long ago. Word spread as quickly as a wildfire when he purchased his home on Charleston, one block away from her. Louise was the first to tell her of his home, and that he had joined the Nortons' church. Carrie felt an irrational jealousy at the news. She chided herself: What right did she have to be upset? He was a single man and she was not a single woman. So she began to brace herself for the conversations about the eligible John Browning.

One afternoon, while Carrie was visiting with Louise, the subject of John arose. Louise watched Carrie closely, noticing how she stiffened at the mention of John's name. There was a change in Carrie that Louise didn't like, but she didn't quite know how to approach the subject without offending her. She loved Carrie and would never risk their friendship. Carrie had become very guarded since Edward's death. Louise knew that this attitude of indifference had turned

Logan completely around. As a result, he had finally gotten rid of
Ruth Pruitt.

Carrie sat motionless, waiting for Louise to confide the latest news
about John. What would it be this time? she thought. His new house
around the corner or the new business he had relocated to Houston?
However, she was not prepared for what was to follow.

"You know that Ruth Pruitt resigned from the church council last
month," Louise began slowly.

"Yes, who cares!" Carrie replied impatiently, wondering why Louise
would bring up that dreadful woman. She had nothing to do with
John.

"Well, she has been hired by the Browning Company, as John
Browning's personal assistant," she continued, allowing time for this
fact to sink in. "She's been telling everyone that he is in love with her
and it's only a matter of time before they're married. Of course, most
don't believe her, what with her reputation and all. I just wanted to be
the one to tell you. I didn't want you to hear it at the luncheon tomorrow."

"What do you mean? Ruth's got to be almost ten years John's senior!" Stunned, Carrie could not hide her reaction. She burst into
tears, sobbing so hard that Louise became alarmed. She had expected a reaction—however, not this one.

"Carrie, calm down. What is this all about?" She tried to console
Carrie, but to no avail. She waited as her friend cried it out. Louise
held her hand, uncertain how to proceed. "How do you know him,
Carrie?"

Between gulping sobs, she told Louise about John, how they had
met as children and fallen in love as teenagers, how she had shunned
him because he was a common laborer and too dark. She recalled
how she had sought acceptance among the light-skinned Negroes,
and, although she had always loved John, she never allowed it to surface for fear of always living without acceptance from her family and
what she thought of as colored society. She didn't understand that
money or position opened all doors, and that the only color people
saw was green, until she met Thomas and Louise, but by then it was
too late. Carrie told Louise about Devereaux and how her grandfather, who was really Edward's father, had raped her. How she had
eventually allowed Logan to go to Ruth because she couldn't stand to
be touched by him. Each time he came to her with his white skin, she

was reminded of Robert Devereaux and rejected him. Finally, she ended by telling Louise about the lunch with John months before, in Prairie View.

Louise, stunned by the revelations from Carrie, sat quietly thinking. "What can I do to help? I know you must see him again!"

Carrie looked up at her friend through swollen eyes filled with hope. "I don't know how I can make that happen. He lives right around the corner, yet I never see him," she said, disheartened.

"I know of a way," Louise whispered in a conspiratorial tone. "John will be meeting with Thomas and the church elders in an hour. They'll be in our library. All we have to do is wander in a few minutes before, and I'll distract Thomas."

It would have to be Carrie's decision. She knew she had opened a dangerous door; Carrie would have to decide if she wanted to travel through it.

To her amazement, Carrie brightened immediately. "How do I look? Are my eyes too red and swollen?"

Louise studied her momentarily. "Nothing that a cold towel and some rouge won't fix." Not wanting to be an accomplice, but knowing that her friend needed closure with John, Louise assisted as a coconspirator. As Carrie freshened up, Louise went to the library to engage Thomas in conversation.

Thomas sat at his desk, preparing for the meeting that was about to take place. He was surprised when Louise entered, distracting him with purposeless questions. Nevertheless, he put his pen down and gave her his undivided attention, hoping that this would be quick and he could go back to his preparations. However, it was not going to be that easy. Louise sat down and settled in.

Next, Carrie knocked at the door, and Louise invited her in as if they were having a social occasion, instead of its being the middle of his business day. Irritated, Thomas remarked, "Ladies, I hate to be rude, but Louise, you seem to have forgotten I have an important meeting in a few minutes and I still need time to finalize this paperwork." Before he could convince them to leave him alone, he heard the chime of the doorbell, followed by John Browning being escorted into the library.

Thomas immediately stood up. "Welcome to my home, John."

"Well, thank you for the invitation. I look forward to today's meeting." The two men shook hands.

"May I offer you a seat and introduce you to my wife, Louise, and her closest friend, Carrie Daniels?"

"Good afternoon, ladies," John responded easily, not allowing his surprise to register in his expression.

"May I offer you a seat? The elders are running a few minutes late. Do you mind waiting to begin the meeting?" Before he could engage John in further conversation, Louise excused them both from the room, surprising him by her firm grasp as she led him through the door.

John stared at Carrie, knowing he had to take advantage of this chance encounter. He had tried every way he could to see her. On the occasions that he had his secretary call, the housekeeper always said she was out or with the children and couldn't be disturbed. After months of trying, he had almost given up hope of ever seeing her again, until his good fortune this afternoon. Who would have guessed he'd run into Carrie at a business meeting? As usual she was stunning. She no longer looked like the country girl he'd known. Carrie was poised, refined, everything that he wanted in a wife.

"Carrie, why have you been avoiding me?"

Her mouth fell open in disbelief at the question. "Avoiding you? Why, how can I avoid you when you've never even tried to see me? As a matter of fact, it was you who said we would see each other again, and soon. At least, I think that was what you said." Feeling her anger rise, she thought, *How dare he think that I'm going to run after him! After all, I am a married woman.* Before he could reply, she went on: "By the way, I hear congratulations are in order!"

John looked puzzled at her statement. "Congratulations for what? The new factory?"

"No, of course not! Congratulations on your anticipated marriage to Ruth Pruitt!" she said, not able to defeat the tears that flooded her eyes.

Shocked at the outburst and grasping the magnitude of her remark, he threw his head back, laughing heartily.

"You have the wrong person. Ruth Pruitt is my personal assistant, nothing more," he said in a tone of finality. "The only wife I've ever wanted, then or now, didn't want me. As I remember, I was too poor, too dark, a common laborer. 'I want love, Daddy! Why do I have to settle? Because I'm not bright enough?' "

Carrie, stung by the emotion in his words and remembering that explosive argument with her father, looked at him questioningly. "How did you know? How did you hear?" she asked. "Your father asked me to come over that evening, because he knew that I had been in love with you since we were children, and my love had only grown over the years. After you had not married, he assumed it was due to the fact that you also loved me and didn't know how to tell them. He thought that if he and Megan arranged the marriage, you would be relieved and happy. Instead, you considered it a put-down, as though they didn't love you, because of who and what I was. What you didn't understand was that they were more sensitive to you and your feelings than they were to any of your sisters or brothers combined." Carrie's mind raced at the enormity of her mistake; she had ruined two lives and hurt her parents.

Aware of the pain and confusion on her face, John longed to hold Carrie close, to comfort her. But he also needed to let her know that she was not the only one who had been scarred in Devereaux. The town had taken its toll on many, and she could not be blamed for her beliefs. He knew that together they would be the salve for each other's festering wounds. But he just stood planted on the other side of the room. He hesitated to move closer to her for fear of discovery, and the consequences she could suffer. Instead he stood directly in front of her. Fervently he whispered to her, "I have always loved you, Carrie. I am here in Houston because of you. I came to right the wrong that was done to us years ago. I know about your husband and Ruth. I also know you don't love him, if you ever really did! I'm here to make you mine!" With that he took her fingers, caressing them with his, and placed a lingering kiss on the tips.

Carrie stared longingly into his eyes, wanting him with every cell in her body. "I need to see you alone," he insisted. Unthinkingly, Carrie nodded her consent, not trusting herself to speak.

John placed his calling card in her palm. "Call me night or day, no matter the time. You can come to my house; I purchased it with you in mind." He lightly planted a kiss near her lips. "Please don't make me keep waiting for you, Carrie," he whispered as he turned to join Thomas and the elders in the parlor. At that moment Louise reappeared in the doorway, clearing her throat noisily. Startled, John straightened himself and made a show of searching for a pen. Carrie flushed guiltily and mumbled something about the powder room. She hurriedly made her exit. Louise escorted John to join Thomas and the elders in the parlor, then excused herself and returned to the sunroom, where she found Carrie sitting staring despondently out the windows. Louise took a seat next to her. Carrie turned to her friend, her eyes full of sorrow.

"I don't know what to do, Louise! He loves me and I love him. He wants to see me alone and I want to be alone with him." Carrie gloomily pondered her circumstances.

Louise had not expected this reaction from either of them, and her mind raced, trying to stop what she so innocently believed she had started.

"Carrie, you've got to come to your senses!" she demanded. "You can't leave Logan—or your children, for that matter. If you see him alone, you know nothing good will come from it."

Carrie turned and looked at her friend sadly. "Nothing good, except I would be happy for once in my life. For only an hour of happiness, I could exist fifty years without complaint. At least I could say I experienced true happiness," she said, her voice full of sorrow.

After a few minutes had passed, Louise asked, "Is a moment of happiness worth a lifetime of sorrow?"

Carrie just continued to stare out the window, as if she had not heard Louise's last question. "It doesn't matter anyway," she said, breaking the lengthy silence. "I found out I am pregnant again. Once he finds out, I'm sure John will go on with his life, wherever that takes him."

Louise slowly released the breath she held in relief. "You see, Carrie, God will help you, even when you can't help yourself. He puts obstacles in our way to deter us. And then He leaves you free will to either let the obstacle remain, or go around it. You didn't choose John when you were free to choose. I know that you have been in pain over the loss of Edward, and over Logan's infidelities. I have watched you suffer. As your friend, I'm just not sure that leaving Logan to go away with John is the answer for you."

Carrie sighed in frustration. "You just don't understand how I feel! You can't! You've always had Thomas; he's always been there for you. I want someone who is there for me. I'm sick of this charade. Logan is remorseful now, but how long will that last? Until he decides he misses Ruth or finds someone new?" she said emphatically. Feeling stifled, Carrie jumped up from her seat and rushed out without a backward glance. She had never exposed herself the way she had today.

Louise continued to sit and stare, engulfed in a torrent of thoughts. *If it were me, what would I do? What would I want Carrie to do, as my friend? Support me in my decision, or determine right from wrong?* Torn between many leanings, Louise began to move her mouth silently in prayer, seeking out the only way she knew to put an end to her indecision and find an answer she could live with.

Carrie rushed blindly from Louise's house, pausing at the end of the walkway to get her bearings and walk home. She didn't know that John was standing and staring out the window, oblivious to Thomas and the conversation among the church elders. He was startled as he noticed Carrie leaving the house, obviously in great distress. Pardoning himself from the group of men, John immediately left the house and followed her. Stopping near the sidewalk, he called after her.

Turning to look back, Carrie halted in her tracks at the sound of his voice. There was no better time to tell him than now, she decided. After all, why have him wait for a call she didn't dare make? As he approached, Carrie resigned herself to see this thing through, although she was unable to mask the sorrow in her eyes that overflowed from her very soul.

Alarmed at her expression and wooden stance, John rushed to her. "What's the matter, what happened in there? Did Louise see us? Does she know?"

"Yes, she knows. Not because she saw us, but because I told her about us. Louise told me you were coming to meet Thomas today, so I stayed. I wanted so desperately to see you again, even if it was only for a moment. I've waited and wondered why I haven't heard from you. Then I began to hear the rumors about you and Ruth, and I was so envious that it couldn't be me." The words seemed to tumble out of their own accord. "I felt so happy when you said it was me that you wanted and not Ruth. I wanted to forget everything, my marriage, my obligations, and just pack up my children to go with you. But I know it's not possible. There's no future for us," Carrie replied between sobs that couldn't be suppressed.

John, mindful that they were standing in the middle of the sidewalk, led Carrie slowly to his car, taking care that they would appear innocent to any unseen onlookers. Driving toward her house, he continued past, turning at he corner and circling back to his home. Parking the car in the rear of the house, he led her through the rear entrance. Once inside, he lifted her into his arms and carried her through the grand hallway to the den. Placing her gently on a chaise longue, he turned to light the fireplace to chase the chill from the room.

Pulling up a footstool, he knelt in front of her, gently kissing her, lingering to enjoy the feel of her skin and the sweet taste of her mouth, a taste he had yearned for. Touching her face tenderly, his fingers began the exploration of a blind man; she returned his kisses and caresses with a passion and enthusiasm that matched his own.

Carrie reasoned that she must tell John about her pregnancy, before they went too far.

As if he read her mind, he put his lips next to her ear and whispered, "Carrie, there is a future for us." He continued as if they had not been interrupted from their conversation on the sidewalk. "I knew when I came that it wouldn't be easy. I know you are married. I also know you're not happy. I would gladly accept the responsibility of raising your children as mine. I would also like us to have children of our own someday."

At his confession, Carrie knew she had to tell him. "You don't understand, John! I'm pregnant now!" she blurted out miserably.

Gazing at her lovingly, he continued to stroke her back with his hands, pondering her last statement and the ramifications of what he was about to say. For Carrie the silence seemed to draw out for hours, when in fact it had been only minutes. Finally John seemed to have reached a decision. Turning her face to look directly into her eyes, again he proceeded.

"I'm a patient man, Carrie. I can wait. I have been looking at possibilities for a new business in New York. I had put it off to stay in Houston near you, but now instead I will leave soon." He gave her a penetrating stare as he continued: "I will busy myself and stay away from you until shortly after this child is born. During that time I will stay in touch with Louise Norton, in case I need to return sooner. When I return it will be to make you mine at any cost. We are not finished. We can't be finished until we are one, Carrie. I need you to complete me." Tenderly he pulled her gently to him.

Molded to his body by his embrace, Carrie wished for more, but she was thankful for his patience and another chance at happiness.

Placing a hand on each shoulder, caressing her eyes with his, he leaned down to kiss her, sealing his intentions upon her lips.

Afterward, they dressed soundlessly. Then John took her hand and wordlessly led her back to the car. They made the short drive in continued silence: words were no longer necessary. As she got out of the car he gazed at her lovingly and told her he would see her next year. She acknowledged with a brief nod and turned back to enter the house that until an hour ago she had thought of as home.

Carrie was unaware that Logan had decided to surprise her and had come home early. He had watched in surprise from the hall window when he saw a car turn in to the drive. He was disturbed to see Carrie in the passenger seat, and even more disturbed to see that John Browning was the driver. Of course, he knew of John Browning. Everyone in colored society knew of him. But what was he doing with Carrie? Logan became frustrated that the trees that lined the drive hindered his view. Carrie stayed in the car a little longer than was normal, and she looked upset as she got out and closed the door. He continued watching her as she strolled up the fieldstone path to the front door. Before she could put the key in the lock, Logan flung the door open, looking past her at the car pulling out of the driveway. "Is anything the matter, Carrie?" Logan inquired, unable to mask his insecurity.

Startled out of her reverie, Carrie replied. "I was visiting Louise and became ill. Mr. Browning offered to take me home, since it was on his way," she said, lying easily.

Logan was very possessive of Carrie and didn't like the idea that another man—especially John Browning, a man who was not only single, but rich as well—had driven her home. Logan eyed her suspiciously. She did not look well, and the color seemed to have drained from her cheeks. His attitude quickly shifted to concern, and he became preoccupied with seeing to her comfort. He went over to assist her to the bedroom. After she was settled in and relaxing, he sat on the side of the bed, worry written all over his face. "Is there anything I can get you?"

Carrie smiled, seeing the concern in his eyes. "It is nothing I haven't endured three times before, Logan. Dr. Washington said I should be fine in about six months."

As the enormity of her statement dawned on him, his face lit up. "You're pregnant? I'm so happy! Lord knows I wanted another child."

Carrie was surprised at Logan's reaction: she never knew he desired another child.

12

Five and a half months later, Carrie gave birth to a son. Logan named him Eddie, after both his father and his deceased son. At first Carrie started to object; then she stopped short. She understood Logan was trying to bury his own ghosts. Eddie was a beautiful baby who captivated anyone he came in contact with. He was fair-skinned with coal-black hair and eyes. Her precious son entranced Carrie. His disposition was so pleasing that before long he had managed to overshadow the grief they had all held on to from the loss of Edward.

Shortly after Eddie's birth, John Browning returned to Houston, as promised. Over the months of her pregnancy, he had maintained contact through Louise. Each month he would send her a dozen long-stemmed red roses to remind her of his undying love for her. Again, many mothers who were trying to match him with their unmarried daughters received his return to Houston with much attention. The list of single women vying for his attention grew longer. But to their growing chagrin, he engrossed himself in his business and bided his time, waiting patiently until things quieted around him. When Eddie was four months old John contacted Carrie through Louise. By now Louise despised her position as a liaison, but she felt obligated after Carrie had pleaded with her to give her any message from John.

Once Carrie and John were together, they knew they could not bear to be apart again. She began to devise plans and excuses for her many trysts with John. Often she would put Eddie in his stroller and take him for long walks alone. During her walks she would always detour to John's home. As Eddie would nap, she and John would luxuriate in their erotic rediscovery of each other. They found enjoyment not only physically; they reveled in each other's company. John was completely at ease with her and talked to her about everything from his businesses to his dreams and childhood. Carrie was also able to open up to John in a way she never had with Logan. She told him about the rape and about Edward, and why she had not wanted to marry him when they were in Devereaux. In many ways she was his soul mate; they shared a bond shared by few people in life.

When the subject arose time and again of Carrie's leaving Logan, it was always distressing. Although Carrie loved John with all of her heart, she also loved her children, especially Eddie. Fearing the repercussions if she denied him his father, she constantly tried to make John understand. But as time passed, he could not hide his pain or disappointment at her decision to stay. She became ever fearful that he would leave her; she knew she couldn't stand the void that would be left without him. But since Carrie had given birth to Eddie, she felt a love and possessiveness about this child that was all-consuming. She rationalized that it was due to the loss of Edward. But deep down she knew that wasn't true. Eddie had a uniqueness that overshadowed any past grief. His love was all-encompassing, making everyone vie for the position of his favorite—everyone but Carrie. He constantly reinforced his love and admiration for her almost from birth.

By the time Eddie was six years old, rumors about Carrie and John were bandied about in colored circles all over Houston although the realtionship had cooled for several months since her refusal to leave her marriage. One afternoon Logan overheard several women from the council discussing Carrie and John. They could barely contain their humor at the fact that Logan was getting cuckolded and it was his just desserts for his affair with Ruth Pruitt. Now that Logan was met with same hurtful rumors that had been a way of life for Carrie, he found it unbearable. He raced home to confront Carrie. Blinded by his jealousy and consumed with rage, he struck her repeatedly as she refused to deny his accusations. Hearing her cries for help, then mercy, Eddie ran to defend his mother, only to be caught in the onslaught of his father's self-righteous rage. Battered and bloody, Carrie lay on the rug in the middle of her room. Fearful of being killed, she had assumed the fetal position to protect herself. At the sight of Carrie bleeding and the bruise coloring on the side of Eddie's face, Logan's sanity and reason returned. He was beside himself with sorrow for his actions.

When he tried to help Carrie to her feet, she cringed in fear of another blow. Her fear of him stung like a whip and, unable to curb his emotions and what he perceived as rejection, he brutally picked her up and carried into their room. Dropping her unceremoniously on the bed, he tore her clothes from her body and brutally raped her.

Realizing his intent an instant too late, Carrie began to thrash and fight with all the strength she could muster. This only agitated the angry excitement Logan felt. Finding his release, he pulled up his pants, leaving her alone in her pain and misery.

After violating Carrie, Logan left the house to go to Ruth. Frightened of his return, Carrie called Louise and asked for her help. Shocked by the unexpected call and the revelation that followed, Louise and Thomas rushed over immediately and took Carrie and the children to their house. When Louise saw Carrie's condition she burst into tears. "What type of brutal animal would do this to his own wife?"

"I deserved it. I should have been more careful. I shamed him."

"You shamed him?" Louise exploded. "What about the years of shame you endured? And he's still whoring around! Except you don't care anymore!" At this Carrie burst into uncontrollable sobs.

Louise called Dr. Washington to look at the cuts and bruises on Carrie and to make sure that her ribs had not been broken. She had to put some distance between herself and this situation, because right now she wanted to see Logan hurt.

By morning the scandal of Logan's attack on Carrie had spread from Third Ward to Studewood Heights. As Logan prepared to leave the church for home that evening, John Browning met him. Louise had called John to tell him of Carrie's condition before he heard it from the gossips.

When Logan saw John, he was filled again with a rage so strong he desired to kill him. What he didn't know was that it was John's intention to do him bodily harm. He had not been able to rest at the thought that Logan had harmed Carrie. He would ensure that Logan would never touch her again. Before Logan could raise a hand in defense, John was beating him savagely. Fortunately for Logan, some of the church volunteers saw what was going on and broke it up. It took four men to keep John away from Logan. A dazed, bruised, and bloody Logan lay in the dirt, suffering further humiliation in front of his church members.

As John pulled away from his captors, he leaned over Logan and spat out, "The next time you want to fight, find a man. I'm right up the block, preacher." Getting into his car, he hurriedly drove to the Nortons' only to be turned away by Thomas, who was still angry with Louise for her involvement in their affairs. She had tearfully confessed her role after she realized that Carrie could have been killed. Thomas wanted no part of this mess spilling over into his life. He deplored Logan, but it was up to Carrie to end her marriage or make it work. He knew there was much more involved; he just didn't know how deep the involvement was. He also had heard the rumors; he chose to look the other way. As a man of God, he put it in His hands to straighten out.

During Carrie's recuperation at the Nortons', John sent fresh long-stemmed red roses daily, accompanied by a card with *John* written on it. Daily, Thomas refused to accept delivery, and the flowers were returned. Logan came each day to visit and try to make amends for his irrational behavior and to ask his wife to return. Eventually Carrie returned home with Logan, thinking John had forsaken her. Although she returned to her own home with Logan, things had changed dramatically between them. They were polite strangers again. Due to his insecurities about John Browning, Logan was no longer able to perform sexually with her. What he didn't know was that the love and affection that had developed between John and Carrie both transcended and encompassed the act of making love.

As time passed, Carrie became depressed and despondent from her self-imposed exile from John. But she had decided that further contact between them was unfair to both John and her children. She did not intend to cause her children any more embarrassment than they had already suffered because of her. She knew that if she were to see John again, she wouldn't have the strength to leave him. She would be caught in a web that would entangle her without release. Carrie changed her whole lifestyle. She dismissed the help, with the exception of a weekly housekeeper, and spent all of her time with

Odele, Sofia, and Eddie. This was one of the happiest times of their young lives, until Carrie found out she was pregnant again.

This time Logan was not pleased when told of Carrie's pregnancy. Oblivious of the night that he had violently raped Carrie, he did not believe this child was his. Although John had moved away from Houston several months prior, Logan was still suspicious of Carrie and unsure whether she and John were still having clandestine meetings. He became increasingly distant after he found out she was pregnant, eventually moving into another bedroom in the house.

Carrie withdrew even further, limiting her outside communication only to Louise. She knew the gossips were going wild with rumors about the questionable paternity of this child. Although Carrie knew for sure that the child was Logan's, she felt confident that after the child was born, all rumors and insinuations would be put to rest when the gossips saw the child looked like the rest of the Daniels clan.

13

Thanks to Louise, Carrie made it through the loneliest period in her adult life. She spent her time writing letters to her mother, who would apprise her of the varied lives of her siblings who were passing for white and still remaining in contact with Megan. She had written to her mother about John and her undying love for him when he had first contacted her several years before. It came as quite a surprise to find out that John always visited her parents on his frequent visits to Devereaux. She was thankful for the special bond that still existed between herself and her parents.

Whenever she wasn't writing to her parents, she would often sit with Louise, making quilts from clothes the children had outgrown. Many times they would sit together in silence in the parlor or on the veranda as they sewed, enjoying their closeness.

When Carrie went into labor, Louise was there, as she had been for Edward's birth, this time without Logan, who failed to come home when Louise sent for him. On a warm spring day in late May, Carrie gave birth to a beautiful caramel-colored baby girl. When she saw the baby she was surprised by her complexion. It was the same color as Carrie's, only richer. Her hair was also brown with auburn highlights, and she had the same almond-shaped brown eyes. Carrie smiled at Louise and said, "I'll call her Ana Carrie, because she's another me."

When Logan saw Ana he turned angrily and left the room. He only saw her rich caramel complexion and thought of John Browning.

Logan despised Ana from the moment she was born. He refused to give her the paternal love and affection that he so freely gave to Odele, Sofia, and Eddie. He penalized her constantly. As a young child she strove for his affection and acceptance, much the same as Carrie had done with her mother. Instead she was rewarded with only insults and contempt. Odele and Sofia would often follow Logan's lead and treat Ana cruelly. She learned as a toddler to keep a safe distance from her older sisters. But where they were cruel and ill-tempered, Eddie was loving and patient. He was her knight in shining armor, always close enough to protect her. Ana loved him dearly. Although she knew Ana was Logan's child, Carrie would sometimes look at her, imagining that she looked like a child she could have had with John.

Carrie was pleased with her children. Odele would be graduating high school and going on to Spelman College next year; then Sofia would follow. Eddie was almost fourteen and the apple of many a young lady's eye. She'd have to keep a close watch on him. And her baby Ana was already seven. Time had flown by, and for that she was grateful. Not a day went by that she didn't think of John longingly and lovingly. But there was no time for regrets or remorse. John had finally married a doctor from New York last spring. He wrote to Carrie a week prior to the wedding to see if she'd had a change of heart. In response she sent him a letter of congratulations. It was the hardest thing she had ever done, but she knew the only fair thing for her to do was completely release him. Carrie had learned to coexist with Logan. It was no longer a strain; she was happy for his distraction with Ruth. No longer wanting his touch or companionship, she was comfortable in the uniformity of her life.

The only sincere source of displeasure and resentment toward Logan came as a result of his cruel behavior to Ana. He refused to allow her to call him Father, and he callously referred to her as Black Gal. This caused many confrontations in the Daniels household. Fortunately, the Nortons adored Ana. Of all the Daniels children, Ana was the one who won Thomas's heart. He paraded her around and would proudly tell anyone that she was like his own daughter.

Ana fondly referred to him as Papa T, and followed Eddie in calling Louise, Mama Louise. In Thomas's and Louise's eyes Ana could do no wrong. It was due to Thomas and his ever-growing stature in the Church Alliance Council that Logan refrained from publicly expressing his contempt for Ana. Whenever the Nortons were present he would behave sullenly, excusing himself shortly after their arrival.

As news of Logan's flagrant indiscretions became widely known, the once popular Ebenezer Church's large congregation diminished until it became very modest in size. To his embarrassment Logan was called in front of the elders of the church council and warned of severe repercussions if he failed to get his personal life under control.

Logan was not able to handle the stress of the decline of the church and soon his health began to fail. One afternoon, when he was at the home he had purchased for Ruth, he began complaining of dizziness. Ruth, thinking he was referring to their tryst, shrugged him off. "Leave your conscience at church, Logan. It only surfaces when you think it's convenient."

Hearing a thud, Ruth turned and saw Logan on the floor, convulsing violently. She immediately called for the colored ambulance and the aging Dr. Washington. Logan was rushed to Hermann Hospital's colored-only emergency ward—he'd had a massive stroke.

Carrie was at home with Ana and Louise when she received the call from the hospital. Driving as fast as she could, she entered through the hospital doors and immediately felt transported back to the evening of Edward's death. Overcome by a chill, she began to shiver. The shift nurse watched her, recognizing the beginning stages of hysteria. Motioning to an orderly, she took Carrie into a room and waited until she calmed down and the anxiety attack passed.

Carrie was not prepared for the immensity of the grief that battered her when she saw his crumpled body under the sheets. She felt the breath leaving her body in short gasps that prevented her from catching her breath. Clutching her stomach, she felt the bile rise in her throat, and her head felt as if it were floating above her body. This could not be! Not Logan, the man she had once loved and adored as much as she now despised and sometimes hated him. Her dream man who had saved her from what she thought was a wretched life, the father of her dear, dear babies, the one who inflicted pain, suffering, and disappointment. The provider who'd given her what she thought she had wanted, who gave and then took away any hope of love and joy. The whirlpool of emotion all came full circle in that room at that time: the love, the hate, the wanting and waiting for what she no longer could have or would have. She felt the scream bursting forth from deep within her very soul and couldn't stop it. She felt herself drowning with no desire to tread water. . . . She was pulled into a whirlpool of despair.

PART TWO

Traveling . . .

14

Closing the journal, Mignon leaned back to rest her eyes. She was enjoying the long drive back to the West Coast more than she would have believed. The children entertained them with songs and stories, and now they were less than two days away from California. Despite the reason for her exodus, this was a surprisingly peaceful time for Mignon because she was given uninterrupted time to spend with her father. They talked endlessly about everything from her decision to leave to his undying love and affection for her mother. The latter really made more of an impact on her than he could ever have known. When he spoke about her mother, Ana, he became animated in his description of her and their love for each other. His love and affection were so strong that he made the feelings almost palpable. This was what Mignon wanted, and she was confident that someone special was out there waiting just for her. Someone who offered a love that was content, devoted, and uncomplicated.

After reading about the circumstances surrounding her mother's birth, she began to understand her and the relationship that she and Carrie shared as mother and daughter. Reflecting over the years that she and her mother, Ana, had shared, Mignon recalled how what she had once considered Ana's ending had really turned into the beginning of living. Her life changed when she met, fell hopelessly in love with, and married Richard Warner, the man Mignon referred to as her dad. He was not her father by birth, but he had come into their lives when she so desperately needed guidance and fatherly love. At the time she did not realize her mother was teaching her one of the most meaningful life lessons she'd ever learn: sometimes you have to get through it in order to get to it.

Mignon remembered feeling a distracted sense of happiness for her mother when she first met Richard. She liked Richard, as she had called him in the early years, and she was glad her mother was remarrying. After all, she thought, Ana was the marrying kind. This was due in part to the fact that Mignon always saw Ana as a mother and wife, never really understanding part of her was a woman too. It was funny, she reflected, how she never thought of her mother as a woman until she became a mother herself. Now she realized how juvenile her assumption that Ana "needed" to be married really was.

As a young teenage girl she tried to understand the sadness her mother must have felt when her marriage fell apart. After many years in an unhappy marriage, Ana decided enough was enough, and one morning Mignon awoke to find that her father no longer lived there. She would never forget the pain and humiliation that her mother faced when she moved to Paris to resurrect her singing career, only to learn the show had been canceled. Mignon had been only thirteen at the time, but she still remembered it as if it were yesterday. To complicate matters, her father had decided to pass for white and didn't want Mignon around to complicate his life. She vowed at fifteen years old that she would never marry or have children. She could endure this type of pain only once in her life. That was, until Dad entered their lives and changed them all, helping to heal the gaping wounds that had been unintentionally inflicted, but remained nonetheless.

As Mignon rode through the Arizona desert, she looked at the vast surroundings and appreciated the beauty of contrasts. God was good. Her life had been a myriad of contrasts, and she had never noticed or acknowledged it. She had spent so much of her life in pursuit that she had never paused and observed. Never allowed beauty to be absorbed and recognized. It had been a blur, whizzing past like most scenery did when you found yourself engrossed in your own problems. She glanced over at her dad, watching him, adoring him, acknowledging who he was and what he had been in her life. She attuned her ears to listen to the harmonic intake and release of the snoring of the three precious souls asleep in the backseat. Silently she thanked God for opening her eyes and her ears, but most of all her heart. For the first time in her life she felt as if she were capable of physical absorption. She loved with every pore. It didn't feel symbolic; it was satisfaction at its purest level.

Looking back on her life, she saw clearly how God had shaped her, shaken her, and supported her, and she realized it was not her strength that had set her free. It was not her cries of hurt, anger, or despair that gave her wings to float, flee, or fly. It was God who had planned this day, this time, before time itself. She wondered how anyone could question One so great?

Deliverance was not a term appropriately defined. Webster should have given it the same definition as *time*. He should have prayed on the meaning before he placed pen to paper. Deliverance came from those she knew and most she didn't, all placed like dominos side by side by the Master's hand. As they fell they touched another, and another, and another, until they touched Maman, then Megan, then Carrie, then Ana, then Mignon, then her children, then theirs. . . . Tears of joy flowed freely from Mignon, cleansing and preparing her for the next phase.

Mignon's father reached over, covering her hand with his. "He'll always take care of you baby," he said, confirming to Mignon what she would always believe: she had been in His presence.

Mignon and her father rode along in silence, each lost in their own thoughts. It was only after Ana had married Richard Warner that Mignon began the process of change, acceptance, and forgiveness. She recalled how corny she had thought Dad was when he and Ana first met and eventually married. He'd greet people by saying, "The Lord is my shepherd; I shall not want," and he departed saying, "God bless you."

Now Mignon knew what he meant and why it was his testimony. She closed her eyes, thinking of what the next days, months, and years would bring. In her mind she began to pray . . . *The Lord is my shepherd; I shall not want; he maketh me to lie down in green pastures: he leadeth me beside the still waters. He restoreth my soul: He leadeth me in the paths of righteousness for His name's sake. Yea, though I walk through the valley of the shadow of death, I will fear no evil; for Thou art with me; Thy rod and Thy staff they comfort me. Thou preparest a table before me in the presence of mine*

*enemies: Thou anoinest my head with oil; my cup runneth over. Surely good-
ness and mercy shall follow me all the days of my life: and I will dwell in the
house of the Lord for ever. . . . Amen.*

As she prayed, bits and pieces of her life flashed across her mind. It
was as if God was clarifying her prayer visually with her experiences. It
was a confirmation and a cleansing of her spirit taking place . . . she
was returning not quite to home, but from a long journey. She would
have a moment to rest, and then the journey He had been preparing
her for all of her life would begin. Now it was clear why He hadn't allowed her to die in her sitting room months before as she bled profusely from a miscarriage.

Each time the memory of that evening surfaced, her senses were
assailed by the sound of her disembodied voice pleading, as she
prayed to God, "Please, please, don't let me die now." She continued
her plea until she began to feel the life slowly slipping from her body,
struggling desperately to hold on to consciousness. As time passed,
her plea changed to, "If it's my time now, please, God, please don't let
my children discover me!" She later found out that Gerald was the
one to find her unconscious and bleeding. *No more babies . . . not now
. . . not ever again.* But instead of remorse she felt release. Smiling to
herself, she relinquished her past with a keen understanding that she
had gone through it . . . the next step was getting to it. Her destiny
was inexplicably tied to her ability to overcome the obstacles in her
past. Turning to her father, she thought about how he had been
through it all with her, from when she was a teenager to now, when
she was a woman. "Dad, did you ever give up on me?"

"Which time, baby?" he asked, winking at her.

"You know . . . did you think I had given up on myself and would
stay?"

"No, honey . . . you're made from stronger stuff. You're the daughter of a marine; you don't give up because the battle's hard. But once
you realized the ship was destined to sink, you took your crew and
headed for safe territory. You realized that you were responsible for
this precious cargo," he finished, nodding to the backseat.

"Yeah. I guess you're right." Mignon turned back to her place in
the journal, contemplating how her father always seemed to see
strength in her, where she felt only weakness. She smiled when he
turned up the Al Green CD and began singing "I'm Still in Love."

"Come on, baby, sing with Dad; your mom and I love this song."

"Okay, okay!" she smiled and joined in singing.

As they finished the song her father became reflective. "You know, baby, you can hear those words over and over in your lifetime . . . and they mean absolutely nothing to you. There may even be times when you wish the person telling you they love you, wouldn't. But when you finally hear those three words from the one person in the world you feel the same way about . . . it erases all the past and you began to consider the possibilities of a future that you will not have to experience alone. Now, when this happens to you . . . believe me, you will know your prayers have been answered. You may not remember now, but Dad had been single so long that everyone had given up on me. All of my friends and family were convinced that it was my personal destiny to remain alone, a confirmed bachelor. Then I met your mother and we fell in love, and you were adorable even though you tried hard not to be. I just knew this was where I fit, where I should be, and my life has been richly blessed since the first day I met Ana."

"I know, and eventually I hope to find the same quality of love and happiness I have seen between you and Mom. But right now the last thing I want or need is to hear those three words from anyone other than my family. The way I feel now, I may be an old lady before I put myself in a position for someone to fall in love with me."

"I agree; now is certainly not the time for you to fall in love. You have to finish this chapter of your life, and you have a lot of healing to do. I believe your healing has to happen before you can love, not before you can be loved. The rest of your healing will take place when you meet someone who will truly love you for the woman that you are. You have a lot to offer any man, baby."

"Oh, yeah . . . me and a ready-made family. I don't think I'll be that enticing to many men, Dad. I think my best bet is to focus on raising my children and deciding on a new career path."

"I disagree. I walked into a ready-made family, didn't I?"

"All right, but the ready-made family consisted of just me, and I was almost grown."

"Which made it harder for me. I was the intruder, and I had absolutely no experience with a child—especially a headstrong teenager like you."

"My point exactly. If you hesitated because I was a headstrong teenager . . . And you are far above average. Can you imagine what I'm facing?"

"Baby, you slay me the way you will always try to change my thoughts and words to take the opposing view . . . which is normally your view."

"I know, I know . . . it's just overwhelming to think about all of this now with so much facing me."

"Don't worry. God knows what's in store for you and when you'll be ready. Until then, whoever He has for you will not come to you. For years I watched as you've given love, only for it to be misused and abused. Now you've shut down, afraid to love anyone but your children and us. Your mom and I have watched the life slowly being choked from you, amazed that you didn't know you were gasping for air. For us it was like watching someone drowning in shallow water and not being able to make them understand that all they have to do is stand up and walk to the shore. So when you asked if I had given up on you it wasn't in the way you thought. Your mother and I had given up on trying to tell you the water was shallow and land was near. We just decided to keep a lifeboat nearby in case you stopped fighting and decided to allow yourself to drown . . . but never had we given up on you, baby. We prayed daily for you that you would feel the life being drained from you and fight back to save it. It was impossible to be in your presence and not feel the thickness around you, as if your sadness contaminated the air. It seemed to seep from your pores like a cancer, except that this affected your spirit. But you're a winner, baby. You got a lot of good fight in you, and like any champion you might get stunned. But we never counted you as being out."

"I never thought you guys felt like that, or even noticed my sadness. I just thought you focused on our success and the possessions that accompanied that success, not on me."

"Well, for a time we did. We were proud that you had achieved so much and had such a comfortable life. But understand one thing; none of that means anything to us if you're not happy and healthy, both mentally and physically!"

"I'm finally on my way now, though . . . on dry land." Mignon sighed, feeling a little melancholy.

Sensing the downward shift in her emotions, Richard played "Love and Happiness" and began singing loudly, comically encouraging her with his enthusiasm to join in. Caught up in the moment and one of her favorite artists, Mignon sang Al Green with her father, until the children awoke and tried to join in.

Leaning her head against the headrest, Mignon enjoyed the beauty of the sunset as she ruminated over the similarities between her grandmother Carrie and the challenges she had faced many years later as a child growing up during the civil rights movement. What a sad testament that although Jim Crow laws were abolished as slavery had been, and so many black people had died fighting for their civil rights—rights that should have been inherent at birth—as a race her own people still alienated one another within their own race based on complexion. House and field, would it never end? Or would they forever as a race strive to be accepted and absorbed by the majority? Sadly, many people still lived their lives based on the myth that the percentage of white blood that flowed through their veins, causing white features and complexions to surface at birth, in fact validated and elevated their existence.

15

When Mignon was six years old her parents moved from her beloved home in Watts, California, to the upwardly mobile View Park area. The year before in 1965 an incident involving the police and local residents resulted in riots throughout Watts. It seemed as if overnight the pockets of close-knit neighborhoods, well-kept homes, and communities were destroyed and scattered like the ashes from so many burned businesses in the devastated aftermath of the riots. Suddenly the only home that Mignon had ever known, her school, and her community had all changed overnight, or so it seemed. For the first time in her young life she felt genuine fear. And for the first time since she could remember the kids in the neighborhood did not stop by her house to hang out after school for snacks and homework. Their parents had warned them all to walk straight home from school to avoid trouble, afraid of their child being out after the four-o'clock student curfew. Everyone was frightened of the tanks that cruised their streets and the soldiers who drove them or stood posted at the corner. Just boys themselves, they stood at their posts staring blankly, with their expressionless faces seeing these people only as a dark "Charlie," not as the young boys and girls that they really were, seeking only the same rights that these soldiers took for granted as their unspoken birthright.

So the small communities of young professionals who had purchased homes in South Central made plans to move where they would be safer, trying to distance their children and wives from the fray. It was not that they feared the rioters, for the most part. These residents who considered themselves a cut above and on their way to achieving the American dream fled their beloved community when the armed guards took over the streets with bayonets. This college-educated group that enjoyed the sense of community in Watts fled not because they feared poverty. On the contrary, many had been raised in or near enough poverty to understand and accept their less affluent neighbors. They chose Watts; it didn't choose them. Mignon's neighbors consisted of young lawyers and physicians, professionals with specialized vocations. Many of the homes had swimming pools and were beautifully landscaped; most of the wives did not work outside of the home.

This was the only neighborhood and home Mignon had ever known; her parents, Ana and Clark, had moved to Los Angeles from Houston in 1961 to escape the racism they faced daily, only to meet it again in a much more terrifying way. The struggle they faced resulted from the perception that Ana was married to a white man. She was brown-skinned, and Clark, although colored, had white skin and gray eyes. He was always mistaken for white, even among colored folk, who were always able to spot their own, even in a crowd. When Mignon was a year old, they settled and bought a home in a quiet middle-class neighborhood in South Central Los Angeles. The Pattons lived a quiet family-life with their daughter Mignon. Weekends were spent entertaining friends and neighbors, having backyard barbecues and pool parties. They were among a growing group of young black professionals who had migrated west and were living as close to the American dream as possible. With one exception: Clark was passing for white to attain the executive position that he held. His colleagues thought he was single and kept to himself due to his shyness, which was an endearing trait to many of the women he worked with, especially his secretary, who had her eye on him.

When the riots broke out, her father was unable to leave the house to go to work for fear of being mistaken for a white man. So Ana would take Mignon with her to do the shopping and run errands. Mignon recalled being frightened at the sight of the National Guard as they lined the streets, holding their bayonets in threatening stances. She asked Ana why they had guns with knives on them and if they were the ones who had set all of the fires that were burning. She remembered her mother's solemn reply: "They're here to keep the white folks safe, baby. To make sure we keep burning down our own neighborhoods." That remark caused the first stirrings of resentment in Mignon that afternoon toward the faceless "white folks," as she rode through the familiar streets that she had grown to know and love, now consumed by fire.

During the days that followed the riots, arid smoke from gunfire and burning buildings permeated the air, hanging like a dingy tarp cloaking the area around their home. Sometimes in the evening she'd hear the cracking and popping sound of shots being fired, followed by the wailing of sirens. After a week, the sound of gunfire became uneventful. Instead of residents taking a customary evening stroll, they were held hostage by a six-o'clock curfew. This quickly canceled the backyard gatherings they had all grown accustomed to. Residents were frightened to shop for food, for fear of being mistaken for a shoplifter. One of the kids down the street had unwittingly made the error of going to the liquor store on Avalon Boulevard for candy. The store owner incorrectly thought he was one of the looters and pulled out a gun, shooting him at point-blank range. The incident sparked five more days of riots, and ended in the demise of the store owner.

The death of this young man marked the beginning of a growing turmoil between her parents as a result of her father's reaction to the child's murder when her mother explained the details of the shooting to him. Mignon knew her mother was still very upset; she had walked with her to Dougie's house to offer sympathy to his grieving parents. As they walked quietly back home, she held tightly to her mother's hand, trying in her childlike way to soothe her mother's pain. Her father had merely glanced up from his newspaper and commented that the boy should have been home and not at some liquor store. His remark sent Ana on a tirade unlike anything Mignon had ever witnessed. And for the first time her father did not sleep in the bedroom with her mother. Instead he moved into the den, sleeping on the couch. They did not speak to each other for several days after her mother's accusatory outburst. Dougie's death impacted the lives of the Patton family and caused a division in their home based on the irrational emotions that surfaced when the subject of race was raised and the participants were on opposite sides of the issue. Until then skin color had never been an issue in their home. They were all different colors. She looked like her grandmother, Carrie, with tan skin and wavy, waist-length black hair. Her father looked white: his skin was white, his eyes were gray, and his hair was straight. Ana was America's description of a "black beauty." Everyone always said her mother looked just like Lena Horne, the actress, and they were right. Her skin was a perfect shade of caramel, her nose was aquiline, and she had perfect teeth and, as her father described them, heart-shaped lips. Not only that, but her mother had been a famous singer in Europe before Mignon was born.

The neighborhood children would sometimes ask, "Mignon, is your daddy white?" She'd reply, "Naw! Crazy!" and they'd laugh and continue to play. Her life had been perfect prior to the riots. In the evenings when her father came home from work, Ana would always be dressed nicely, waiting dinner until her father was seated with his drink. Only then would her mother place the food on the table and call them in for dinner. It was customary for her family to sit and have dinner together and listen to anecdotes about her father's day at work. After the murder of Dougie, Ana became withdrawn, often exclaiming in exasperation, "Clark this is just too white for me. Do you think we could discuss the issues at hand . . . like all of the riots that are happening across this country because white folks don't want to give us equal rights? What type of life is our daughter going to have if you and I are not willing to become part of this revolution?"

This outburst typically caused Clark to withdraw in silence. Leaving the table, he'd sit in the den and watch Jerry Dunphy report the evening news. Mignon could never understand what brought the arguments on, or why her father would have such a pained expression and cut his story short. Nevertheless, she remembered only good times in this home, and how the riots caused her once-ebullient parents to become subdued. As time passed the conversations ceased to be animated and fun and there were no more parties, no more friends stopping by, because of the National Guard, the curfews, the palpable feeling that slavery had returned. The homes and neighborhoods that had once been coveted now felt like shanties, and the overseer carried a bayonet instead of a whip. Emasculation of the many men who were heads of households was the unspoken intent, and in many instances the result. Those who had moved to the West Coast with the intention of fleeing the oppressive subjugation of life in the South were transported back each evening as they returned to their south central community, eyes downcast, heads slightly bowed, not meeting the soldiers' eyes, in the age-old slave position—not wanting to be singled out by the trigger-happy police as a potential troublemaker. The return of this behavioral defense reverberated through these families, recalling an instinct that was ancestral in spirit. Without consciously realizing it, they all were looking for the Underground Railroad that would take them to freedom. Within a year most of the homes had been sold to the city to erect a freeway that would not be completed for twenty years. What had once been considered a utopia was now as barren and deserted as Egypt had been after the Israelites fled in search of the Promised Land. These families scattered also in search of their promised land.

For Mignon and her parents it meant not only a forced move that had unexpected repercussions on each one of them. For her father it also called up a familiar instinct—to pass. What had at first been a defense mechanism to help him get through the day with his white colleagues and return to his blackness at night was no longer comfortable. As time passed, he felt his comfort zone switch. Without being aware of precisely when or how it happened he knew he was more comfortable around his white coworkers than his black friends—or even his own family. He was torn between his love for his wife and his daughter and his desire to pass for white.

For her mother it was a confusing time; she loved her husband, but could not forgive him for his insensitivity to her feelings. He had never been subjected to all of the racism she had been confronted with throughout her life, and she not only resented her husband's white complexion, but she also knew that he was secretly passing for white. Over time she grew to resent all people who were white, without exception. Her transition was almost immediate as she discarded her typically well-coiffed hair for an Afro. Because she was very fashionable, most people never understood the depth of her statement in the abandonment of the established norm. Her mother became a black militant and her father became the establishment; lines were drawn in the sand and Mignon tried to walk it like a tightrope. To trip and fall on either side would certainly mean estrangement or even worse.

As their neighbors began to move due to the devastation of the riots, her parents feared remaining in south central Los Angeles.

Hoping to regain the sense of family they once had, the Pattons sought a promised land in a home on Mt. Vernon Drive in the coveted neighborhood of View Park, nestled in the hills of west Los Angeles. Their home was a lovely trilevel brick perched atop a hillside, boasting a view of the city from the back. Her parents had not spoken one word about the impending move, planning to surprise Mignon and hopefully help her to forget the war zone she was leaving.

One morning her parents called Mignon into their room. After she was seated, her mother smiled and said, "Get dressed; we're taking you to see our new home!" Mignon felt uncertain; she didn't want to leave the few friends who had not yet moved, or her home. Ana watched her daughter knowingly. When Clark left the room, she pulled her daughter onto her lap. "You'll love the house, baby, and you'll meet new friends; just wait and see—there's even a pool! You'll love it! So don't look so down; put on your pretty flowered sundress . . . you're getting ready to meet new friends!"

Feeling elated, Mignon jumped up from her mother's lap and ran into her room to get dressed. Returning so that her mother could braid her hair, she even took with her the pretty satin ribbons that matched the dress. She wanted to look her best when she met her new friends. When they arrived at their new home, she couldn't believe her eyes. It was the biggest house she'd ever seen. Walking through in amazement, she couldn't believe the house was theirs. There was even a grand piano in the living room, and white carpet; she ran from room to room, bursting at the seams with excitement at her new home. To get to the family room you had to step down in deep shag carpet that surrounded a circular wooden floor. There was a fieldstone fireplace dominating the center wall, with a television and stereo system built into the wall. Completely in awe, she walked down the hallway and stopped in her tracks, staring in amazement at the colorful fish swimming in a huge aquarium that was also built into the wall. When she finally came to her room, she was out of breath from excitement. Her mother and father stood by the door of her room waiting expectantly, grinning from ear to ear, anticipating her reaction. They were not disappointed as she gleefully shrieked in surprise. It was decorated just like Gidget's on television . . . the perfect room for a little girl. The furniture was white, trimmed in gold; there was a canopy bed with a pink bedspread and matching curtains.

Turning back to the door, she ran to her parents, hugging them both fiercely.

She couldn't wait to get back and tell her best friend, Raymond, about the new house. At her age, Mignon didn't comprehend the enormity of her surprise new home. To her distress, not only was she parted from her friends, but also she soon found that this area held none of the warmth or charm of the community they had left. The beauty of their home could not make up for the loss of fellowship she had once felt. On top of this, she was not welcomed by the children the way she had been in Watts.

In the afternoon of her first day in her new home she went outside to meet some of the children who lived on her street. Waving shyly, she walked a couple of doors down to play hopscotch with a group of girls her age. As she approached, the group became quiet and stopped playing. Turning to Mignon, one of the girls stepped forward. "Stop right there and don't come any closer!"

Shocked, Mignon stopped dead in her tracks, not sure if this was some sort of new game.

"Now turn right around and take your funny-looking self home . . . my momma said we can't play with no Oreos, 'cause you ain't nothing!"

For a moment Mignon's mind went blank; then she yelled back, "I am not an Oreo, you stupid girl. . . . That's a cookie, and anybody can see that I am not your food!"

"Who are you calling stupid? We know you're not food . . . you're just all mixed up—white daddy and colored momma gave you funny-colored eyes, good hair, and black skin. As my momma said, what a waste! Go home!"

Mignon retreated back to her home, her pride wounded by the girl's assessment of her. Reaching her door, she broke down in tears as she told the story to her mother. Later that evening she overheard her mother telling her father about the incident.

Although Ana rallied for her daughter, her refusal to join any of the social clubs that the women in this community considered important resulted in exiling Mignon even further from her peers. They had standards by which they determined if a playmate was acceptable or not. Mignon was in the "not" category, because she looked too different, and on top of looking different she was taller than the other kids, which drew even more negative attention her way. Grimacing, she reminisced about her mother's constant reprimands not to slouch or to stand with her shoulders slumped. Ana never seemed to understand that she was just trying to blend in. After being threatened with wearing a back brace if she didn't stand straight, Mignon finally relented and kept perfect posture from her waist up. However, from her waist down she tried to shorten her stature by standing bowlegged. Eventually the neighborhood kids settled on comparing her to an Indian and teased her mercilessly. As a result Mignon spent the better part of her adolescence and well into puberty attempting to prove she was purely black, never caring about the extremes she would eventually have to go through to convince everyone she was just like him or her.

She smiled at the unexpected recollection of her attempt to prove her blackness at twelve years old. Her biggest goal was to resemble as closely as possible a black-light poster of the female warrior. Even to this day she remembered her idol and cousin, Danny, taking her to her first head shop on Crenshaw Boulevard, and buying the poster with her allowance. Mignon still recalled the effect that poster had had on her self-perception. Staring at the poster on her wall, she admired the strength emanating from the warrior woman, who held a spear in her hand as she stood on the cliff, appearing to stare out at the orange sunset over some unknown valley. Mignon had convinced herself that except for the Afro she looked exactly like the woman in the poster. This thought inspired her to bravely take the next step. Sneaking into her bathroom with her father's scissors and clippers, she proceeded to cut her waist-length hair, calling to mind how Danny's girlfriend had confided that it was vinegar mixed with Jergens lotion that would make her otherwise good hair nappy enough for an Afro. Naively she prepared the concoction and put it in her too-straight hair. Half an hour later, her hair had turned a bright copper with orange highlights, courtesy of the vinegar, and for all intents and purpose was nappy as a result of being robbed of all its oil and stripped of its natural color. The end result was that Mignon had an Afro, which everyone knew you could only have if you were black. Proudly she went downstairs to join her parents for dinner and surprised them with her new look.

Walking into the dining room she took her seat, her heart beating so fast she felt as though it would explode. Her father looked up with his normal greeting of "Evening, prin—" stopping in the middle of his greeting. She watched as the blood drained from his face, his eyes simultaneously filling with tears. Feeling something was amiss, her mother peeked in from the kitchen and exploded. "What in the hell happened to your hair?" she demanded.

"I guess you can look in the mirror and answer that question yourself! She's obviously imitating her mother. Why else would she mutilate herself like this?" Her father's explosive response shocked them both into momentary silence. Regaining her wits, Mignon sat silently, her head bowed as the storm between her parents escalated into a full-blown argument that opened a door that should have remained closed. The uncomfortable silence to follow lasted for days, seeming to permeate the house and its inhabitants. Among her peers, this act, nothing short of courageous, won her short-term acceptance, but long-term disgrace with her parents, particularly her father. Instead of acknowledging it as a teenage attempt to act out rebelliously, her father took it as a personal affront. His whiteness both physically and mentally contrasted with her blackness. His efforts to make her into the Negro version of Gidget were undermined by both Mignon and her mother.

The psychological effects of the riots on her parents were lasting. It was as if a container of emotional baggage had been packed and moved to Mt. Vernon as an infant, growing more each year, and taking up more space in their home as it grew to giant proportions. Her father was constantly reminded of the sense of freedom he experienced each time he left home, escaping the boundaries of Negro life to the tree-lined streets of west LA. Parking his car in the garage of his office building, he was greeted by the Negro garage attendant and the lobby receptionist in the formal tones of deference that were reserved for white people. Clark never thought to correct the oversight; as time passed he came to expect it. Among his peers he readily and easily fit into their group, laughing heartily at the coon jokes, never taking it personally. At home he and Ana frequently argued over his intense appreciation of the television show *Amos 'n' Andy*, or the way he delighted in the antics of comparable shows with Negro actors. After the riots Clark, heedless of the consequences, decided he had been right in keeping the fact that he was a Negro to himself. It was easier to pass during the day and return to his questionable heritage each evening.

Ana had also grown weary with her marriage to Clark. For years she had tried to accept her position as his wife and had really done her best to portray the perfect "white" wife she knew he craved. When they were first married she felt it was the least she could do, considering her betrayal. And for years she had been tormented by guilt, but now she had reached the point of no return again. After fleeing Paris brokenhearted, Ana had found that Clark was waiting, still in love with her after all the years they had spent apart. Instead of weathering the storm on her own and healing, she allowed herself to be comforted and drawn into the belief that she could erase Paris and build a life as Clark's wife. She had unsuccessfully denied her yearning for the limelight of the stage and for the one who sat just beyond, watching her performance, enthralled by her song. Mignon was her child and she would go wherever Ana went; no longer was it impossible to raise a child alone or be a single mother.

After the riots and the move to their new home, Ana's interests changed dramatically. She was as involved as ever with Mignon, but now her purpose was to ensure that her child understood and was proud of her heritage. She insisted that Mignon's bookcase consisted of a broad range of books on black history and stories by black authors, and was always quick to point out discrepancies in the treatment of black versus white people, as well as the self-loathing of some black men who overlooked the beauty of black women in search of a white woman. Every Wednesday night, Ana would hold "rap sessions" at their house. On these evenings her father would always find an excuse to work late. But to this day, Mignon remembered the energy in her house on those evenings. The den was full with about twenty men and women wearing Afros and dashikis, sitting on large floor pillows casually placed around the room. The fireplace was always burning real wood, regardless of the season, with the stereo system that was built into the wall playing Miles Davis and Nina Simone on the reel-to-reel tape player. One wall in the den had a built-in two-hundred-gallon aquarium with saltwater fish, which seemed to add to the surreal atmosphere. Mignon would find a pillow close to her mother and listen to the opinions and manners of expression of this group. Typically she would lose interest in some long-winded discussion and fall asleep on the pillow until her mother would gently nudge her, nodding in the direction of her room, their silent exchange that it was time for her to go to bed.

Mignon deeply regretted what she naively believed to be the rift be-

tween her parents over her decision to wear an Afro. But she rationalized that it was well worth it at the time to see the shock-filled faces
when she walked to the bus stop. For the first time in the six years that
she had lived in View Park she was minus the two long braids that had
once been her signature hairstyle. Overnight Mignon became the
epitome of a bold soul sister; at twelve years old she could easily pass
for sixteen. She was as tall as her mother and fully developed; she also
carried herself with an assurance that was not typical of a child her
age. Constantly she could be found reading either Eldridge Cleaver's
Soul on Ice, The Autobiography of Malcolm X, or the works of Richard
Wright, Langston Hughes, Nikki Giovanni, and Sonja Sanchez. It was
from this source that she developed her self-awareness. When she
turned thirteen she rallied for Angela Davis, even leading a demonstration in middle school to protest the incarceration of her idol,
proudly wearing her "Free Angela" button, even as the girls' vice principal called her parents to pick her up after she had been suspended
for three days as a result of the protest.

After that her father refused to speak to her for several days, looking through her if they passed in the house. Twice now she had fallen
from the tightrope. She also learned that the tightrope of acceptance
among her peers was never a certainty, so she eventually became hardened against the insults and able to ignore the instigators. Strength replaced weakness, and a desire for acceptance was soon replaced with
indifference. She learned to both despise and appreciate her people
and culture, although like her grandmother, Carrie, she never desired to be anything other than what she was—a black girl who would
someday be a black woman. Instead of faltering or seeking solace in
acceptance elsewhere, Mignon's transformation could be tracked on
the walls of her room. It no longer reflected the taste of her parents;
the walls were filled with posters of the people she read about:
Malcolm X, Dr. King, Eldridge Cleaver, Stokely Carmichael, Jimi Hendrix—"'scuse me while I kiss the sky." Unlike other girls her age she
didn't have posters of the teenage heartthrobs—the Jackson Five or
the Five Stairsteps—although she did enjoy their music. Instead she
listened to Jimi Hendrix, the Last Poets, Al Green, and Nina Simone.
Spending much of her time alone writing revolutionary poetry, she
had ceased to be the princess of her father's dreams.

Again her world changed. Her father could no longer stand living
among strangers. He had to seek his freedom to be who he felt he

was—a white man. So he did the unthinkable: he left Ana and Mignon for a white woman. He may as well have fallen dead, because the day that Ana found out about his betrayal, she pronounced him dead. She mourned him as she would someone who had unexpectedly died. Then she took account of where she was and moved on. His name was not mentioned; it was as if he never existed.

Within six months she had returned to the stage, performing regularly at the Coconut Grove. She called Sammy Martine, her former agent, who was quick to take the reins to reestablish her singing career. He immediately planted several strategic articles in the local black newspaper, the *Sentinel*, and Ana's return to her singing career had been announced. As it had done in the past, her career took off. The last thing she had time for was crying over a man she had tired of years ago. Her responsibility was to herself and her daughter.

In contrast, Mignon's reaction was complete devastation. She took her father's rejection personally. When he left, he never returned to see his daughter or invited her to stay with him. His reasoning was that she would be too difficult to explain. He left her with all the material things she could want—the only thing she was missing was him, which she couldn't seem to reconcile herself to the way her mother had. Ana had been able to move on. Mignon was not like her mother; she didn't mourn and move on. Her pain turned to anger and then hatred—her heart was festering like a scab that would not heal. So she distanced herself from love; her father, her first love, had shown her firsthand that love could not be trusted. Now, on top of it all, her mother had announced they were going abroad to live in Paris for a year; she had signed a contract to perform in *Le Revue Negre*, a remake of the 1920s stage show performed by Josephine Baker. This was an opportunity of a lifetime. Ana assured her that she would love Europe and would probably hate returning to the States.

"They love our people in Europe, baby . . . it's so different from here—just wait," Ana stated, smiling at her daughter reassuringly.

Ana bought books on the life of Paul Robeson, Josephine Baker, and James Baldwin to prepare her daughter for another outlook, telling her that black people like Nina Simone and others had sought refuge and made their homes in Paris. Ana also told her that black people lived all over the world and generally were treated with more respect in other countries than in the United States. So Mignon traveled with her mother to Paris, determined to return to the United States one day. She relished the thought that her father would miss her and realize what a mistake he had made by abandoning her.

As Mignon returned to the present, preparing to continue reading the journal, she was most surprised when she flipped through the pages and found the journal also contained her mother Ana's biography, and that the remainder was blank pages, left for a story yet untold—her story. It was kind of funny, Mignon thought. Who would have ever thought her story would be worth telling, even in a family journal? Returning to the present, she listened to her father singing to Chaka Khan, then Aretha Franklin. Reclining her seat, she found her page again and returned to the journal.

16

The next time Ana saw Logan it was almost six months after his stroke, when Carrie wheeled him into the house. She was shocked when she saw how his once handsome face was drawn down on the right side in a permanent sneer, and his right arm seemed to have folded itself in toward his body. She hid behind Eddie, holding his hand tightly, afraid of the man whom Mama had brought back. This was the first of many harsh new changes in the lives of the Daniels clan, the effects of which would have a lifelong impact on them.

Shortly after his stroke, it became apparent that Logan would be unable to return as senior minister of Ebenezer Church. Members of a once strong and wealthy congregation slowly departed, leaving only those of humble means from the Heights. As a result, the Church Alliance Council decided to replace Logan and relocate his family from the elegant church-financed Third Ward home back to the modest Studewood Heights home. The church could no longer support their lifestyle with the reduction in offerings. This meant a drastic change from the lifestyle of privilege and acceptance that they all had become accustomed to.

The two-bedroom house in Studewood Heights now held six people. This sudden and unexpected change in their lives caused a dramatic shift in the bonds that could bind or strangle a family. They became a group of strangers, with Carrie as the thread that held them thinly together.

Odele, the eldest, grew more distant from her family, refusing to acknowledge the change in their lifestyle. It was a source of disgrace and humiliation that resulted in her becoming a social outcast within her close-knit group of well-to-do teens. As a result, Odele completely withdrew from her family. With her looks she knew she could pass for white. She began to plan her departure.

Ana was very unhappy in Studewood. The neighborhood children teased her incessantly because she was so skinny and dark. They teased her for being the darkest child in her family, although most of them were much darker by comparison. However, they didn't compare her to themselves; instead they compared her to her brother and sisters. Ana's siblings were unanimously considered the most beautiful in the Heights, because they were light-skinned. Many of these children's parents did day work in colored homes in the Third Ward for meager pay. Treated like second-class citizens whenever they left Studewood, they were subjected to Jim Crow laws everywhere, even in the Third or Fifth Wards. The same Jim Crow laws applied, except it was not colored-only, it was light versus dark skin that distinguished them. So Ana became their "whipping boy," and they took their frustrations out on her.

After moving to the Heights, Ana was left to fend for herself. Eddie was never around and Carrie was distracted, always busy searching for work and overwhelmed by the recent changes in their family. Odele barely spoke to anyone, and Sofia was at Logan's beck and call. Ana immersed herself in the choir at the Nortons' church. It was there that she gained acceptance and confidence as week after week she sang solo, always amazed at her ability to make grown folk cry or catch the Holy Spirit. When she was not at church she tried her best to stay as far away from her frightening father and hostile sisters as she could. No matter how hard she tried she could not forget her father's cruelty toward her. Nor could she quiet the way her stomach lurched each time she heard him call her name with his slurred attempts. Now when he tried to smile at her with his monstrous countenance and asked her to sing for him, she often thought that the monster in him had finally surfaced. The horror of dealing with her father when he had been well had left an unforgettable brand across her mind.

She remembered the beginning of the school year when she started the second grade. She stood proudly in line with her siblings, holding tight to Eddie's hand. Her father, Reverend Daniels, as she was instructed to call him, ordered them into the parlor after breakfast for inspection before they left for school. They all stood at attention, with straight posture and knowing smiles; this game usually ended in a treat. As they stood in line, each child eagerly anticipated the treat—all except Ana. She stood nervously grasping Eddie's hand, hoping this time she'd be included. Logan looked at each child, smiling, until he spied Eddie's hand grasping Ana's firmly. "She can stand by herself, Eddie," he said sternly.

"I know, Father, but she's scared of lineup, so I hold her hand," Eddie replied, hoping his father would understand and respond with kindness. Logan ignored his last remark and turned to Sofia. He affectionately touched her long, straight braids and moved to Odele, remarking on how proud he was that she was going to be graduating high school this year. Completely passing over Ana, as though she weren't in the line, he smirked when she dropped her head, dejected, fighting back tears, again feeling the pain of being excluded.

Looking at her older sisters admiringly, she also thought they were beautiful with their near-white skin and straight, long hair. She often wondered why she had been born darker, with her shoulder-length hair that was neither kinky nor straight, just plain unruly. All she knew for sure was that she was the only child not allowed to refer to Logan as Father. Instead he insisted she refer to him as Reverend Daniels. Ana could not suppress the butterflies in her stomach as Logan reached into his pocket. Waiting breathlessly, she watched as he pulled out three shiny half dollars and placed one each in Odele's, Sofia's, and Eddie's waiting hands. Her stomach fell, as did her hope of being included. Not knowing what else to do, she continued to stand with her hand outstretched. Her mind raced as she tried to control the tears that threatened to spill down her face. *I'm his child too; why does he always have to be so mean to me? What have I done to him?* Ana wondered in her childlike way. She continued trying again and again to win his approval, but she was always met with cruel remarks or harsh repercussions for any mistake she made.

Eddie looked over at his baby sister, his heart aching at the pain that was in her eyes. He looked at her thin body; she had a delicacy and frailty, unlike his older sisters. At that moment he realized he had just touched the one person he loved more than anything.

Standing alone in the middle of the room with her hand bravely outstretched, Ana waited. Logan sat in his chair, holding the morning paper in front of him so he wouldn't have to look at her. Eddie cleared his throat to gain his father's attention. Logan looked up from his paper. "Yes, son, what is it?" His voice was edged with impatience.

"You forgot Ana's coin, Father," he replied hastily. Logan stared at his son long and hard, willing him to back down. Eddie stood his ground and returned the stare with equal firmness. Logan shrugged and said, "I only had three half dollars, and this nickel." With that he tossed the coin in Ana's direction. It slid under the table, so she had to lie on her belly to retrieve the coin. Logan sat and watched with a cruel smirk on his face. He turned back to Eddie. "Is there anything else, son?" he inquired. At that moment Eddie hated his father intensely, and wished in his childish way for some harm to befall him; he never wanted to be like him.

Eddie turned to help Ana get up and dust her knees off. He looked into her face and saw the tears from the humiliation she suffered from Logan's constant need to berate her. But Eddie held his head up with a pride he did not feel, so that she would imitate his actions, as she usually did when confronted by Logan's cruelty. Turning her palm up, he placed his coin in her hand in exchange for the nickel. As they left the room he turned to find Logan closely studying him, unable to mask his irritation. Eddie gave him his brightest smile, feeling victorious as he departed. Eddie and Ana left as they had entered, with his hand cupped protectively over hers, protecting her as he had done since her birth.

Now all of that had changed, and Ana often felt left alone and unprotected. Whenever possible she sought the shelter and loving home of the Nortons and their church family.

17

After Logan's stroke and the decision of the Church Alliance Council to take away the Third Ward house, everyone expected Carrie to fall apart. Instead she responded as she had all of her life to adverse conditions: with strength. She knew that the change in lifestyle would have negative repercussions on her children. She was more concerned with their well-being than with her own. After they were all settled in Studewood Heights, she became responsible for managing the household and its finances. The council provided a monthly stipend to cover their expenses. However, after reviewing the books, she realized too late that it was barely enough to cover living expenses.

Carrie immediately began seeking employment, but soon became discouraged when she discovered she was qualified for very little. She had never prepared herself during the years of her marriage to do anything other than volunteer work. During her adult years, she taught Sunday school or worked on various committees and raised her children. She always thought she had all the skills she would need to be a good wife and mother, never imagining she would be called upon as the provider too. Now she was faced with supporting her family, with no skills other than housework, which she had learned many years ago working for her grandmother and Robert Devereaux. She had resented servitude then, and loathed the idea that it might now be her only alternative.

Carrie wrote often to her parents, describing the changes that had occurred over the span of the last six months. She also told them how she was looking for work and it seemed she would have no option but to do day work or take in laundry. Despite Megan and Jesse's attempts to entice her to move Logan and the children to Devereaux, Carrie flatly refused, although her parents made it clear she could have had the main house for her family. However, she never wanted to return to Devereaux.

After seeing that Carrie would not change her mind about returning to Devereaux, Megan wrote to her daughter, Stella, who had been living in Houston and passing for white. Stella was married to a rich Jewish man, David Goldstein, and lived in River Oaks, the richest section for whites in Houston. Stella had been so afraid of having a child for fear that it would reach back that when she gave birth to a son she gave the boy to her maid to raise as her own child. According to Stella, she provided for the boy, who was almost eleven years old now and financially took care of his parents. This arrangement allowed Stella to visit the boy weekly. It was very painful to Megan and Jesse when Stella confided her story to them, although they never questioned her actions. They didn't understand why she hadn't asked for their help. Surely she knew after all these years they could be trusted with her secret and might have raised their grandson.

When Stella had first found out she was pregnant, she was elated. A child would keep her company when David traveled. And it would surely be the answer to his prayers. He wanted an heir to take over the chain of department stores they owned. As the pregnancy progressed, she began to have nightmares of the birth, dreaming that the doctor handed her a brown baby. Stella would awake terror-stricken. At five months she was convinced that the baby she carried had reached back and would be brown. She began to plan. It was too late to abort without possibly losing her life. Tormented by her options, she thought her luck had surely changed when her maid, Maggie, who also happened to be pregnant, had a miscarriage in her eighth month. She began to hatch her plan, with Maggie as her willing accomplice and confidante.

Unfortunately for Stella, she had distanced herself from her family through years of lying about her birth and background. The thought never occurred to her to seek them out in her time of need. During Stella's eighth month, David was scheduled to go to New York for an annual buying trip. He argued against the wisdom of taking a trip so near to the delivery date; he even suggested postponing the trip until after the birth. But Stella wouldn't hear of it, insisting that he was being overprotective and that the baby wasn't due for at least another month.

After David left town, Stella and Maggie put their plan into action. Maggie used a potion given to her by a Creole woman from Fifth Ward to induce labor. But things did not go as smoothly as planned. When Stella drank the mixture to induce labor she had a violent reaction. First she began throwing up, then cramping. Within an hour she found herself in the throes of labor. Then the unexpected happened: she began hemorrhaging. Maggie grew fearful of the amount of blood that Stella was losing, so she literally yanked the baby free from the grasp of his mother's body, causing Stella to lose consciousness from the excruciating pain of birth.

Hysterical with fear, Maggie recalled the Creole's retelling of a "bleeding birth" and how she had scraped the woman's womb. In a feeble attempt to stop the flow of blood, Maggie used the blade of a butter knife to scrape Stella's womb. As if in a daze she used diaper cloths to pack her womb to stem the blood loss. She had completely forgotten the baby, until she realized it was the baby's cries and not her own that filled her ears. The child was yelling at the top of his lungs from the shock of separation from his mother. She looked at the baby and back at Stella, instinctively knowing that if she didn't react quickly Stella would die. Maggie ran to the phone and called Dr. Stein. Then she wrapped the baby in a blanket and put him in a shoe box in a room reserved for the servants.

By the time the doctor arrived, Maggie thought Stella was already dead. She hadn't moved, and Maggie wasn't sure if she was even breathing. Afraid of being caught, Maggie told the doctor she found Stella in that condition. Dr. Stein was shaken at the loss of blood, but after some effort he found Stella's pulse and was able to slow the bleeding. As the attendants placed Stella in the waiting ambulance, Dr. Stein assured Maggie that Stella would be okay. Once the ambulance had driven away, Maggie returned to the house to take her baby home.

Not long after the ambulance took Stella, David received a call from his parents informing him Stella was in River Oaks Hospital in critical condition. When he arrived at the hospital, his grieving parents and Dr. Stein met him. The doctor informed him that Stella had hemorrhaged severely from premature labor.

Shaken at the terrible loss and the critical condition of his wife, David was inconsolable. Stella remained in critical condition for almost a month. During that time David rarely left the hospital or her bedside. She remained hospitalized until she had fully recuperated.

According to plan, Maggie took the baby to her home to raise as her own son. To Stella's everlasting sorrow, after she finally recuperated and visited Maggie at her home, she discovered the child was not brown at all. He was white like Stella and David. But it was too late; everyone believed Stella's baby had died during the miscarriage. Now she had to live with the lie of his death. She knew she could never tell David he had a son, an heir. Instead she tried to remedy this tragedy by ensuring that her son had the very best that money could buy. She bought Maggie and her husband Clyde a lovely home in the Fifth Ward and a new Buick; she furnished the home and took great pains with her son's nursery and, eventually, bedroom. Stella convinced herself that things would turn out for the best.

It was Megan's hope that Stella would be able to maintain her sanity in the tangle of lies that she had told. She knew firsthand how bad decisions could come back to haunt you. Who would have thought her firstborn child, Ruth, would have become so entangled in the life of her firstborn by Jesse? Megan recalled how attached Stella used to be to Carrie when they were children. She thought the Lord had provided an opening for her to help them both. Stella and Carrie both had their load of grief. Megan decided it was time for the two sisters to reunite. She would ask Stella to help Carrie by giving her a job.

When Stella received the letter from her mother she was stunned by her request. Her life was so removed from Devereaux and her family, but now she was besieged by the carefully buried memories that threatened to overwhelm her. Should she dare bring Carrie so close? Certainly no one would ever see a resemblance. But could she be certain that Carrie would not betray her and destroy the lies of background and history that she had so craftily built? In Megan's letter she wrote that Carrie had a family and that her husband was ill. Another surprise for Stella—she didn't realize Carrie had a husband or children.

Stella continued to ponder the possibility of hiring Carrie. She needed a companion; David traveled so much, which often left her alone in their sprawling estate. She remembered how loving Carrie had always been as a child—sometimes more so than Megan, who had too many children and was so devoted to Jesse. She decided to meet with Carrie. The meeting would tell her what she should do. She called Maggie, scheduling the meeting at her house when David left in two days. That way if it didn't work out, Carrie wouldn't know where or how to find her. After she'd made the arrangements with Maggie, she made the next call to Carrie.

Surprised at receiving a call from her younger sister, Stella, after so many years, Carrie was nervous as she prepared to go to the house in Fifth Ward to meet her. She was confused because she knew Stella had been passing as white for years. She didn't know of any white folks who lived in Fifth Ward; the area was mainly populated with Creoles and Geechees. Maybe time had brought about a change; however, she couldn't imagine Stella changing that much. She drove up to the neat white frame house, which was surrounded by a picket fence with a perfectly manicured lawn. It was one of the nicest homes on the block, with the exception of the well-tended home across the street, which Carrie was painfully familiar with because it was the home Logan was rumored to have purchased for Ruth Pruitt. As she opened the gate to the yard, she noticed a boy a few years older than her Ana, playing alone quietly. Even though there were other children his age playing nearby, he seemed not to notice. There was something vaguely familiar about him, but she couldn't put her finger on it until he turned to look at her. The blond hair and gray eyes that seemed to mix with green and blue were the same color as Stella's. He was also white like Stella.

"Hello," she said, smiling at him. Carrie was surprised Megan had never mentioned Stella's son. The boy held her eyes with his momentarily before hesitantly smiling and returning to his silent game. *He's beautiful,* she thought. When she reached the door, it was opened before she could ring the bell. She stopped short, puzzled by the huge woman standing before her. She was certainly not Stella. Thinking she had mistakenly gone to the wrong house, and confused by the little boy, Carrie showed her puzzlement.

The woman standing at the door smiled kindly, "I'm Maggie. You must be Carrie; come on in," she said, motioning for Carrie to enter.

As she moved her ample body aside so Carrie could pass, she called out, "Son, don't get too close to those rosebushes. You know what I'll do if they cut you!" The boy looked at his mother solemnly and moved toward the center of the yard, away from the bushes.

Maggie turned to Carrie. "Have a seat. Miss Stella will be right along. Would you like some ice tea?"

"No, thank you," Carrie replied, perplexed. She looked around the room at the pictures of the boy and his parents. This child had apparently reached back to his white kinfolk. His father was a very dark man and, although Maggie was fair-skinned, this child looked white. *You can never tell what you'll get when you put so many different dyes in the mix,* she thought. *Sometimes it reaches back and chooses black; sometimes it reaches back and chooses white.*

As she sat immersed in her thoughts, the boy's happy yelling interrupted her: "Miss Stella! Mama! Miss Stella's here!" Hearing her son's screams of delight, Maggie came from the kitchen to open the door for Stella. As she stood at the door waiting for Stella to enter, Carrie watched the play of expressions on Maggie's face. Her expression had noticeably softened as she watched Stella bending to speak with her son. Although Carrie could not see Stella from where she sat, she could tell from Maggie's response that Stella was a frequent visitor, and she had the impression that she came to visit Maggie's son. Although she greeted Stella warmly, it was evident that Maggie was not considered Stella's equal. Carrie silently observed the exchange between the two women.

Carrie was dumbfounded! Was this white woman her sister? Stella had never been considered beautiful in a cookie-cutter way; *unique* was more descriptive of her look. But she was undeniably white, and in the midst of almost plain, unremarkable features were the most remarkable eyes, so unique they were like a signature. Stella had always been distinguished by her doelike gray eyes with flecks of green and blue. Her clothes were obviously expensive. Even Carrie recognized clothes designed by the unrivaled Coco Chanel. Stella was a visual announcement of her wealth. Carrie had not been prepared for Stella the woman; she remembered only Stella the baby, the little girl that she helped to raise. Momentarily lost in memories, Carrie recalled how Stella would follow her around, asking seemingly unending questions. Then she remembered how Stella had turned her back on her entire family when she became an adult. It seemed that Stella had discovered, after years of being mistaken for white, that life had given her an option she could not resist.

Why would she want to see me now? Carrie wondered. She decided to let Stella start the conversation; after all, she had initiated the meeting.

For the first time in her adult life, a colored woman intimidated Stella. Carrie seemed totally unaffected by her obvious wealth and the difference in their positions. She had taken great pains in her appearance to show her big sister what she had missed and could never have. However, Carrie had apparently lived very well. Stella was confused and unsure how to proceed. She had expected Carrie to be submissive and practically begging for help. The last thing she expected to find was this composed woman who seemed to think she was on the same level as Stella. Taking a seat in the chair opposite from Carrie, Stella greeted Carrie formally, as polite strangers, certainly not as long-lost sisters. "It's so good to see you again, Carrie. What a pleasant surprise; you're so"—her voice trailed—"elegant." She was unable to mask her amazement.

"Thank you, Stella. It is also good to see you again," Carrie replied, wondering why Stella was being so formal and why she had called this reunion.

As though reading her thoughts, Stella came straight to the point. "Megan said you were having trouble and you might need help." Recalling too late that Carrie had always been very proud, she knew that if rubbed the wrong way, her sister would get up and leave. Unexpectedly, Stella found she was intrigued by her older sister and wanted to get to know her better. Of course, they could never be known as sisters, but she just might work out as her companion—that was, if Carrie was not opposed to being in a position of subservience. She found herself hoping it would work out.

For a moment Carrie was puzzled, her mind racing. *Of course, Mama would be the only reason Stella would have contacted me after all of these years,* she thought miserably before replying, "Yes, Stella, I am in need now. My husband had a stroke just over six months ago. We have four children, and it is a hardship on us because he is unable to work." She hesitated. "I have not worked since I've been married." For the first time she truly despised Logan for letting her and their children down and putting them in this position.

"Hmmm, I see," Stella murmured thoughtfully. "I am in need of an assistant, someone who can keep my affairs in order, manage my schedule, and oversee domestic staff. There is some travel involved. My husband owns a chain of department stores. I'm sure you've heard of them—you see, my last name is Goldstein." Stella paused a beat, waiting for the enormity of her wealth to dawn on Carrie.

Although she was stunned at the revelation, Carrie merely nodded her head in recognition of the store she had shopped in frequently over the years, never guessing her baby sister was married to the owner of the Goldstein empire.

"I guess I don't need to say we can never acknowledge our past together," Stella said, interrupting Carrie's thoughts. "I need someone I can trust, and you need a steady income. I will pay you twenty-five dollars per week."

Carrie was filled with disgust as she thought how Stella would have to disguise their relationship in order to live among whites. She could not fathom the depths of the deceit Stella had created in order to erase who and what she really was: a colored woman. This was in itself repulsive and foreign to Carrie. She had always longed for lighter skin, but never with the desire to be accepted by whites. She had always longed to be accepted by the colored folks who looked like Megan and Jesse.

Carrie wanted to turn Stella's offer down regardless of the generosity—most colored professionals didn't make that much money. Swallowing her pride, not for the first time in her life, Carrie nodded her acceptance of the job her sister offered.

Secretly delighted at her capitulation, Stella had not failed to notice the struggle of emotions on Carrie's face. Giving Carrie an advance on her first week of pay and the address of her home, and reminding her to use the servants' entrance, Stella said she would start work on the following Monday. Stella stood to indicate that the interview was concluded. As they walked toward their cars, Stella caught Carrie off guard. Instead of the formal parting that Carrie expected, Stella caught her in a tight embrace, whispering, "I'm so happy, Cara; it will be like the old days." *Cara* was the pet name Stella had used to refer to Carrie when they were children. Unbidden tears sprang to Carrie's eyes as she tried unsuccessfully to fight them back. Although separated by race and class, they would always be tied by blood.

*   *   *

Carrie sat in the library at Louise's house later, fidgeting with her hands as she told her friend about the meeting she'd had earlier with her sister, Stella. Louise sat unmoving, riveted to her every word. She had heard of light-skinned coloreds who passed for white, and even knew a few who lived Back East. But she'd never heard of the type of family that Carrie had been raised in. Several of the children had chosen to live a lie and forfeit any familial ties. How hard it must be for Carrie to have siblings in name only; how difficult for them to have to live their lives as lonely strangers. Louise listened, watching Carrie intently as she told of the closeness that had existed between her and Stella as young girls, and how Stella had left home at seventeen to live among whites and be accepted as one of them. Stella had no contact with her family for years after she left. From time to time Megan received a hastily scrawled note stating, *Healthy and happy. Stella.*

What Carrie didn't know and so couldn't share with Louise was that Stella had begun to write Megan detailed letters after she became engaged to marry David Goldstein. She wrote begging for their forgiveness because she could not invite them to be a part of her life. She had created a background of two lovely—white—parents who died in a fire, which consumed all of their worldly possessions, thus leaving her to fend for herself, which was how she ended up working at Goldstein's department store.

18

Monday morning came faster than Carrie was prepared for. She cursed herself over and over for accepting the money and the job. The last thing she needed was to have to live Stella's lie. She thought of calling Stella to tell her she wouldn't be able to work for her. She almost convinced herself that Stella had also had a change of heart; then she remembered how good it felt to hold her sister and the way she felt transported back to less complicated times. Anyway, she needed the money, so she really didn't have a choice at all.

As Carrie drove down Westhiemer Road to the entrance of River Oaks, she was amazed at the enormous estates. This made the homes in Third Ward look like outhouses, she thought. Stella had really done it. She'd passed for white and was the grand lady she had always pretended even as a child to be. Even though she had other siblings who were passing, Carrie was sure none had reached the lofty heights of Stella's lifestyle. Swinging her car into the spot marked *Servants and Deliveries,* Carrie parked next to three other cars, obviously employees of her sister. She noticed the same Buick that had been parked in Maggie's driveway. *Something strange about that one,* she thought. Making a mental note to observe Maggie a little closer, Carrie got out of the car slowly, straightening her hat and buttoning her jacket. She was fashionably dressed in a bright red knit suit. *I am not a maid!* she had thought that morning while deciding what to wear. *And I'm sure not dressing like one!* She stood for a moment survey-ing the well-kept grounds, thinking how lovely it was. As she reached the steps, again the door opened before she could ring the bell. It was Maggie.

"Good morning, Carrie! Miss Stella asked me to look for you and bring you up as soon as you arrived!" she said, smiling brightly.

"Good morning to you, Maggie! You startled me; I didn't expect the door to open until I rang the bell," replied Carrie, trying to hide her irritation.

"Oh, I'm sorry; I didn't mean to startle you. It's just that when I'm in the kitchen, I see everyone who uses the servants' entrance."

Carrie could not decide if Maggie was being a smart mouth, so she decided to ignore her last remark and asked, "Can you show me to Stella, Maggie?"

The large woman stopped dead in her tracks and turned like a bull ready to charge. "Don't you mean *Miss* Stella, girl?"

At that moment Carrie knew what it was about Maggie that was so strange; she was sure Maggie was crazy. She saw the glazed expression in her eyes and instinctively knew that she had to tread lightly around this woman.

"Yes, I meant to say Miss Stella, Maggie. Would you be kind enough to show me to her?" Carrie asked softly, standing very still. Maggie stood in a hulking stance, scrutinizing Carrie closely to discern whether she was sincere. Carrie returned her gaze. After seeing no threat, Maggie turned to show Carrie the way.

As they entered the grand hall, Maggie turned back to Carrie and said, "I don't take to no colored gal disrespecting Miss Stella; you un-derstand me, gal?" Carrie nodded slowly to indicate that she under-stood. Again Maggie turned to lead Carrie past the great hall down a corridor to the rear stairs. "These are the servants' stairs," she said brightly, as if she were giving a guided tour. "These stairs be for us—you may neeeever take the front stairs." She guffawed loudly at her pronunciation of the word *never.* "Come on, hurry up—I got breakfast to make. I make the best pancakes around, but you can't eat any 'less'n some left over and I ain't hungry. . . . Well, no, sirree, you ain't getting none, 'cause I'm always hungry." This time she doubled over in laughter. Carrie paced herself to stay at least five steps away, in case of another mood swing. Noticing that Carrie did not join her in her laughter, Maggie straightened up and walked the rest of the way in angry silence. "Miss Stella is right this way."

Carrie followed, keeping a safe distance as they approached the double doors that marked the entrance to Stella's suite of rooms. She maintained her distance as Maggie knocked softly on the doors before opening them to announce that Carrie had arrived.

To Maggie's surprise, Stella invited them both to come in. It had been almost a year since Stella had invited Maggie to join her in the privacy of her sitting room. Maggie recalled that unforgettable occasion, when she had made the mistake of confessing her affection for Stella. Now Stella avoided close contact with Maggie as if she had to tread carefully or else Maggie would explode like a bomb. Stella maintained a respectful distance from Maggie at all times, never allowing her to forget her position as the family cook. At first Maggie was confused and hurt at Stella's response to her. Maggie had assumed her confession would bring them closer as a family. In her warped mind that was what they were—family—and Clark was their son, their secret. Now Stella was bringing in this intruder, and Maggie just couldn't figure out why. *What does she need with her?* Maggie thought jealously. *I'm all she needs.*

Obviously not used to being invited into Stella's boudoir, Maggie could not hide her discomfort as she shifted her weight from foot to foot.

"Maggie," Stella began, transporting her back to the present. Maggie blinked twice with her myopic stare, looking mildly perplexed. "I want to formally introduce you to Miss Carrie; she will be my assistant, and as such, she will be addressed according to her position. She will take meals with me, so please prepare a breakfast tray for the two of us, and I'm sure you know to handle all other meals accordingly."

Carrie watched Maggie closely as Stella gave her instructions. She did not fail to miss the struggle Maggie had trying not to betray herself by showing the rage she felt.

Maggie nodded, confirming that she understood Stella's requests. "May I be excused now, Miss Stella?" she inquired through clenched teeth.

Stella, appearing completely unaware of the rage held so carefully in check by Maggie, consented, dismissing her with an absentminded nod of her head. Carrie waited until Maggie, left closing the doors firmly behind her, before she shivered in reaction to her.

Stella observed Carrie's reaction. "Yes, Cara, she is very strange, but completely harmless," she explained, although her voice lacked conviction. "Maggie has been with me for almost fifteen years; she is loyal, dedicated and very possessive. She's been through a lot with her crazy husband, but she's completely reliable."

Carrie replied, "I agree with everything but *harmless*. She is frightening, and if you don't mind, I'll wait until I go home to eat. Somehow I don't think my food will be as tasty as yours."

Stella shrugged her shoulders. "That's entirely up to you, Cara," she said ambiguously. Quickly switching subjects she said, "Cara, I hope you don't mind my using my pet name for you . . . or I will call you Carrie, if you prefer." Stella obviously hoped she would not insist on being called the latter.

"Cara is fine," Carrie replied, smiling and feeling relaxed in Stella's elegant home. Carrie realized what the term "nigger rich" meant now. There was a difference. "Your home is lovely, Stella. I've never seen anything quite like it," Carrie said, openly admiring its beauty.

"Yes, it is," Stella agreed. "I wanted *all* of this" she said, sweeping her hand in a wide arc to encompass her surroundings. "Let's take a walk through the gardens, Cara, so we can talk. Sometimes I think the walls have ears." Stella led Carrie through the enormous mansion out past the swimming pool and tennis court to the informal gardens. Finally they came to the gazebo surrounded by weeping willows, luscious plants, and colorful flowers whose scent filled the air.

The two sisters sat for minutes just enjoying the surroundings and each other's company in a contented silence. They took pleasure from the closeness that only a sibling can feel for another after years of separation. This was the first time that Carrie had felt totally relaxed since John's departure. Unaware that Stella was watching, she shook herself, as if it would help to remove the images of John that filled her mind and made her heart race. She had tried unsuccessfully over the years to put him out of her mind. It seemed nothing, not even time, would help her to forget him.

Stella continued to scrutinize her older sister until Carrie became aware that she was being studied closely. Stella silently contemplated the repercussions of telling the truth. She decided she had to be honest if this arrangement was to succeed. Breaking the silence that had shifted and begun to feel uncomfortable, she said, "I want to talk to you in confidence. I thought it would be best to bring you up to date on the events that have transpired in my life. Other than Mother, no one else knows the truth."

Her curiosity whetted, Carrie sat still, remaining silent until Stella was ready to proceed. Stella took a deep, calming breath and told Carrie about her life since leaving Devereaux. She finished by telling her about the strained marriage, and her husband's departure to Galveston. The couple had only recently reunited in the past few months. She even confided her fear that it had been too little, too late. Her instincts told her there was someone else, and that someone had won her husband's heart.

Sitting quietly, trying to digest Stella's story, Carrie asked, "What about Maggie? Don't you think she's figured it out?"

"Oh, heavens, no! Cara, she's not that smart. Maggie thinks she has a white child; you see, she thinks I had an affair and the child is the result. But you're right in assuming she can be dangerous! She is greedy, and that greed could make her very dangerous."

"She is dangerous, Stella! Why do you think she can be trusted?" Carrie became frustrated at the senselessness of Stella's predicament. Was being white worth all this? she wondered.

Stella responded as if she had read Carrie's mind. "No, it's not worth it. . . . I just don't know how to get out! I love David—I have from the moment I laid eyes on him—and believe it or not I love my son. I made a mistake because I thought . . ." Her voice trailed off as she tried to form her emotions and thoughts into words. For the first time she was hit by the full force of her loss. Stella moaned with grief from the void she felt without her baby, and knowing her fear had cost her the chance to have another.

Incredulous and dismayed by the unexpected turn in Stella's story, Carrie felt unsympathetic. "You gave him away because you thought he'd be brown like me." Her shoulders slumped, as if a great weight had been laid upon them as the realization of why Stella had given up her son fully dawned on her. "You gave him to a crazy woman instead of your own flesh and blood. We would have taken him, Stella, be he dark or white! Me or Mama—yes, Mama—she didn't give me away, and she is as white as you, Stella!" Carrie knew she was screaming, but she couldn't quiet herself. Was she supposed to understand? Feel sympathy for Stella? She got up to leave and found she couldn't go; everywhere she turned was filled with lies and deceit.

Carrie watched Stella, doubled over sobbing, releasing years of grief and guilt that she had skillfully held in check. Instead of leaving, she gently pulled Stella upright, looking her directly in the eyes to see if she could fathom the measure of her regret. "You can't undo what's been done, but you can try to fix what's broken inside of you. It won't be painless or easy, but you won't be happy until it's done, Stella." Carrie spoke these words with a sincerity that struck Stella to the core. She knew Carrie was right; she just didn't know how to go about it. She knew that things would change, although somehow she knew it would not be for the better. Stella and Carrie sat together in the gazebo well past the lunch hour, each sister silently engrossed in her own plight and each weighing her options. It was Stella who noticed the shift in the sun's position and suggested they return to the house before the servants became suspicious. However, they both knew she was speaking of Maggie.

19

Maggie had wanted a child all of her life, or so it seemed. As an only child, Maggie had been the result of a first and last night of mindless, unprotected passion. She was an unwelcome addition to her hardworking parents' lives. Neglected as a child, she filled her days and nights pretending to be a mother as she played with baby dolls well into her teens. Often she daydreamed about how she would become the perfect mother to a houseful of children. As a teenager she filled her days devouring books about romance, and listening to the soap operas on the small radio in the parlor.

Maggie's parents worked as domestics in the small town of Big Springs, Texas. They rarely had time to spend with Maggie because of the ceaseless demands of their employer. As a young girl she learned to play quietly so as not to disturb her parents' employers or embarrass her parents. Although big-boned and slightly overweight, she had a wholesome appeal. But due to the lack of attention from her parents, she was extremely shy and lacked any degree of self-confidence. As the child of domestics, she became accustomed to servants' entrances, and she even had a servant's demeanor, trying not to be seen or heard.

In the summer of her fifteenth year, the course of Maggie's predictable life changed dramatically. On the day of her father's birthday, Maggie's mother, Mary, suggested Maggie go to work with her.

They had planned a surprise for her father. Mary thought that if Maggie helped her clean, then she could wash and iron the clothes. She instructed Maggie to clean the master bedroom and baths, and then check with her once she had finished. After an hour had passed, it occurred to Mary that Maggie had not come back down to get her next assignment. Thinking that Maggie had forgotten, Mary went in search of her lazybones daughter. Mary walked impatiently into the master suite, expecting to find her daughter daydreaming. Instead, she was horrified to find her employer in a state of undress, his member becoming limp at the sight of Mary, as Maggie lay spread-eagled, her face flushed, on his bed. Startled by Mary's entrance the man looked from mother to daughter. "Get up and get outta here, gal!" Disoriented, Maggie feverishly tried to clothe herself. Revolted and fearful of losing her job, Mary apologized to Mr. Samson for her daughter's unruly behavior and apologized for her getting in the way or causing him any trouble. She then looked at her wayward daughter, demanding she dress herself and finish cleaning the room. Maggie was frightened and confused; she tried to explain that Mr. Samson always played the nasty game with her, but her mother refused to listen, finally threatening Maggie if she didn't keep quiet, and as usual Maggie complied and did what she was told: she kept silent.

That evening her parents decided she had caused them enough trouble; they made plans to send her to Houston to live with her aunt Geneva. They could not bear to suffer the humiliation of their only daughter bearing some bastard. After all, they were hardworking, churchgoing folk. According to Mary, teenagers in the neighborhood where she lived surrounded her sister Geneva. She was sure Maggie would quickly settle in, meet other teens, and develop friendships. While living with her aunt, Maggie became acquainted with the mail carrier who delivered the mail to her home. His name was Clyde Patton, and although he was at least ten years older than Maggie, she was charmed by the special attention and interest he displayed. She found herself hanging around the front porch awaiting his arrival each day to make small talk. After six months their relationship blossomed from exchanging pleasantries to Maggie sitting quietly to listen to Clyde's big plans. Clyde began returning after he finished his route to visit with Maggie and Geneva.

Geneva was not very fond of Clyde but she hesitated to speak against him, because he was the only friend Maggie had made since she'd arrived in Houston. One evening Clyde asked Geneva if he could speak with her alone. Not surprised by his request, she invited him in. Sitting quietly in her chair she waited for him to begin. She had expected Clyde to request permission to court Maggie. Instead, to her surprise he requested permission to take her hand in marriage.

Maggie had been eavesdropping near the doorway and overheard his request. She was so elated at the prospect of getting married and having babies that the fact that she really didn't know this man never crossed her mind. Seeing the delight on Maggie's face at the request, Geneva consented to Clyde's request on the condition that Maggie's parents approved.

Clyde and Maggie were married a month later in a small ceremony at Geneva's home. Maggie soon found out that Clyde was not the gentle, considerate man she thought him to be. Clyde was physically a very unattractive man. He looked like a weasel, and his eyes constantly darted around the room as if looking for an escape route. Black as Maggie was fair, he wore his hair in a greasy conk and had a belly that announced the number of beers he consumed.

Clyde was both attracted by her fair skin and resentful of it, because he thought her fairness made her superior to him. For that reason he felt he had to control Maggie and everything she did or said. Clyde felt powerful and complete only through force and control. His favorite pastime was to use force on his wife to control her actions.

Although her parents had never been loving or affectionate, neither were they physically abusive. When Maggie was first confronted with Clyde's anger, she immediately tried to make amends. However, the harder she tried to please him, the angrier he became. The first time he hit her, she was so dumbfounded that she begged his forgiveness, telling him she would do better next time.

Clyde thoroughly enjoyed humiliating and physically dominating her in this way; it aroused him. Grabbing her roughly, his stale breath coming in short gasps, he unzipped his pants, entering her with brutal force, taking her roughly. Once he was finished he'd push her away, zip his pants, and go to sleep in the other room. Many nights Maggie would lie awake, stunned and in great pain, bruised both on the inside and the outside. Rocking herself to sleep she would think, *I'll do better next time. I was a bad girl again.*

As time passed Clyde became more abusive and the slaps turned into beatings. Maggie was seventeen the first time she became pregnant. Thinking this news would cause Clyde to forgive her for being bad, Maggie excitedly met Clyde at the door as he came home from his route. Stopping short, he stared at her suspiciously through bloodshot eyes. "What are you grinning at, stupid?" he barked.

"We're gonna have a baby," she said, smiling broadly.

To her alarm, he didn't think it was good news. Glaring at her angrily, he began cursing her. As usual, Maggie immediately became apologetic, seeking forgiveness, not understanding why he didn't feel as overjoyed as she did. Her submissiveness only infuriated him more, causing his anger to grow. On this occasion he beat her until her face resembled a well-used punching bag, but she didn't mind as long as the baby was safe. *This must mean it'll be okay,* she thought. No sooner had this thought passed than the next punch landed directly in her belly. He hit her so hard she thought her navel had exploded. The pain was blinding in its intensity. Doubling over, she tried to throw up, hoping it would give her some relief from the excruciating pain. Then she felt the warm, sticky flow as her first child left her body, seemingly screaming and fighting its way to the floor. As the child departed, so did her consciousness and her will to live.

When she finally awoke, Aunt Geneva was sitting at her bedside. Noticing that Maggie had come out of the coma, Geneva took her hand and began to weep softly. Geneva pleaded with her to leave Clyde and return to her home. But Maggie looked at her in disbelief. "He is my husband, and he will be the father of our big family," she replied. "You just don't understand; he's a good provider. He'll be nice, you'll see." As far as Maggie was concerned the subject was closed.

After Maggie returned home, Clyde was careful not to get too rough with her. He began staying away for days at a time, returning late at night, generally falling into a drunken stupor in his room. But after a few months their lives returned to normal, the beatings resumed, and Maggie was repentant. Since she had never really known anything different, this lifestyle became normal to her. As time passed she became less frightened of Clyde and grew to understand his moods. Sometimes he would become talkative, and Maggie would use this time to try to find out when he wanted to start a family. After all, this was the only reason she could think of to be married, and the only good reason she could think of for doing that foul act she called the nasty.

One evening when Clyde was in a talkative mood, Maggie questioned when they were going to have a baby. Looking up from his paper, he studied her with interest. "What do you want with a child, when you're just a child yourself?"

Maggie did not falter in her response. "If I am grown-up enough to be a wife, then I am grown enough to be a mother. I want a baby from you; I want to give you a son or a daughter," she finished with a self-satisfied smile; she was pleased with her response.

"Hmmm, you sound mighty sure of yourself," he said feeling magnanimous, which was rare. "Tell you what: when you get a good job paying decent money we can afford to have a baby, but not until then. I told you I have plans, Maggie. I can't afford you and a baby unless you have a job. You understand . . . right?" he asked.

"Yes, Clyde, I understand," she said, filled with renewed hope.

Clyde was amazed when Maggie informed him four days later that she had a job in River Oaks. As the child of domestics she learned the fine arts of cooking and cleaning as a child. None other than the Goldstein family had hired her, and they were paying her good money. He knew he would have to keep a firm hand on her now so she wouldn't get uppity, like most of the high-yella women he'd known. Clyde had completely forgotten his promise of having a child. So intent was he on keeping the upper hand, he neglected the real reason Maggie had taken a job.

What Clyde didn't anticipate was that Stella Goldstein would be drawn to Maggie by her sweet disposition and willingness to please. They became as close as an employer would allow an employee to become. Since Maggie's parents were domestics, she instinctively knew the right things to do to endear herself to her employer. Over time, Stella began to notice the bruises, and the pained expressions as she moved about the house. One evening she called Maggie into the study and questioned her about her home life. After Clyde had caused her to have her fifth miscarriage, Maggie bitterly told Stella about him.

It was a release for Maggie to finally be able to talk about him and his cruel ways. She told everything—everything except about the blackouts and the spells of unreasonable anger that she couldn't seem to control. Something told her to hold this back; somehow she didn't think Stella would understand. Maybe she would become fear-

ful, and Maggie certainly didn't want that to happen. Instead, to
Maggie's surprise Stella offered to give her the baby she carried. At
first Maggie thought she was hearing things; that was, until Stella repeated her request. Of course she readily accepted, although she kept
expecting it to be some sort of cruel joke. When the night came and
her son was born, she kept waiting for Stella to wake up and ask for
her baby back—especially once she saw the boy. But Maggie had been
lucky; by the time Stella regained consciousness it was almost a month
later. She was in the hospital and her son was with Maggie. It dawned
on Maggie to wonder why she was giving her baby away. Maggie was
shocked when she realized Miss Stella must have been having an affair, just like in the stories on the radio. She sure had been fooled; she
always thought Miss Stella was a faithful wife.

When Maggie came home with her son, as she called him, Clyde
confronted her, telling her that nobody's bastard was living in his
house. Instead of cowering, as she had done in the past, she turned
on him like a mother bear defending her cub. Maggie had put on
nearly one hundred pounds; her weight combined with her anger
made her a more than formidable opponent. Afraid at the outcome
of a physical confrontation with her, Clyde turned on his heel, cursing her and warning that the boy had better stay out of his way. She
accepted his terms and he hers. After that day the beatings stopped.
Clyde had seen the glint of insanity in Maggie's eyes and feared for
his life.

Shortly after the boy was born, Stella Goldstein bought a beautiful
home for them in the Fifth Ward and a new Buick. The house was
completely furnished, and Maggie ensured that every room was im-
maculate. Every room but Clyde's—she put the old furniture in his
room and kept the door closed.

Maggie lived for her boy. She would destroy anything or anyone
that hurt her son or prevented her from giving him what she felt he
needed. Last year she'd proven that to the neighborhood kids, who
often heckled and made fun of her child. They pushed him into
the rosebushes in the yard and then laughed uncontrollably when the
thorns entangled him. But she'd shown them all; she went into the
shed and got her husband's ax. When she returned to where her son
was caught, those urchins thought she had gotten the ax to use on
them. That thought did cross her mind. Instead, she turned her
anger on the rosebushes as she chopped and slashed at them until

nothing but debris from the bushes remained. By the time Maggie was through, the rosebushes had been completely destroyed. As the haze of anger slowly left, she looked at the startled faces of the children and noticed several of them had peed their pants. She began to laugh uncontrollably, which was even more frightening to the children, who turned and ran in fear of their lives.

Maggie stood rooted to the spot, cackling as her hair lay in limp clumps loosely around her face, breathing heavily, her hamlike hands still holding tightly to the ax. Before the end of the day the story of Maggie and the rosebushes had traveled all through Fifth Ward. The children nicknamed her "Crazy Maggie" after that day.

Over the years she had been able to tell when her rage was close to exploding and tried to contain it. However, more and more often, as of late, she couldn't control it. She'd come to her senses after the storm of anger and rage had passed. All too often the boy felt the outpouring of her rage and was beaten unmercifully. He tried to do things to please Maggie, to make her smile, hoping maybe then she'd forget the beatings. But she had become like Clyde. The boy's pleas only incited her rage. As he grew older he prayed to live to see the day when he could leave.

As time passed, Maggie could feel her sanity slipping away from her and she knew she was barely holding on by a thread. She could almost visualize the thread breaking; it had come close this morning with that uppity nigga bitch, Carrie! But she'd show her. Maggie was in love, had been since the day Stella had asked her about her home life. She wouldn't let anybody take her Stella from her—or their son. Stella had given her the family she had always wanted. They were a family; she was gentle and kind, and Stella loved her too. She had just hired this woman, Carrie, so David wouldn't be suspicious of whom she really loved. Maggie felt herself relax for the first time in days, since she realized that Carrie was not an immediate threat to her or her family—but she would keep an eye on her, just in case.

20

After the first day, Carrie began to look forward to going to work, although it was hard for her to think of it as work. In many ways she felt as if she'd returned to her childhood and she and Stella were young girls again. They would frequently find some silly thing that tickled them and burst out in laughter. She had been working for Stella almost a month and had become adjusted to her routine. When she met David, Stella's husband, Carrie understood why she had fallen in love with him. He was very kind and gentle toward Stella. When he returned from his trip Back East, he surprised both Stella and Carrie with gifts. He told Carrie that Stella did not speak of her childhood often, due to the painful loss of her parents. But whenever she did, she would talk of the maid's daughter, Cara, whom she had grown to love as if she were a sister. As Carrie listened, tears of regret filled her eyes. She couldn't imagine having to live the lies that Stella had built her life upon. Poor Stella—she had it all, and she had nothing at all.

The only time that Carrie resented Stella and her job was when Stella's friends visited. She found it hard to stomach Stella's transformation; within a moment's notice she would change into a pretentious, overly animated version of herself. Carrie was accustomed to the snobbishness of these women. Although they were white their attitudes were no different from those of the colored women who socialized in the circles she had once frequented. Whenever Stella's friends visited she would take her seat in the rear of the room and await Stella's slightest bidding. Sitting quietly, she would listen to these women who lived a world apart from the colored socialites and she realized that although they were separated by race, they were the same: the same concerns and insecurities about their husbands, the same unfulfilled dreams, the same ceaseless boredom and fear of aging, dread of being a less-than-perfect parent and mate. If she closed her eyes she would not know if she was at a women's auxiliary luncheon or River Oaks bridge club gathering. All of her life she had imagined there to be some great difference that separated white from colored, other than the obvious. To her great surprise she found the differences to be insignificant; it was the sameness that she realized was the most frightening truth to both sides. One evening Carrie told Stella of her assessment. To her surprise Stella responded haughtily and told Carrie she was getting out of her place. After that incident their relationship became very strained, and Carrie became very closemouthed, determined to stay in her place.

Carrie was so busy with work and trying to keep up with the kids and the demands of Logan that things began to fall apart around her without her even being aware of it. Unfortunately, she didn't take notice until it was too late. One afternoon Sofia called Carrie at work. When she came to the phone she heard Sofia sobbing. "Baby, is everything okay?" Carrie asked, trying to contain the fear that began to creep up her spine.

"Mama, come home. It's Odele—she's gone," she stated, crying hysterically.

"Sofia? Sofia? Calm down!" Carrie demanded, trying to remain calm herself.

Stella hurried into the room after overhearing the controlled panic mixed with anxiety in Carrie's voice. "What's wrong, Cara?"

"I'm not sure. It's my daughter Sofia, and she said Odele's gone!" Carrie replied, obviously distressed and trying to restrain her threatening hysteria.

Seeing that Carrie was in no condition to drive, Stella futilely tried to calm her. "Hold on; I'll get David. We'll drive you home—you don't need to face this alone."

Carrie rode in silence, her lips moving silently in prayer. She couldn't bear the thought of losing another child, and she was too afraid to ask Sofia any more questions, afraid of what she might answer. Gone? How could Odele be gone? David, Stella, and Carrie rode along in silence, each preoccupied with their own thoughts. As they pulled up to the house, Carrie noticed that all the lights were on. Before David could come to a complete stop she leaped from the car and ran up the short walk to the front door. It was thrown open by Ana, who appeared anxious and frightened. "Where's Odele?" Carrie demanded. "Where's my baby?"

"She's gone," Logan replied in his raspy voice and slurred speech, standing in the parlor, his crooked body positioned over the walker he now used. "She can't stand living in Studewood no more, she can't stand being colored no more, she can't stand Black Gal no more, and she sure can't stand you and me no more. So she packed her things and left for Hollywood!" Logan spat out the last words as if he tasted something foul. "I say good riddance to the ungrateful wench." He finished by dropping Odele's letter, which he had been holding to the floor. Carrie felt the earth go out from under her; the last thing she saw before passing out was David's bloodless face as he stared, mouth agape, at Sofia.

Carrie awoke to find Stella and Sofia bending over her, holding a cold towel to her temples, trying to bring her around. Sitting up slowly, she saw Ana crying, softly rocking herself. "Come here, baby" she called. Carrie held Ana gently, whispering, "Mama's all right; everything's gonna be just fine." She gently held Ana's face in her hands so she could look her in the eyes. "My promise, okay?" Ana visibly relaxed at her mother's words. Carrie looked around the room, perplexed. "Where's Eddie?"

"I'm not sure, Mama. I'll go look for him," Sofia volunteered, seeming nervous and edgy.

David decided to take advantage of this opportunity to be alone with Sofia. "Relax, Carrie, I'll drive her around the area. I'm sure we'll find him faster, and it will be a lot safer."

"That'll be fine," Carrie agreed hesitantly. She didn't recall introducing David and Stella to the children, or to Logan for that matter. She knew she had blacked out, but she was sure it was for only a minute or so. For some reason she felt uneasy as she turned to watch David and Sofia as they left the house.

Carrie quickly pushed this thought aside; she had no time for foolish musing—she had to find Odele. She had lost a son; she wouldn't lose any more children, not if she could help it. Carrie turned to Stella. "I will need some time off—I have to find my child. Once she's found, I'd like to return to work for you."

Stella couldn't bear the thought of being separated from her sister again. "There has to be some way other than this," she replied thoughtfully. She told Carrie they would work it out together. "With my resources we have a better chance of finding Odele."

But before Stella could continue, Logan bellowed, "I know who you are!" triumphantly, as if he had just solved the riddle of the ages. "Carrie, just 'cause I'm crippled doesn't mean I'm stupid. Fine white lady, all right—or is it really high-yella nigger jus' pretending! Don't this beat all. Just wait till that fancy white husband of yours finds out he's part of my family!" Logan sneered, his face even more contorted than usual. Stella could feel the blood drain from her face and felt her stomach fall. So this was where and how it would finally come out, she thought.

"If you so much as speak a word of this, Logan Daniels," Carrie warned, waiting a beat before dropping the blow, "I will swear you're crazy and have you committed. It wouldn't be hard, either. Then I'll be free—free of you and your ugly ways. I'm sick to my stomach of you! All these years I've wasted . . . I should've left after Edward died, but no! I stayed and put up with you and your whoring until it damn near killed you! Now you think I'm gonna sit by and watch you destroy my children, my family, and any chance I have at happiness? For you? The once great, light, bright, damned near-white preacher! No, sir. Your day is through in this house, and with me! You can't hurt us anymore! And you sure can't hurt me! I won't let you!" she yelled at him, her chest heaving in an attempt to restrain the anger welling up inside of her.

"Call Ruth!" Carrie demanded, pulling the phone to him and putting it in his hand. "Call Ruth! Or better yet, I'll call." Grabbing the phone, Carrie dialed the number she had committed to memory over ten years ago. She turned back to Logan, and this time it was her turn to sneer. "I always knew, Logan. I never bothered her because she was doing me a favor. She kept you from bothering me most of the time."

Ruth picked up the phone on the fourth ring, wondering who could be calling so late. She was surprised and alarmed by the familiar voice on the other end. "Ruth? Carrie Daniels. Logan and his belongings will be ready for you to pick up in one hour," the voice stated matter-of-factly.

Shocked, Ruth stumbled around for a response. "There must be some mistake, Carrie. I have no way to care for Logan. After all, he is your husband."

"Oh, don't be so quick to hang up, Ruth," Carrie responded smoothly. "You see, Logan *is* my husband, and everything that he owns also belongs to me—including your home. As I said, I'll see you within the hour." Carrie hung up and returned the phone to the cradle.

Looking up to find Ana standing with her mouth agape and Stella wearing an expression of combined shock and astonishment, for once Carrie didn't care what anyone else felt or thought. She felt liberated after years of enslavement to a man she had ceased loving after the death of her son. She looked at Logan, his head hanging and his shoulders slumped in defeat. He was pitiful, but she felt no pity. Turning to Stella she said, "I have packing to complete; let me know when Eddie and Sofia get home, or Ruth comes, whoever is first." With that she turned on her heel and went in the back room to get Logan's traveling case and pack his belongings.

Stella sat down heavily. "Come, Ana, sit with your aunt. Let's sit and wait." Ana silently took the seat on the sofa next to her aunt Stella. Stella reached for Ana's hand, and they sat together in a silence that was at first awkward and then comforting as they both contemplated the events that had taken place that evening and wondered what paths the future would take.

Logan slumped miserably on his walker, feeling the full effect of his defeat. He knew not to confront Carrie now, not when she was like this. He'd wait and get better. He knew he could; he just hadn't really tried. He had grown comfortable with the attention and lack of expectations he now received. Carrie was just upset; he knew she didn't mean the things she had said. This might be just what they needed, and now he could see Ruth too. This might not be as bad as it seemed, he thought, a bitter smile playing at the corner of his mouth. Carrie would be back, and this time it'd be on his terms. After all, he'd been a good provider and husband. Of course, he had a wandering eye, like most men. But so did Carrie, and he had even accepted John Browning's bastard daughter. "Yep," he murmured to himself, "she'll be back in no time; then I'll call the shots."

21

David and Sofia rode through the dirt-paved streets of Studewood in silence, both fearful and stunned, in disbelief at the chain of events that had caused their personal lives to cross paths. After Galveston, David had made the arrangements for their assignations, and Sofia would concoct weekend visits to friends' homes. This was easy in the fractured condition of what once had been her family. David knew she was colored; what he didn't know was that she was only sixteen years old.

At fourteen years old, Sofia had developed the voluptuous body of a temptress. This had caused both Carrie and Logan great concern, but Sofia had always been honest and not fast like some of the other girls her age. So they put their concerns to rest. This was true until Sofia felt abandoned by both Odele and her parents. She became best friends with Peggy, the daughter of a prominent colored doctor. Peggy did everything a proper, well-bred girl shouldn't. She didn't care; she knew her pickings would always be ripe because of her wealth and her father's reputation. She enjoyed Sofia's friendship. Because of Peggy's aloofness and social standing, true friendships with girls her age had always been elusive. Now she and Sofia were as close as sisters, and both enjoyed the attention they received from the college-age boys they met on their trips to Galveston. The night that she met David after taking a swim on one of their trips and mistakenly coming to shore on the whites-only section of the beach had caused Sofia to fabricate who she really was, much as Stella had done.

David was obviously much older, but when she emerged from the waveless ocean he came to her as if she had called him. Standing right before her, he gently brushed her hair from her eyes, saying he thought she wasn't real. He immediately began to apologize for taking the liberty of touching her; such behavior was completely unheard of in the South. Sofia assured him there was no harm done and nervously looked around to make sure no other whites had seen her on their beach. She apologized, turned, and dove back into the water to swim to the colored-only section of the beach. To her surprise and secret delight, David ran the entire length of the beach, crossing into the colored-only section, and again met her as she emerged from the ocean onto the shore. This was the first time anyone had been so captivated by Sofia. Unsure how to respond, Sofia excused herself and turned to leave.

David knew she was young, but her shyness had the same effect that a match had to fuel—He returned to the beach house with his mind in a guilty dilemma. David thought of the loss of his child and the emotional distance Stella had put between them. The best solution at the time was to retreat to Galveston in the hopes that the time apart would bring them closer together. Now he was filled with angst as he thought of his wife, and his burning desire to see the beautiful woman named Sofia again.

The next day David strolled casually along the colored-only section of the beach. As the day wore on he grew flustered when he did not find her. Then he began searching in earnest. With single-minded determination he moved unself-consciously among the sunbathers, seeking the beautiful woman whom he had met the night before. David would not rest until he saw her again. She had been the sole subject of his dreams last night, and she was all he could think about today. He had no idea what to do or say when he found her; he just knew he had to find her. Just when he had almost decided to look elsewhere, he noticed several young men who looked to be around college age surrounding two sunbathers. He knew by instinct that only Sofia would command this type of attention. David decided to take his chances and approach the group. He noticed Sofia lounging on her stomach reading, while her friend, who was also attractive, entertained the group with anecdotes about the night before.

As he drew nearer a hush fell over the group of merrymakers when they saw a white man approach. Sofia looked up, a puzzled expression on her face. She turned to see what everyone was looking at; then a broad smile of delight lit up her face. She had hoped he'd look for her. She had hoped that what she saw in his eyes the night before had not been a figment of her imagination. She hadn't been sure until now. Slowly she stood and ran to meet David, to the complete amazement of Peggy and their newfound friends.

As they met he took her hand, smiling. "I'm David." He was so happy and relieved to have found Sofia that he could not suppress the grin that split his face from ear to ear. "Would you have lunch with me?" he asked.

His question broke the spell for Sofia; she became painfully aware of the fact that he was white. Looking around self-consciously, she grew embarrassed by what she thought the other colored sunbathers were thinking. "I'm afraid that would not be possible," she heard herself saying, even as her heart sank.

David then realized the ignorance of his request; it would be impossible for the two of them to have lunch at any of the beach restaurants. But David was not so easily defeated. "How about if I make a picnic lunch—will you have lunch with me then?" he suggested, hoping she would not be able to resist.

As he had hoped, Sofia consented with a nod of her head. The dimple in her chin and her perfect face captivated him; in all his life he had never been this close to physical perfection. They walked side by side to his beachfront home; he talked while Sofia listened intently. As they came upon his home, Sofia was in awe at the size of the home he referred to as a cottage. It was as large as the home she had been raised in when she lived in the Third Ward. Sofia did not betray her astonishment to David and behaved as if she were accustomed to this type of lifestyle. She joined him in the kitchen as he put together items for a picnic. Leaving the house, they sought the shade of a fig tree that sat at the farthest end of his property, which overlooked both land and ocean. Sofia would always remember that day as the day she fell in love with David. He never touched her; they just talked for hours, and when all had been said they lay on opposite sides of the blanket in silence, enjoying the closeness and the distance, the peace and the anticipation. There was no doubt for either that it was only the beginning. The need to belong to someone had always been

Sofia's greatest desire; she lived in Odele's shadow, trying to be a part of her life, and always seeking to be Logan's favorite, even though she knew he loved Odele more. Now she didn't need either. She'd found where and with whom she belonged.

Sofia Daniels and David Goldstein fell in love, as only two lonely strangers who saw their fantasies in each other could do. At the end of three days, when they both had to return home, David gave her his office number, saying she could always reach him there. He made her promise to call him as soon as she arrived at the dorm. David asked Sofia if there was a way he could contact her at the dormitory. To make him think she was older, Sofia had told David she was a freshman at Texas Southern University. Thinking quickly, she told him her parents couldn't afford a phone. He told her to call him as soon as she could, holding her closely, slowly and seductively brushing his lips against hers, regretting that any minute he had to be separated from this gentle beauty. "I'm going to have to do something about the phone situation," he said regretfully. Taking a step back, he turned and watched as she walked away. For the first time David regretted being married.

When Sofia returned home, she thought about David night and day. She wanted to call him, but feared she could not get away to meet him. She had begun to despair that she would never see him again; then she devised a plan. Two weeks passed before Sofia was able to call David. She was shocked when the operator answered, "Goldstein's department store." She was even more astonished when she was put through to the president's office and David's voice came through. Her stomach filled with butterflies when she heard his familiar masculine voice saying, "Hello? Is it really you, Sofia?"

She released a sigh of relief because he sounded sincerely happy to hear from her. "Yes," she replied, feeling her nervousness and apprehension slowly slipping away.

"I thought you'd never call. I've been going out of my mind. When can I see you?" he blurted out. They made plans to meet each other. This was the beginning of a relationship that they could not seem to end.

Sofia had not told either David or her parents about the baby. She was four months pregnant and she had to wear girdles to flatten her growing tummy. The clock was ticking and time was running out. As she and David drove slowly through Studewood she decided now was as good a time as any to tell him the truth. "David we need to talk. We have to talk."

David slowly turned toward her, his eyes red from unshed tears. "I never meant to hurt you. I love you so much. I never told you that I was married because I did not want to hurt you. I knew it didn't interfere with the way I feel about you. I know that you're pregnant." He grabbed her hand tentatively, holding it as if she were fragile as glass. "If that's what you were going to say, I already know. I have already begun to prepare a home for us. It was supposed to be my surprise to you whenever you got your nerve up to tell me about the baby," David finished, looking at her expectantly.

Sofia sat in stunned silence, her mind racing. It hadn't even registered until now that the woman in her house—her mother's employer—was her lover's wife. He already knew she was pregnant? How had he guessed? Had her parents arrived at the same conclusion? Should she tell him she was only sixteen? Fearing his rejection, she decided to wait. "David, I love you, but I'm scared. If I stay here, my parents won't let me have this baby. They'll call in Miss Sukie—she works on any girl that gets knocked up when they're too young—"

"Then I'll take care of it, Sofia!" David interrupted. "I love you, and I love and want our baby!"

David was so sure of himself that Sofia felt safe and protected. She decided that, just like Odele, she would also leave. Turning to David, she said, "I just want us to be together as a family." Leaning against him, he took her in his arms, gently smoothing the stray hairs around her temples. Planting a passionate kiss on her waiting lips, he could not hide the force of his lust. Sofia forgot about all else except David and this kiss. At that moment, time stood still. David knew that he could not completely fulfill her wishes, but he would do his best to give her all the things that would make her happy.

By the time they returned to the house, Logan was no longer there.

22

The boy was now a man. C.P., as he was called, stood six feet, four inches. He was tall, well built, and fine. C.P. had a boyish charm that had a magnetic pull on the opposite sex. He attracted women and girls effortlessly. A natural athlete, he played center for the TSU Tigers. His goal was to play professional basketball, and everything was going as planned. His coach expected him to go first round in the draft. C.P. was lucky because he was an only son, which meant he was not automatically recruited to fight in the Korean War. He loved campus life and looked forward to leaving Houston after college to play in the pros. He knew that it was the only way for him to escape the suffocating attention of his mother.

C.P. had been thinking a lot about his mother lately. Sometimes he felt overwhelmed with guilt for wanting so desperately to leave. At other times he was plagued with concern for her mental well-being. She had been behaving very strangely, talking out loud to herself and laughing as though she were having a conversation with someone unseen. Changing his plans, he decided to head home and check on his mother today instead of hanging out after practice with his teammates, as he would normally do. For some reason he had a sense of urgency to get home. Instead of waiting for the bus, which was unpredictable, he began to jog home. As he jogged his sense of unease seemed to grow with each step. Without realizing it he had begun to run at a full sprint.

As he ran he thought about his mother, and for the first time the idea he had always repressed finally surfaced. C.P. hadn't realized his mother was crazy as a young boy, even though the kids nicknamed her "Crazy Maggie" after she chopped down the rosebushes in the yard. He always thought she was cruel and mean-tempered, but not crazy. The realization came to him as he ran, recalling how she'd always ask if he was doing the nasty, then walk slowly around him, sniffing the air, staring him straight in the eye, and saying, "I can smell the nasty from ten feet away, boy. You'd better not ever let me smell it on you." She'd finished with a menacing glare full of an unspoken threat. Each time he thought of that day chills went down his spine as he recalled her glazed expression while she continued sniffing the air like a dog. He ran on, his lungs burning with each intake of breath, tears streaming from his eyes as he was assaulted with another memory: his mother cutting down the rosebushes with an ax, threatening the neighborhood children, his father, and Miss Stella's assistant, Carrie. Sometimes she would hold him too closely and whisper how she loved only him, Ruth, and Miss Stella.

Maggie became worse after Miss Stella let her go almost two years ago. This came on the heels of threats she made against Carrie. Although Miss Stella continued to pay Maggie weekly, as she always had when she was working, it seemed only to anger her more. There were times that his mother's anger and cruelty to him caused him to despise her. But C.P. had always loved Miss Stella, and he always would. As a child he thought she was the prettiest lady he had ever seen. He would sometimes daydream that she was his real mother; he even thought he looked like her. One day he even told his mother that he thought he looked like Miss Stella. Maggie beat him unmercifully at that remark. He never commented after that day on any resemblance he might have to anyone other than her.

Running at breakneck speed, CP turned the corner of his block. As he approached the house his stomach lurched. *Why are all of these people standing in front of my house?* he wondered. Feeling tingles of fear creeping up his spine, he pushed past the spectators and stared in astonished disbelief at his father. Clyde was sitting on the porch swing taking shallow drags from his Camel cigarette, calmly staring back at the growing crowd as if he were not aware of the butcher knife that was lodged to the handle in his chest. C.P. felt his knees turn to water as he pushed his way through the crowd. He bent to ask his father if he was okay. It felt as though he were being pulled into a horror story. His father continued puffing on the cigarette, staring past him. Then C.P. recalled the stories he had been told as a child of his father's violent history and how he used to beat Maggie. Propelled into action, he ran past his father, throwing the screen door ajar, looking for his mother.

Filled with horror and dread, he ran to her room, expecting the worst. Then he heard her humming in her tuneless way in the kitchen. Woodenly, he turned and walked with leaden steps into the kitchen, toward the sound. He found Maggie standing over the cutting board putting crust into a pie pan. When she looked up from her work, she nonchalantly told him, "Clyde has my good knife. Run and fetch it for me so I can trim the crust on your favorite pie. Go on!" she demanded. Bubbles of spittle filled with blood formed as she spoke. Not knowing what to do, he stared at the bruise on her cheek and the blood running from her mouth. Her apron was decorated with splashes of blood that continued to the roll in her stockings. "Don't just stand there, boy; do as your mother says!" she again demanded.

C.P. felt disembodied as he turned to go back to the front porch. By the time he made it to the porch the police had arrived and his father was dead. Pushing past him, they went in to get his mother, guns drawn. To their surprise she stood at the door of the kitchen offering them homemade cookies and telling them she'd serve them fresh pie as soon as her lazybones son returned from fetching her knife. C.P. stood on the porch as the police escorted Maggie into the car without restraints. "Son, I'm going to talk to these men about your bad daddy. Dinner is ready. I'll be back to tuck you in," she said, smiling. He realized her front teeth were missing. *That's where all the blood came from,* he thought absently.

The police officer looked at him with pity. "Son, the morgue will be here within the hour to pick up the body. In the meantime, I would suggest you stay with a friend. Don't touch a thing—police work, you know." He closed the door of the cruiser and resumed his post at the front gate. Numb and detached, C.P. turned to go to his room. In less than an hour his world had tumbled in around him. Not knowing what else to do or who to call, C.P. called Stella.

*   *   *

Stella hung up the phone; she could not believe that Maggie had finally snapped. Nor could she comprehend the effect it would have on her. She knew only that her child, the child she had denied, was in need and had called her. Stella told him to pack a few things and come over. She immediately called David and retold the story C.P. had told her. She asked his permission to let the boy come stay awhile with them, already knowing he would agree. Over the years David had grown quite fond of C.P., and had even written him a letter of recommendation to assist him in attaining a full scholarship to Texas Southern University. Stella busied herself waiting for his arrival. She had a room in the servants' quarters prepared for his stay.

Sitting on the bed in his room C.P. looked around, knowing it would be his last time in the house. Once he left his home he would never come back. Packing his bag, he decided to look for work immediately. He would not impose on the Goldsteins any longer than he had to. Mentally he began to list the people he needed to speak to. His coach would be first; he had to break the news that he would be dropping out of school. C.P. occupied his thoughts with trivialities; he didn't want to allow the devastation to seep in.

Taking a long look at his home, he turned and walked away, not looking back, not even once. As he turned the corner he knew it would be his last time in the Fifth Ward. He walked along without regrets. Boarding the bus for River Oaks, he began the slow process of shutting out his many unwanted memories. Looking out the bus window, he enjoyed the scenery of the beautiful trees flowering in spring. For the first time C.P. noticed the progression in the scenery from Negro middle class to the affluent neighborhood of River Oaks. Standing at the door marked *Servants and Deliveries,* he waited several minutes to compose himself before ringing the bell. As expected, Carrie answered the door. Hugging him tearfully, she led him to the library, where Stella impatiently paced the floor, awaiting his arrival. C.P. stood just inside of the door until she directed him to be seated. Tentatively he sat down. For the first time in his life he felt shame and embarrassment in front of Stella. Somehow he felt responsible for and soiled by his mother's violent behavior. Not knowing what to say, he began by apologizing for calling.

"Nonsense!" Stella responded, impassioned, as she tried to bottle her emotions. "Clark, you have been like a son to us. Your mother has brought you around since you were born. I would have been upset if you had not called us. I can only imagine how devastated you must be to have come home to that scene. Sadie will take you to your room; try to get some rest. I know it's hard. When David gets home we'll talk about your future," she finished.

At this Clark's eyes filled with tears. "I've already decided on my future. I'm quitting school. I appreciate your hospitality, but I'll only stay for a few days until I find a job." As he tried to rearrange the plans he had made for his life, the emotional strain he had tried to contain exploded, and Clark crumbled under his heavy burden.

Unprepared for the maternal tug she felt, Stella hesitated momentarily before going to his side. Taking him in her arms, she held and comforted her son until his sobbing ceased. "There'll be no more talk about quitting school, Clark. I want you to go to your room and rest. It is not time to make or change plans. It is just time to rest." Clark willingly allowed himself to be led to his room. He didn't realize how exhausted he was until he lay down on the bed and immediately fell into a dreamless sleep.

The next morning he was awakened by a knock on his door, followed by Sadie entering with a breakfast tray. Placing the tray on the table next to the bed, the soft-spoken maid told him, "The Goldsteins want you to meet them in the gazebo after you've had breakfast." Sighing deeply, he wondered whether he would have to move right away. To his surprise they offered to allow him to live with them until he graduated. Mr. Goldstein informed him they would employ him as a handyman.

As time passed, the Goldstein household adjusted to its new addition. However, instead of Clark's being treated in the detached manner of an employee, they all settled into a familiar and comfortable routine of taking meals and long walks together. Clark focused all of his attention on basketball and his studies. He was determined to have a successful career and a wealthy lifestyle. For the first time in his life, he lived without fear. The Goldsteins treated him well. To his surprise they both displayed a sincere interest in his courses, and Mr.

Goldstein made a point of attending all of his home games. The more time he spent with the Goldsteins, the more he realized how abnormal his childhood had been. As a result of his affection and admiration for Stella, he found he was attracted to girls who looked like her. The only problem was that girls who looked like Stella were normally white, with few exceptions. This especially posed a problem for a Negro man living in the South during Jim Crow days. As a result, Clark did not date often, unless he found that rare Negro girl who was as white as he was. Stella would often joke with him about how she knew he was really a ladies' man. At times he longed to tell her how he dreamed of marrying a girl who looked just like her, but he never did. He feared offending her, or worse.

Sometimes he would look up to find Stella and her companion Carrie studying him intently as he finished a chore that had been assigned to him. Clark was very fond of Carrie; there was a gentleness and sadness about her that caused him to feel protective of her. There was also something very familiar about her, but he could never put his finger on it. He enjoyed her company, and he was intrigued by the stories she would share with Stella about her children. There was a lilt in her voice as she tried to suppress her smile when she recalled something they had said or done. It was obvious she loved her children dearly. Again, Clark would feel pangs of loneliness. He never recalled moments of closeness or the kind of shared joys that Carrie spoke so fondly of. He especially enjoyed the anecdotes she told about her daughter Ana. He would laugh heartily, imagining a pig-tailed, mischievous preteen who fell madly in love at a moment's notice.

Although Stella mentioned that Ana had just turned sixteen, Clark still thought of her as barely postadolescent. That was, until he met Ana. The first time he saw her he was walking at a brisk pace to get out of the frigid winter air. He had parked his car, the Buick Stella had given to his mother, in the space designated for staff. As he rapidly approached the door, it bolted open as Ana, also trying to stay warm, ran toward Carrie's car. Entranced by her beauty, Clark tripped over the ledge of the door, almost falling to his knees. Fortunately, Carrie was just leaving and put out her hands to steady him. Embarrassed, he laughed self-consciously, apologizing for being so clumsy.

"Nonsense," Carrie replied. "That daughter of mine hates the cold so much, I'm surprised she didn't knock you down trying to get to the warmth of the car!" Carrie shook her head in mock disgust.

"Your daughter?" Clark inquired, wondering if this was Sofia.

"Yes, that's my Ana." Carrie bade him good-night as she also left for the warmth of her car.

After that day, he made a point to try to find out more about Carrie's daughter Ana. To his surprise, he found she was never far from his thoughts, and he looked for the chance to see her again. One afternoon he overheard Carrie and Stella discussing plans for a debutante party in Ana's honor. This was the opportunity he had been waiting for. Appearing to be only mildly interested in their planning, he asked when the party was to be held. As he anticipated, Carrie and Stella both exchanged startled glances and told him the party was to be held the following Saturday. Then Carrie apologized for not personally extending an invitation to Clark; she had assumed he would come with the Goldsteins, as Stella had mentioned they were bringing a guest to the party. "There will be lots of young women of quality for you to meet!" Carrie informed him pointedly.

"Good, it's settled, I'll be there!" Clark responded cheerfully, anticipating the opportunity to meet Ana face-to-face. He had to find out what it was about her that intrigued him so much.

After Clark left the room, Stella complimented Carrie on her observation. "It's high time he met a nice girl," she said thoughtfully.

23

Ana swung her hips in the mirror, watching her gown swirl around her delicate ankles. She was preparing for her debutante party on Saturday night. It had taken Carrie and Stella nearly a month of arguing over who had a keener fashion sense before they finally settled and let Ana choose her own gown for the ball. As usual, things always worked themselves out, as Mama Louise was so fond of saying. And when Ana looked back at their lives she realized how true that saying really was.

After Odele ran away to Hollywood and stardom, Sofia followed close on her tracks. Except, as Carrie later learned, Sofia left home because she was pregnant by an older man. They never learned who the man was, but from Sofia's letters he took good care of Sofia and their daughter, Angel. Sofia frequently called and sent pictures of Angel, even offering to send Carrie and Ana train tickets to come and visit her in Los Angeles. Although Sofia painted a rosy picture of her life, Ana had the idea that Sofia's life had not worked out quite as she'd planned. But one thing she knew about the Daniels clan was that they were all big on denial. Sofia told them Angel's father had bought them a mansion, but Ana remembered how Sofia could exaggerate. Ana had decided that as soon as she graduated from Yates High School she would visit her older sister and niece.

Ana's lifestyle had changed tremendously, thanks to Aunt Stella, a

relationship she still had to keep secret. As a birthday present for
Carrie several years ago, Stella had purchased one of the smaller
homes in the Third Ward. But compared to the home in Studewood,
they were living in splendor again. Ana was elated to have returned to
the Third Ward. She had never been happy in Studewood. Even as a
young child, she had decided she wanted a life of wealth and position.
Lena Horne, the movie star, was her idol. They both had the same
complexion and similar features. Lena had been hailed as a rare
beauty among Negroes and white folks alike. So Ana wore her hair in
the same style as Lena, and reveled in the open admiration she received about the resemblance. *Not bad for Black Gal,* she would think
from time to time, calling to mind the pain and confusion the name
had caused when Logan used it, refusing to acknowledge her by her
given name.

Now Black Gal, the nickname she had so venomously hated, was
commonly used by her friends and family alike. Eddie had begun calling Ana Black Gal shortly after they moved to Studewood. He knew it
infuriated Logan because it undermined his malicious attempt to be-
little or humiliate her. Soon everyone used the name when they referred to Ana. But because Eddie had made it clear that she was his
favorite sister, she wore the name as her medal of honor. During the
previous ten years of her life she recalled how she had needed the
closeness of her brother to get her through the turbulence that encompassed their lives. She also remembered how hurt and disappointed she was when he refused to move back with them to the
Third Ward. He adamantly refused to cut all ties to his friends and
lifestyle in Studewood. Eddie had fallen prey to the seduction of the
fast life. He had no interest other than carousing, gambling, and
drinking. Frequently he'd make his way over to their home, often-
times smelling of whiskey, with some starry-eyed girl hanging on to
him. Each nameless girl he brought—they all answered to "baby"—
was obviously hopelessly in love with Eddie. Ana was accustomed to
the steady parade of adoring females and always wondered why
Carrie never tried to hide her hostility or disgust at Eddie's lifestyle or
his choice of women. Ana generally ignored the girls and directed
her conversation entirely to Eddie, as if the two of them were alone.
Carrie would always make a cutting remark about his choice in
women. "Eddie, you need to leave these whores alone and find a decent girl to settle down with!"

"I like my life, Mama!" Eddie never defended the women whom Carrie so grievously insulted; he only defended his right to live his life and make his choices as he saw fit. The argument would always end with Carrie fighting back tears, telling him she could not stand to lose him. Sometimes she would unthinkingly or unknowingly finish her plea by saying "again." Ana knew that her mother was referring to the first Edward. This thought always gave her chills; she could not bear the thought of anything bad happening to Eddie any more than her mother could.

As time passed, Carrie never gave up on the hope that Eddie would change his mind and come to live with them. Each day she always made enough dinner for three, always in the hope that Eddie would stop by. On the rare evenings that he joined them alone, Carrie and Ana would bask in his undivided attention. Eddie had a way of making them feel special and beautiful. Secretly, Ana was happy he had not fallen in love and settled down. She enjoyed having her brother's attention and knowing she held a special place in his life. Generally, after they had eaten dinner, they would sit together in the family room to listen to the latest 78s on the new stereo console that he'd bought for Carrie as a housewarming gift. "Black Gal, sing something," he'd implore. And sing she did! Ana enjoyed the evenings when she pretended to be a famous singer. Using a candle as her microphone, she'd serenade them tirelessly. After a while Eddie would begin to get restless. This usually was an indication that it was time for him to get on the streets.

Just before walking out the door, he'd hug Carrie tightly, kissing her on the forehead. Then he'd take a wad of money folded over once in his pocket and give Carrie and Ana what he called spending money, usually a few hundred dollars. Each time Carrie would refuse it, as Ana held on to her share, hoping her mother wouldn't insist she return it. As expected, she always did, and then Eddie would place it right back in Ana's palm or in her pocket when Carrie wasn't looking.

"Okay! Okay, Mama! Just put it away for me in case I run out!" Carrie would look at him intently, trying to discern some hidden meaning to his words. Not ever finding any, she'd take the money and tell him where she was hiding it.

Eddie was Ana's heart of hearts. She idolized him and made sure she was always home as if by unspoken agreement around the time that he would drop in. Before leaving he would hug and kiss both

Carrie and Ana, looking them over as if it would be his last time. Then he'd say as he was leaving, "I got to go make some bread. 'Cause you the only nigga women gonna pimp me!" As he'd walk away, Ana would watch, thinking how handsome her brother was. She'd admire his Cadillac and his sharkskin suit, fascinated by the colors as they seemed to dance over the fabric. One thing about Eddie—or Fast Eddie, as his friends called him—he was always dressed sharp and always drove a fine car, even though he was just twenty-three years old, which was unheard of for most colored men his age in the South.

"Don't forget my party Saturday night!" she called out to him as he pulled out of the drive.

"Wouldn't miss it for the world; I'll be there!" he promised.

By Friday night Eddie was on a train to Los Angeles to escape One-Eyed Lonnie, a small-time hood in the Heights. He'd put a contract out on Eddie for getting his wife, Daisy, pregnant.

The remainder of the week moved at a snail's pace for Ana. When Saturday arrived, she was excited and nervous at the same time. Ina May and Lena, her best friends, spent the night with Ana, talking and primping all night long, discussing how they'd look and act at the party the next night.

The following morning Carrie knocked firmly on the door, smiling to herself as she heard the three girls groan collectively. Waiting a few minutes and still not hearing any movement, Carrie opened the door. "Ana, you girls get out of bed now! Tonight is a big night, and we still have a lot of things left to do."

Ana sat on the side of the bed and stretched, trying to pull herself out of a deep sleep. She turned and nudged Lena and Ina May. "If I have to get up, y'all definitely are gonna get up too." The three girls dressed and went downstairs, to find Carrie standing next to the phone, hands on her hips.

"Mama? Is everything all right?"

"It's that meddling Stella. She and David have decided to play matchmaker with some widower from Back East."

"What's wrong with that?" the girls chimed in, as if on cue.

"When are we going to meet him?" asked Ana, forever the romantic, excited at the prospect of her mother meeting a man.

"Tonight, if Stella and David have anything to do with it. They're bringing him to your party," Carrie replied in mock exasperation. The phone rang again, interrupting Carrie. As she hung up the phone, she looked even more exasperated. "That was Louise. She insists that we go and get our hair done—and to make matters worse, she's on her meddlesome way! I have never seen so many busybodies in my life. You would think it was my party, instead of my youngest child's." She sighed, unable to mask the irritation she felt at her sister and friend.

Ana whispered to her friends with a shrug of her shoulders, "She's just nervous about tonight. Let's go and do our nails; then I want to go to Rexall. I saw the prettiest red lipstick—I've got to have it for tonight!" she exclaimed excitedly. Ana couldn't wait for her party to begin; she prayed that both the boy Aunt Stella called C.P. and Don would be there. She had not mentioned one word about C.P. to her two closest friends yet. On the other hand, all they had talked about was Don in town visiting his parents from Southern U. She had made sure his younger sister, Gloria, was invited; now Ana just hoped she'd bring Don.

Until she had seen C.P., Don Washington had been the most handsome boy she'd ever seen in her life. Don's skin was a rich milky chocolate, he had dreamy eyes the same brown as his skin, and his hair was wavy and black. When she first spotted him dropping Gloria off at school after the Christmas break, she'd asked Lena if he was Gloria's beau. She informed Ana that Don was Gloria's older brother. He was also the bee's knees, the absolute dreamiest boy in Houston. Surely she must know that he was the same Don that every girl from preteen to college age wanted for her own, and so far he remained elusive and unattached. After seeing Don, what she did know was that Don Washington would be hers—unless she decided on C.P. instead.

Well, who says I can't be fickle? she thought, continuing to daydream.

At sixteen, Ana Daniels was a rare beauty among Houstonians. She was often compared to Dorothy Dandridge or Lena Horne, and wore her hair in the same styles those women did, to emphasize the resemblance. Ana had come into her own, aware of her beauty but not overly concerned with it—until now. Now Ana wanted to use every advantage she had to win the attention and heart of Don Washington. He was handsome, smart, and well-bred—a good catch and perfect husband material. His father was the first colored judge in Texas, and Don, already in law school, intended to follow in his father's footsteps.

Although bright, Ana had no real interest in academia. She would often tell her friends that she intended to attend Texas Southern University to get her M.R.S. If she didn't get married then she would move to California with her sister and pursue a singing career. She had a lovely voice and won many talent shows throughout Houston. She had even been featured on local radio singing Billie Holiday's "Good Morning Heartache." Ana had her future all planned, and it was all-promising.

Tonight was her debut. Thomas and Louise had spared no expense in planning and preparing for this celebration, and they had even hired a band to perform. Stella had ordered Ana a gown from Goldstein's couture line. Because red was Ana's favorite color, her dress was made of iridescent silk woven with thread that reflected shades of red as the lights touched it.

When Carrie saw Ana's dress she had a fit. "A sixteen-year-old girl should not wear such a bold color." Fortunately for Ana, Mama Louise and Aunt Stella would not allow Carrie to change Ana's order to the more juvenile and virginal white dress that Carrie preferred.

Ana and her friends spent the rest of the day primping in front of the mirror and each other. They practiced their haughty looks, mimicked from *Ebony,* the colored magazine. Then they perfected their smiles by rubbing Vaseline on their teeth so their lips would glide smoothly into what they hoped was a seductive smile. Earlier Ana had insisted Carrie do as Louise asked and get her hair done. It was important that she was as stunning as Ana. Also, Carrie was a bundle of nerves and Ana didn't want it rubbing off; she already got butterflies every time she thought of the evening to come.

Bored and filled with anticipation, Ana suggested the three girls walk to the Nortons' but ended up being shooed away by Papa T, who said they were slowing the preparations and getting in the way. Ana, more than a little perturbed at the treatment from Papa, went away sulking as her friends followed quietly in her wake. Stopping at the Rexall to check out the cosmetics counter, Ana picked up a new perfume called My Secret. Spraying a mist in the air to test the scent, she looked slyly at Lena.

"This was made for me to help me keep my secret."

"Okay, I'll take the bait—what secret do you have?"

"Well, if I just blab and tell you two then it's not a secret anymore."

"I should have known, Ina—there is no secret, because we both know Ana can't keep a secret."

"Well, when my dreamy secret appears tonight I won't have to keep it, will I?"

"You mean Don?" Lena could not keep from prying; she had sensed her best friend was holding back, but even when she tried to call her bluff it failed to work.

"No, I don't mean Don. . . . I mean someone else. He makes Don seem soft, if you know what I mean." Ana could not believe that she had voiced her preference for C.P. over Don. Clearly Don was the better catch; as far as she could tell, C.P. had nothing to offer.

Ana's disparaging comparison of Don and this unknown suitor managed to silence both Lena and Ina, as they wondered if the stress of the party was giving their friend the vapors.

Carrie returned from the hairdresser feeling more relaxed than when she'd left. As usual, Louise had thought of the right distraction to take her mind off the chaos. Carrie sighed; she had become so concerned with everything turning out perfect for Ana's party that she was a nervous wreck. She entered her house with an air of expectancy, and now looked forward to meeting this potential suitor that Stella and David were so excited about. Since she had divorced Logan over four years ago she had not dated anyone. He had finally married Ruth, and to Carrie's own surprise it had absolutely no effect on her.

It was funny, Carrie reflected—she had allowed Logan to disrupt her life for too many years. As a result, she had stopped paying attention and lost her children as they struggled toward adulthood. Odele had run off to Hollywood to pass as white and become an actress. She had bitterly blamed Carrie for the disruption of her perfect life. Now the only time Carrie saw her was in the movies. Delia, the screen name she had assumed, rarely wrote and never called. Her letters were always brief and distant, and she never left a return address or telephone number. The closest Carrie came to Odele or Delia was seeing her on the cover of one of the screen magazines.

Sofia had followed in Odele's footsteps by running away to Los Angeles, except she was not running toward stardom; she was running away from fear of discovery. Not only was she pregnant, but by an older man, obviously white and wealthy. Carrie arrived at these conclusions after photos of her granddaughter, Angel, arrived. She was indeed a little angel. Stella always laughed, saying the child had reached back to its grand-aunt. The child was white, with dark hair and the most beautiful gray-green eyes, strikingly similar to Stella's.

Once Stella laid eyes on the baby, she insisted they take a trip to California to see Sofia. When they arrived in Los Angeles, they were surprised when her chauffeur drove them down a beautiful tree-lined street amid which the new Goldstein's department store stood, along with several other upscale department stores. The driver informed them it was the newly developed Santa Barbara Plaza. They continued past the shops to beautiful modern homes nestled in the hills that overlooked the city of Los Angeles. The area was appropriately named View Park. "Hmmm, Sofia's not exactly in need of diaper-and-milk money, is she, Carrie?" Stella commented, more than a little surprised. So, also, was Carrie, although from her conversations with Sofia she knew her middle daughter was certainly not in need—financially, anyway.

As they approached the front door, Sofia flung it open, running to embrace Carrie tightly, and then Stella. Carrie had informed Sofia who Stella was after they both had gotten past the shock and trauma of her pregnancy and hastily announced departure. They all embraced tearfully as they stood on the walkway that was surrounded by lush tropical foliage and a perfectly manicured lawn.

Finally Carrie and Stella seemed to come to their senses at the same time, asking "Where's Angel? Sleeping?"

"Oh, I forgot!" Sofia explained. "I was so excited to see you both! She's playing in the den. Let's go and find her," Sofia suggested, leading the way. Carrie and Stella exchanged worried glances. To their surprise, Angel was in the den being watched by her nanny—another surprise, as they had expected to find her playing alone, temporarily forgotten.

Carrie and Stella were both impressed with Sofia's lovely home. It was furnished with warmth, and her home exuded love. Sofia had returned to her normal dress size, but the birth had ripened her youthful appearance. She was stunning. Sofia was and wasn't the daughter Carrie remembered. This Sofia was mature, self-assured, calm, loving, and confident. These were the attributes of a woman who was well loved and well kept. Carrie saw only a glimpse of the once-insecure

Sofia as she observed her studying Stella closely from time to time, almost as if she were sizing her up. On several occasions she had behaved rather rudely to Stella without provocation. She seemed to openly compare Stella's magnificent ten-carat canary-yellow diamond wedding ring to her own ring. Sofia's ring was beautiful in its own right, but certainly could not compare to Stella's. Carrie prayed Sofia would learn to enjoy the things she had, for she was certainly blessed. But Carrie remembered that as a child, Sofia always compared herself to Odele, measuring herself against her own private scale. For some reason Sofia always seemed to think the grass was greener on the other side. Unfortunately, it seemed as if Sofia had yet to learn and accept that there would always be others who had more, no matter who you were or what you had. Carrie was happy that her daughter did not have to struggle and had such a pampered lifestyle. She was curious about the man she had chosen. However, they were to leave with no more information about him than they came with, much to Carrie's chagrin.

After their stay with Sofia, Carrie was able to return to Houston in peace. Her daughters were fine. Sofia also had not been in touch with Odele since her stardom. She said that through her friend she had had the opportunity to sit next to Odele at the premiere of her last movie. They made polite small talk, Sofia gave her a photo of Angel, and although Odele promised to call, they had not spoken since. At one time this would have devastated Sofia. Now she merely accepted it as a matter of fact. Even more to Carrie's surprise, Sofia refused to go to visit Logan. Since he had married Ruth, she had no desire to reestablish the close relationship they had once shared.

As Stella and Carrie talked about their visit with Sofia on the flight back to Houston, Stella mentioned that she would make sure David stopped in and checked on Sofia on his trips to Los Angeles. Maybe, just maybe, he would find out who this mystery man was.

That was almost eight years ago, and still they didn't know who Angel's father was.

Eddie now lived and hustled in Studewood. Much to Carrie's dismay, she had not been able to convince him to move back to the Third Ward with them. He said the Heights were in his blood, and he was living and dying in the place that made his blood flow. Carrie knew then that she had lost her only son to a force she couldn't fight with logic, pleas, or tears. Eddie always got around her fears, laughing and joking her out of the depression that sometimes would engulf her at the thought of any harm coming to her only son.

Each day Carrie would pray to God to cover her son. "Keep him safe, Lord, head to toe." Sometimes she'd repeat this prayer hourly until it became a chant.

Ana would hear her mother's prayer and understood the prayer was not for her. However, she never felt offended or shortchanged. She often chimed in, saying the same prayer that Carrie had spoken: "Safe from head to toe, Lord, safe from head to toe!" Carrie and Ana had both heard about the women whom Eddie pimped as he hung out at Bennie's Bar each night, but they didn't care. They'd heard about the drugs and gambling. They didn't care. The only thing they cared about was "safe from head to toe, Lord . . . keep him safe from head to toe." And for a while the Lord was listening.

Ana Carrie, another me, Carrie thought, *another me but not. Stronger than me, more pride than me, more determination than me, more guts than me, and, if I have anything to do with it, if I can help her down the road just a little farther, a better life than me!* Carrie was determined that Ana would not repeat the mistakes she had made. Now, as she dressed for her daughter's party, she thought, *The battle's almost over, Lord; she's almost there.* Carrie hummed a tune and put the final touches on her makeup. Then she called Ana into her room to fasten her dress. She'd heard the girls downstairs giggling for the last half hour.

Ana walked into Carrie's room, unsure why she had been summoned. When she saw Carrie she froze. She had never seen her mother look so . . . *alluring* was the only word that came to mind to describe Carrie's appearance. Although Carrie was now in her late forties, due to personal and family tragedies her hair had turned white, a pure snow white. She refused to allow her hairdresser to put any of the so-called tints in it, saying "This is my medal; I earned it, so I'm wearing it."

Her white hair framed her face, perfectly contrasting with her smooth, tan complexion. To emphasize the color of her hair she wore a platinum satin strapless gown. On any other woman the dress might have appeared a little more conservative than it did on Carrie. Instead, the birth of five children had accentuated the positive, leaving her an hourglass figure.

Ana whistled softly between her teeth. "Gee, Mama, you're going to knock every old man dead," she said in mild astonishment.

Knowing this was intended as a compliment, Carrie took it as one. She turned so Ana could zip her up. "Are you ladies ready?"

"Yes, we're just waiting for you!"

"I'm on my way down then," Carrie replied as she glanced in the mirror, making a final inspection of her appearance. Pleased at how she looked, she grabbed her wrap and purse and joined the girls downstairs.

24

Carrie, Ana, and her friends arrived at the ball amid a throng of people. It was a perfect spring evening for a garden party. As expected, the decor was impeccable: there were bowls and bowls of fresh tulips arrayed in white, pink, and red; bouquets of balloons appeared to serve as the anchor for the white tent that covered the stage and dance floor; tables adorned with the tulip bouquets were placed in clusters throughout the well-manicured yard. Ana could not have wished for a more beautiful and exquisite presentation. She proudly walked into the party arm in arm with Carrie. They were quite a pair—mother and daughter, the perfect complement. Carrie displayed the refined beauty that Ana would grow into. Ana reminded everyone of the youthful and innocent beauty Carrie had once possessed. There were murmured exchanges among the guests as they exclaimed how they were both so beautiful. Carrie and Ana began to mingle, pausing to greet and acknowledge their guests. As they made their way through the room, Louise approached Carrie, smiling broadly. "You both are breathtaking," she stated as she embraced first Carrie, then Ana. "Follow me; I'll show you where our table is before you get lost in the crowd," she said excitedly as they followed in her wake. Although Louise was now in her sixties, she was unrivaled in her elegance and bearing. Carrie still admired the way she managed and moved through a crowded room, constantly smiling and commenting to her guests without pausing, continuing to lead the way. Once they arrived at their table, Carrie and Ana both screamed in unison as Sofia and Angel came around from the rear of the table. With his arm around Louise, Thomas affectionately kissed his wife on the tip of her nose and said, "You did it, Miss Louise."

Returning his gaze lovingly, she said, "No, we did it, Thom, and it was easier than we expected, especially with this last-minute surprise appearance by Sofia and Angel. I needed this distraction; if I had to wait any longer I would burst! Now if I can just hold out a few minutes more!"

Ana and Carrie were so surprised to see Sofia and Angel that for several minutes they embraced, squealing with excitement, momentarily forgetting they were not alone.

For a brief moment Sofia did not recognize the sister she hadn't seen for almost nine years. She couldn't believe she was so beautiful. This couldn't be the child she and Odele had teased and called Black Gal. All the pettiness and pain were forgotten as the two sisters embraced and celebrated the present.

Stella, David, C.P., and their surprise guest, John Browning, arrived shortly after Carrie and Ana. They made their way into the party, finding their way to the table of honor. As they drew near they heard a child scream, "Daddy, you're here!" Stella, C.P., and John stopped short when she ran to David, throwing herself in his arms. Carrie turned to see who Angel was running toward, and her eyes caught sight of John. For a moment she stood unblinking, not certain if she had imagined an older, more debonair John. He stood with Stella and David, strikingly handsome with his gray hair and mustache, the perfect contrast to his creamy chocolate skin. So disconcerted was she by his presence, Carrie tried to battle the butterflies that had taken control of her stomach. By the time she understood the scene that was quickly developing in her midst, it was too late. It occurred to her that the room had grown almost completely silent, and that David was the man Angel had called Daddy. Carrie, stunned, turned to find Stella.

Dazed, Stella was rooted to where she stood. Her mind raced as she struggled to make sense of what she had heard and seen. She looked from Sofia to David and caught their expressions, and suddenly understood that David had caught the girl as she jumped into his arms. Slowly the room began to swim before her; Stella had to escape. Choking back tears, she tore away from the hands pulling at her and ran, pushing through the crowd, for the door. C.P. followed close at her heels, turning back to Carrie. "I'll take care of her," he called back as he turned, obviously distressed, and followed her through the crowd. Carrie looked at Louise, who, for the first time since she'd known her, didn't seem to know what to do.

At Stella's departure, the guests who had been standing in the grand hall quietly excused themselves and headed for the ballroom and gardens, where they could openly discuss the scene that had just taken place. Carrie was still in shock. How could this be? she thought. David and Sofia? It all made sense now: her instincts the night Odele ran away, the older white man whose identity was never disclosed. Carrie looked at Sofia stunned. Sofia was her child, but she didn't really know her after all.

Sofia's face could not disguise her delight at the outcome of the evening. She thought she had won.

Carrie walked to David as he stood looking helpless and defeated. He placed his arm protectively around Angel's shoulders. "Follow me, David, Sofia," she instructed speaking in clipped sentences. "Angel, you go with Ana and Louise," she added. As she walked to the ballroom doors she felt all eyes on her. Instead of ignoring her guests, Carrie stopped and asked for everyone's brief attention. "Ladies and gentlemen," she began, "this evening we are here to celebrate my daughter, Ana, as she makes her entrance into society. Many of you have just witnessed a very painful episode in the lives of my family and friends. If you are here to feed off of our pain, then I ask that you take your leave. If, in fact, you're here to celebrate Ana, I beg you forget this episode, at least for the evening, and enjoy our hospitality with glad tidings." Carrie finished and turned, exiting the ballroom and walking to the library with David and Sofia in her wake.

As the doors to the library closed, John went to speak to the Nortons. "I'm going to leave now," he said, "It is not the time to reunite with Carrie. I'm not sure she would even want to see me under these circumstances."

Louise looked at John in astonishment. "Did you see what she just did?" Louise asked, indicating the announcement Carrie had made in the ballroom. "She has matured in ways you can't imagine, John. Now, if you're leaving because that intimidates you, just say so, and I will wish you well. But if you're the same man who didn't care that she was married, you just had to have her under any circumstances, I'd say now represents as big a challenge as you faced then—with one exception: you're both free to be together." Louise could not believe the chain of events, one after the other. She looked around to find Ana. To her relief she was dancing a little too closely to Judge Washington's son Don. *Hmmm,* she thought. Carrie hadn't mentioned that Ana and Don were an item.

Carrie stood in the library appraising both David and Sofia. When she finally spoke she surprised them both. "David, are you leaving Stella for Sofia?" she inquired in a no-nonsense manner.

"Uh . . . well . . . I love Sofia very much, but . . ." His voice trailed off.

"I assumed that much," Carrie replied, "with the house, jewelry, nanny, and all. However, you haven't answered my question! Do you intend to leave Stella and marry my daughter Sofia?" she asked relentlessly.

David looked helplessly from Carrie to Sofia and back again. "You know it's not possible," he said, finally admitting what Carrie knew all along. "Marriage to a Negro could never happen, not only because I'm white but also because of the Goldstein empire. I would lose everything if I married a Negro girl," he finished brokenly.

Carrie could see the pain of realization wash over Sofia, but it was better she find out the truth now than wait any longer.

Sofia had given up a great part of her youth hoping that one day David would keep his promise and leave his wife for her. Sofia could not believe what he had just said. Because of the pain he had caused she wanted to cause him pain. Sofia turned on David with a ferocity he did not know she possessed. "What you mean to say is you can marry a Negro girl as long as she pretends to be white," she said angrily.

David looked stunned. "What are you trying to say?" he asked.

"What I am saying, David, is that your so-called white wife is my Negro mother's younger sister. One thing I can say for you, David, is that you like to keep it all in the family! My family, that is!" Sofia ran blindly from the room in search of Angel. She intended to leave Houston and never return. This was not the happy ending she had envisioned when she'd called Aunt Louise and asked her to help her surprise Ana at her coming-out party. She had known Stella and David would be there. Now David had made a big mistake. She would make sure he lived to regret it.

Carrie turned back to face David after Sofia abruptly ran from the room. "I'm sorry so many people had to be hurt, David," she said. "The Lord knows I have had my share of pain, and so has Stella. However, Sofia is my child and you took her from me as a baby. She is just twenty-six years old, and now she has to create a life she can live with. Angel has her life ahead of her. She will need you both. But I'm not asking you—I'm warning you to leave my daughter alone. If you couldn't marry her, you should have never touched her. She was a baby and you knew it. You and Stella have made a lot of messes along the way. Now you need to go home and start to clean them up. As for Sofia's ranting about Stella . . . you can believe it or not. One thing you know for sure: be she white or Negro, she always loved you and stood beside you . . . until now." Carrie turned and walked to the fireplace, turning her back on David, silently waiting for him to leave the room.

When Carrie heard the door open and close softly behind her, she assumed it was Louise. As she turned around, her heart caught in her throat. John stood just inside the doorway, erasing all of Carrie's thoughts about David, Sofia, Stella, and their problems. God had answered her prayers. Carrie went to his waiting arms. John stood with his arms open, beckoning for Carrie to enter the place where she belonged. As they stood together he thought of all the things he planned to say to her when he saw her. "I love you" was all that came out.

"And I, you," was her only reply. Their lips joined, seeking the familiar warmth and passion that had been missing in their lives.

They were interrupted by a soft knock on the door, followed by Louise poking her head in and smiling brightly. "I was praying I'd find some happiness in my home tonight," she said.

"You have found great happiness tonight," John replied. "Would you mind if Carrie and I excused ourselves and said good-night so that we can catch up in private?" he asked.

"Not at all," Louise responded before Carrie could interrupt. "Ana is staying with us for a few days, so you're free to go." Carrie smiled her gratitude to her friend. As usual, Louise knew the right thing to say and do.

John turned back to Carrie. "You tell Ana good-night, and I'll have my car pulled around. I'll meet you in front," he said.

"Okay," Carrie replied breathlessly, leaving to seek Ana out in the midst of what had turned into a complete teen party.

Carrie soon found Ana in the middle of the dance floor, dancing very close to a handsome young man who looked vaguely familiar. She was disturbed that Ana was leaning into him with such disconcerting intimacy. She tapped her daughter lightly on the shoulder to get her attention.

When Ana saw Carrie she straightened immediately, putting distance between her and Don. "Uh . . . Mom," she stammered, obviously flustered. "This is, uh . . . Washington . . . Don Washington. Don, this is my mother, Carrie Daniels." Ana faltered, desperately trying to regain her composure. She had been so disappointed at C.P.'s departure, not to mention the embarrassing scene that Sofia had clearly planned. As usual she had only her own interests at heart, uncaring that it was Ana's night, her ball. Now Ana intended to really give everyone something to think about. Don Washington had come to her like a bee to the scent of nectar, and she held him captivated, feeling the penetrating stares of envy of her peers. Oh, well, Don would have to do for now. . . .

"It is a pleasure to meet you, Don," Carrie replied graciously. "I am sure, since we have never met before, that you are not dating my daughter. . . . Is that correct?" she inquired. "Well, no, Mrs. Daniels," he admitted. "I would like to remedy that right now," he said with an air of respect and confidence. "Although we have not been dating, I would like your permission to call on Ana," Don requested confidently, with his most engaging smile. Carrie liked this young man's confidence and straightforward manner. Many young men would have been intimidated; instead this young man had worked the situation to his advantage.

Carrie smiled at Don and agreed to let him call on Ana. Turning to walk away, she touched Don lightly on the arm. "I give you permission to date Ana, not disrespect her. As you dance with her always allow room for the flow of air and light to pass between you. Do I make myself clear?"

"Yes, ma'am, like Waterford." Gallantly he stepped back from Ana, allowing light to pass between their bodies.

"I look forward to having you over for supper soon, Don. . . . Ana, have a good evening, baby. Thomas and Louise insisted you stay with them a few days. I'm tired and I've decided to leave with the rest of the old folks." Carrie kissed her daughter's slightly flushed cheek and departed.

Whistling softly between her teeth, Ana said, "I can't believe you charmed Mama so easily. Permission to call on me and invited to supper! She must really be exhausted."

"Not at all, Ana; she knows a nice guy when she sees one."

"Hmm, either that or, knowing my mother, she's checking to see if there's a wolf under sheep's clothing."

"There's a wolf, all right. I've never been partial to sheep—way too docile."

"Oh, my, Mama warned me about you big college men. Excuse me; I think Mama Louise is looking for me—don't go anywhere Mr. Wolf; Red Riding Hood will be right back." Ana could not believe she was flirting so audaciously with Don. Maybe she would forget about C.P. for a while. Don was turning out to be more interesting with each passing moment. She would see how he fared in the time they had remaining this evening to determine if she would decide to see him again. Now she had to share the good news Carrie had given her with Lena and Ina. Not in a million years did Ana think she would have been as lucky as she was tonight. Staying with Mama Louise and Papa would give her the freedom she desired. They were both deep sleepers, which made it easy for her to come and go as she pleased. Hopefully Mama would need a few more days to herself—obviously the spectacle that Sofia had made of their family tonight was just too much for even her formidable mother.

Almost forgetting Don, Ana turned smiling coyly, knowing he would remain rooted to the spot until she returned. Catching both Lena and Ina through the arms, she startled the pair as they huddled, giggling behind their hands at the antics of Henry Johnson, a classmate they both shared a crush on.

"Our plans for tomorrow night have changed!" Ana announced, bubbling with excitement.

"How?" both girls chimed in unison.

"Mama's not feeling well and she asked Mama Louise to let me stay with them a few days, so that means we all stay here until I have to go back home. Tomorrow night we're gonna go to the Regency Room and see Little Richard and dance all night long!" she exclaimed.

For months all the radio stations had talked about was Little Richard at the Regency Room, but Carrie had forbidden Ana to go and refused to allow her to discuss it anymore. Despite Ana's attempts to negotiate, plead, or cajole to get her way, Carrie stood firm in her resolve: Ana was too young and impressionable to hang at the likes of the Regency Room. Now Ana had found her way out. Rumor had it that there might even be an open-microphone talent search to open for Little Richard; if so, Ana intended to perform.

25

True to his word, John was waiting patiently for Carrie outside. As she descended the front steps he took her hand and suggested they take a stroll and enjoy the warm spring evening. Carrie could think of nothing she'd prefer more, as long as she was with John. While they walked, Carrie became aware that they were heading toward the home that John had purchased over twenty years ago. To her surprise it was still perfectly maintained. "I always kept it," John interrupted, reading her thoughts. "I always hoped we'd return to it one day as husband and wife," he said softly. Carrie's eyes filled with tears as John stated what she had only dreamed.

"Carrie," he began, "will you marry me and be my wife?" Emotion choked his voice to a hoarse whisper.

"I will," she replied, tears of joy running down her face. John pulled a small ring box from his pocket and opened it, offering the ring it held to Carrie. "I bought this ring for you seventeen years ago," he said. "I knew the day would come when you would wear it." Carrie could not believe her eyes; the ring was exquisite. John placed the four-carat, heart-shaped pink diamond solitaire on the ring finger of Carrie's left hand. "I wish we could say our vows tonight." John sighed. "But I want a ceremony so I can announce that you are my wife to the entire world." Carrie beamed at the thought; she would finally be with John. This time nothing and no one would separate them. They walked hand in hand toward their old home and a new life.

"Sssshh, be quiet!" Ana implored, glaring at Lena, who had caught a case of the giggles as the girls sneaked past Thomas and Louise's room. When they reached the stairs Ana whirled around to Lena in mock irritation. "Why do you always do that? Every time we sneak out of the house you always have those crazy fits!"

"You know I can't help it . . . I giggle when I'm nervous. At least I don't get a weak bladder like Ina!"

"Oh, no, you didn't say that, heifer!" Ina chimed in, angry and embarrassed at the reminder. "I can't help it—it runs in my family and y'all know it."

Now it was Ana's turn to catch a fit of giggles. "Stop, y'all . . . let's go before we miss everything."

Releasing the throttle and easing Louise's car silently down the driveway, the girls made their escape and were on their way to the Regency Room.

Getting in the Regency was no problem for Ana—one of Eddie's friends worked the door. Not only did he let them in; he had the hostess seat them at a table up front with a RESERVED sign. Smoothing her new red sweater and matching skirt, Ana strolled to the table as if she were the star attraction. The girls ordered Cokes and tried to appear sophisticated as they waited for the show to begin. Surprising Lena and Ina, Ana reached into her purse, pulled out a pack of cigarettes, and lit one, inhaling deeply.

"When did you learn how to do that?" they asked, impressed and shocked by their friend.

"Eddie."

"Your brother! He gave you the cigarettes?"

"No, he didn't give me the cigarettes—I took them . . . and no, he doesn't know. I learned by watching him. Plus, he told me that whenever he went somewhere and lit up, the women always thought he was older. So I figured if it worked for him it would work for me. Been practicing too, and I'm pretty good at it, I might add."

"You sure are. . . . Can I try?" Lena begged.

"Yes, you can try, but not here—you're not gonna embarrass me when you start choking."

Before Lena could respond she watched Ana's expression shift from surprise to anger. Following Ana's gaze, she watched Don Washington and his date being escorted to a table not far from theirs. Meanwhile the lights went down in the room and the royal blue curtains parted on the stage as Smooth Sammy, the local disc jockey, opened the evening. As rumored, he invited anyone who could hold a note to come onstage. Surprising her friends for the second time that night, Ana got up, slowly blowing a stream of smoke from her heart-shaped lips, and glided confidently up onstage with the other courageous contestants.

As they took the stage it became obvious to Smooth Sammy from the crowd's response to this stunning beauty that if she had enough talent to fill a small thimble then they would crown her. This one definitely had "it," star quality. Quickly selecting three contestants, he whispered to Ana, "Honey, you go on last. You know the old saying, 'save the best for last.' "

Ana looked at him and smiled. She would make that two-timing Don Washington regret his decision to bring a date tonight. She was in her comfort zone . . . nothing felt as good as the energy from a loving crowd. Ana had frequently soloed at church and learned how to work the crowd. As she expected, the first and second act were good, both singing rock and roll along the lines of Little Richard's style. Ana decided on the ballad "That's All I Want from You." Little did she know that besides Don Washington, C.P. had entered the Regency, and both men were watching her with varying levels of interest and intent. Standing in front of the mike, Ana was transformed by the stinging melody that told of emotions she had yet to feel.

The audience was entranced by this sultry beauty whose voice felt like softly scented petals falling from her lips onto their skin. Swaying to the beat, she sang the refrain: "A little love that slowly grows and grows, not a love that comes and goes, that's all I want from you. A sunny day with hopes up to the sky, not a day that comes and dies, that's all I want from you. . . . Don't let me down, but show me that you care for me. Remember when you give you also get your share."

In her husky voice filled with longing, Ana moaned low and long until the crowd could feel her need in the pit of their stomachs. And then as smoothly as she began, she ended. And just as she had dreamed, the crowd went wild, chanting her name, screaming, "Encore, encore!" Smooth Sammy began yelling for everyone to calm down and allow her to return to her seat. To her surprise, Don stood at the bottom of the stage steps, chivalrously bowing before her and offering to escort her to her table. The crowd applauded appreciatively at his gallant gesture—all except his date for the evening, who sat angrily contemplating whether or not she should leave. Still slightly dazed at the audience reaction, Ana looked at Lena and Ina, who were teary-eyed at their friend's performance. Ignoring Don and his feigned chivalry, Ana took her seat, quickly taking a sip from her drink. How dared Don come to the stage as if to lay claim to her? What next? she wondered, attempting to gather her wits.

"Your drink looks watered down . . . can I buy you another?"

Turning her head to follow the voice that offered her a drink, she faced the most beautiful pair of gray eyes. C.P. stooped next to her chair, smiling.

"What are you doing here?" she countered.

"I came to see you," he responded, smiling as he caught her off guard.

"Well, next time please be kind enough to drop a hint and not make it such a big surprise! Really, what are you doing here?"

"Celebrating with a few teammates," he offered. "Now tell me what you would have done differently if you'd known I was going to be in the audience." It seemed as though his eyes glowed, so intense was his gaze.

"Well, I would have sung a song for you!" She was flirting recklessly.

"I thought you did."

Not accustomed to being shut out, Don cleared his throat loudly to regain Ana's attention. Remembering Don, Ana began the awkward introduction to C.P. Just as she finished, Ana noticed Don's date approaching her table. Before she could nod an acknowledgment the woman unceremoniously tapped Don on the shoulder.

"Apparently you forgot your way back to our table after you escorted your *cousin* from the stage." Her voice dripped with sarcasm. Ana took this opening to assist herself out of a potentially uncomfortable situation between Don and C.P.

"Oh, my apologies. I'm so sorry for keeping Cousin Don away from you! Don, you didn't tell me you were here with a date—did you forget your manners?" she said, holding his eyes with hers, knowing he was both embarrassed and contrite. The last thing Don wanted to do after tonight was lose out on dating Ana.

"My name is Ana, and this is C.P., Lena, and Ina. . . . What's your name?"

"Cindy Mae," the girl replied uncertainly.

"Y'all can join us, if you like." She let the invitation fall, confident that neither Don nor his date would take her up on it. As expected, Don suggested it might be too crowded at Ana's table, and he and Cindy Mae returned to their table.

Turning back to C.P., Ana said, "Yes, I would like another drink now."

Mesmerized by her beauty and self-confidence, C.P. signaled a waiter to refill their drinks. He gestured to his teammates to join them, and introduced them to Ana's friends. For the rest of the evening the two talked easily, finding common ground as C.P. entertained her with stories of college life. They were both Little Richard fans, and danced wildly together as he performed.

After the show was over and they were preparing to leave, Smooth Sammy came running over to Ana with his card. "Come down to the station Monday at five P.M. I want you to sing that song on live radio. I'll have some important people there—girlie, you're gonna be a big star."

"I'll be there. Uh, is it okay if I bring my friends?"

"Bring your entire family, girlie, if it makes you happy. Remember I said you're gonna be a star—might as well get used to getting what you want! See you Monday at five!" Sammy hurried backstage.

"Is that what you want to be—a singer?" C.P. inquired, still not quite believing that voice had come from Ana.

"Yeah, I guess I do. I've always loved to sing, but I never sang anywhere much, other than church or for my friends and family. But this is what I've always dreamed of."

"Well, it looks like we're both getting what we've dreamed of." Hesitating slightly, C.P. announced to Ana, "I got a letter today from the Lakers; they want me to come to their camp and try out for the team. That's why the guys and I are out celebrating!"

Squealing with delight, Ana impetuously kissed C.P. full on the lips. "It's our time! And you know what makes it perfect? It's happening at the same time. Do you believe in fate?"

C.P. nodded. "Yes."

"Tonight was supposed to happen . . . we're supposed to be together tonight because our dreams are beginning and I guess so are we. . . ." Her voice trailed off as the enormity of her words and thoughts hit her.

"I'd better go find Lena and Ina before I start rambling." Getting up from her seat, Ana quickly walked away, embarrassed at how much she had revealed about her feelings to an almost total stranger, something she was not accustomed to doing. Instinctively, C.P. followed Ana. Catching up to her, he embraced her tightly and kissed her deeply, momentarily forgetting they were not alone but standing in the middle of a crowded room. "It's okay . . . I feel it too. I don't know what it is, but I've felt it since I first saw you months ago. So let's find our friends together and we'll meet at Juke's Burger Joint tomorrow after church, okay?" he asked intensely.

"Okay," she agreed, allowing him to take her hand and lead her into the crowd to find their friends. For once Ana didn't question the path ahead; she felt as if they were on common ground.

As planned, Ana met C.P. the next afternoon at Juke's. Seeing her in a poodle skirt and matching pink-and-gray sweater, C.P. was reminded that Ana was just sixteen. Last night he had been entranced not only by her beauty, but also by her air of confidence typically found in someone much older. Watching her walk into the diner caused him to have to reconcile himself to the fact that she was still a child and too young for him. By the time Ana had reached the table, C.P. had already decided on a course of action. He was on his way to Los Angeles to become a guard playing professional basketball. There was no room in his life for the problems that would be created by dating Carrie's youngest daughter, Ana.

"Hey!" She smiled shyly, greeting him. "Been waiting long?"

"No, I came a little early so I could think clearly."

"Oh, is it still crazy at Stella and David's because of what happened at my party? I still can't believe it, but Sofia has always been like that. You know, she just thinks about herself."

"Well, yeah . . . it's still a little crazy, but Miss Stella is handling it all pretty well, considering."

Before C.P. knew it several hours had passed, and he had become so enthralled by Ana that he failed to tell her that it would make no sense for them to continue seeing each other. Glancing at her watch and rising from the booth, she asked if he would go with her to WHTX radio station while she sang on Monday, and of course he agreed. Paying the check and preparing to leave, he decided he would tell her after her performance on Monday.

26

Ana's first challenge was to convince Louise that she had been se-lected from the school choir as a finalist to sing for Smooth Sammy at the station after school on Monday. After hours of coaxing Louise finally consented to Ana's request. Though Carrie offered to pick her up and drive her to the station, Ana assured her that she would be okay taking the bus from Jack Yates High School to the sta-tion with Lena and Ina in tow, so Louise reluctantly agreed. The truth was, C.P. was picking Ana up after school let out and driving her to the station. Not for the first time, Ana was too excited to have a con-science; she just prayed to sing well. Fortunately her prayers were an-swered: her performance received more call-in requests than that of any other amateur in the station's history. This time Sammy was pre-pared; he had the station's owner seated in the sound booth paying close attention to this young ingenue.

Ana, after her performance, captivated Saul Berman, the owner of WHTX, as much by her beauty as by her song. For once, he thought, Sammy had not wasted his time. When he had left his office just an hour earlier to witness this new sensation, as Sammy already referred to her, he had thought of it as a waste of his precious time. Rising from his seat to join both Sammy and Ana in the sound booth, Saul had to take a deep, calming breath; he could not believe he was ner-vous.

Entering the room, he noticed the white jock standing in the background, eyes affixed to Ana. Unconsciously Saul sucked in his stomach and tried to add a few inches to his height. As he approached Ana and Sammy, she looked up, startling Saul with a smile. He was mesmerized as he stood in front of her. Feeling drawn by her beauty and captivated by her unique charm, he found himself making promises to help her career that he had not made in twenty years as the owner of the most popular teen station in Houston. Delighted by Ana's response to his offer, he mistakenly assumed her to be interested in him personally. So, stepping out of character a second time, Saul extended an invitation to her.

"Ana . . . why don't you join me for dinner and be my guest to see Little Esther perform tonight at the Regency?"

Ana was momentarily stunned by his offer.

"I'd love to join you, but I'm here with my friends. Uh, I hope that's okay. Sammy said it wouldn't be a problem."

Grimacing at her referral to Sammy and her friends—especially the jock—Saul took a different approach.

"Well, then, you're all invited to be my guest for dinner and the show," he offered magnanimously, impressed with himself at his generosity.

"Well, I sure appreciate the invitation, but tonight is a school night, and my mom will have a fit if I'm out late. But y'all can feel free," she offered to everyone.

"Uh, no, thanks, we've got to get home just like you, Ana. We just came to cheer you on," Ina offered.

"Okay, okay, I get the picture!" Saul responded. "I forgot you're all minors, anyway. But Ana, I would like to get you back to the studio. I'd like to record you and include the song in our rotation . . . you know, see where it goes from there."

"Ooooooh, I can't wait," Ana screamed excitedly. "I'll call Sammy tomorrow and find out all the particulars—if that's all right with everybody?"

"That'll be just fine," Sammy and Saul replied in unison, surprising each other.

As the group left, Saul grabbed Sammy's hand and began to shake it enthusiastically. "That's some girl you found, with big talent—we have to get her in a contract, and soon!"

"We?" Sammy responded, unable to hide his surprise.

"Well, who else do you know? No colored man can get it done without a white man behind him! No offense, Sammy; it's true—that's why we work so well together: we're truthful with each other!"

Without replying, Sammy turned to leave mumbling, "I have to get to the show to introduce Little Esther." The last thing he intended to do was turn Ana over to this cracker.

C.P. failed to sever their blooming relationship that evening, as he had planned. Instead he tried to erect a bridge to maintain closeness, knowing his train was scheduled to leave Friday for Los Angeles and basketball camp. So for four days they were with each other at every opportunity. The night before his departure Ana sneaked out of the house and walked to the corner, where he waited in his car. Instead of displaying her normal exuberance, she was subdued and seemingly distracted.

C.P. also was out of sorts, not wanting to face the separation that confronted their new romance. Arriving back to the place where they began, the Regency Room, they listened to the melancholy songs of Little Esther, dancing in a close embrace, creating a memory to cherish on the lonely nights to come. After closing the club they returned to Ana's home and made plans for their future with each other.

For the first time in Ana's life, she enjoyed a man's company more than the company of her brother, Eddie, who was her idol. She was even more determined to move to Los Angeles after high school and pursue her singing career and C.P. Maybe she would meet with Smooth Sammy and the station owner to discuss her career. She wanted to make it big enough to get to LA—and fast.

27

Stepping from the airplane, Ana could not believe that less than a year after returning to singing and the stage she had been invited to return to Paris, France, to star in the remake of Josephine Baker's *La Revue Nègre*. The last time she had been here she was barely twenty years old; now she was returning with her thirteen-year-old daughter, Mignon, and the secret that this country held that had haunted her for years.

Recalling the first time she had visited France, she remembered how enchanted she had been by the people, the history, and the melting pot of cultures. The traditions and language fascinated her, inspiring her to master the language and become like the Parisians. Her agent, the former Smooth Sammy, had reassumed his real name, Samuel Martine, after signing her to an exclusive contract and leaving radio. He had been true to his word to represent her as his sole act. For her first big tour he had gotten her booked as the opening act for Dinah Washington on her European tour, which was scheduled to open in Paris. At that time her only goal had been to get to Los Angeles, in close proximity to C.P. But instead fate led her to France and all of its enchantment.

It was not long after Ana's first opening performance at Palais de Congress that she soon became the toast of Paris. Her singing style coupled with her beauty produced a loyal following among young, hip Parisians. She was called *"la Foncé Fille"* or "the dark girl," her on-stage reference to her childhood nickname, Black Gal. Not only did it stick, but her saucy, spirited, carefree attitude caused her popularity to soar. Her signature song was "Black Gal in Paris," a song she wrote on the plane to Paris.

When she stepped onstage, the crowd was typically Parisian; impatient for Dinah, they continued to talk at their tables even after the lights had gone down, signaling the opening act. Ana stood in front of the microphone for a few moments, waiting for the noise from the crowd to die down. When the sound died to rustling and whispers, she dramatically reached for the microphone. But instead of grabbing it, she flung her arms in a wide arc, simultaneously discarding the midnight-blue stole that had been wrapped like a sheath around her body, unveiling a silver beaded gown that literally seemed to create its own light. Instead of taking the microphone, she stood in front of it with her arms outstretched, her face seeming to search the audience as she sang out, "What is a black gal doing in Paris?" The audience reaction was immediate; they shouted their approval as she continued to sing in her rich, melodic voice filled with an underlying edge of yearning. The audience was enthralled as she sang the lyrics of her song. By the time Ana had finished her set, she had been dubbed *la Foncé Fille,* and her name began to travel in European circles far and wide.

After the tour with Dinah Washington, Ana's popularity in France had made her a success, and Sammy found himself in a position any agent would envy—he had to turn down engagements. To his delight, he already had her booked a year and a half in advance, with a waiting list to boot.

For Ana, Paris had no rival. Never before had she imagined such freedom as a woman of color. Men of all nationalities would pause admiringly as they passed her on the streets or in restaurants, paying her outrageous compliments and trying to court her. She had kept in touch with C.P. for almost a year after moving to Paris, but had lost touch with him after he had a knee injury that ended his basketball career. The last time she heard from him he had moved back to Houston and was recuperating at the home of Stella and David in the Fifth Ward. Although Carrie and John were busy with their own lives, between traveling and planning their wedding, they had seen to limiting her social life with a chaperon, Miss Marjorie Fonteneau, a spinster from Devereaux, Louisiana. Between Miss Fonteneau and Sammy both trying so hard to protect her, she sometimes felt as if she would suffocate. Her only freedom was on the stage, and during the afternoons, when she would put on a pair of capris and penny loafers to stroll along the banks of the Seine. Some afternoons she would wander aimlessly from the Louvre to the Place de la Concorde.

One afternoon on her stroll, she decided to detour from her path along the Champs Elysées and window-shop on Avenue Montaigne. As she walked from Chanel to Christian Dior she smiled, thinking of the French translation for *window-shopping;* they called it *window licking,* and she guessed in a way it was. Standing almost trancelike in front of Dior, imagining herself in a real Dior gown, she couldn't help but notice the handsome man staring at her from inside the boutique, being fitted by the tailor. Returning his gaze, she smiled in return and continued to study the lines of the exquisite gown on display.

28

Pierre-Michel St. Honore had put off this fitting as long as he could, until his sometimes overbearing but lovable mother had playfully threatened to cut his trust fund if he continued to refuse to have his tuxedo fitted and ready in time for his parents' thirtieth aniversary celebration. It was to be an extravagant affair covered by the media, although his mother was most concerned about the Paris *Vogue* magazine article. They were doing an exclusive on the St. Honore family and the title that was to be passed to Pierre-Michel. It would be the first time that the title of marquess would be passed to a man of mixed heritage. There was also much anticipation due to the attendance of his excellency the prime minister, as well as the fact that Pierre's parents were always being lauded on their endless generosity to one charitable cause after another.

This celebration of thirty years of marriage was, to Pierre's mother, the inimitable Mignon-Marie St. Honore, and father, Jean-Claude St. Honore, an announcement of their undying love despite the odds. Jean-Claude St. Honore was an only child born to parents of noble blood. His father was a marquess and expected to pass his title, enormous wealth, and vast landholdings, which included the Château de St. Honore, where the celebration was to be held, to his only son. That was, until Jean-Claude went against his wishes and married Mignon, an orphaned *Nègre* of French–West Indian descent. Jean-Claude had been stripped of his title and disowned by his family.

Although the marquess did not touch his trust fund, he had his attorney change his will so that his son would not inherit his title as marquess or his lands and château in Marseilles. Jean-Claude was so in love with his wife and new son, Pierre-Michel, that he accepted his father's wishes and moved his family to Paris. Purchasing one of the old mansions near the Parc Monceau, where the family made a loving home. Jean-Claude had always yearned to be an artist, which was how he had met Mignon-Marie. She was a figure model and responded to his advertisement. It was not the first time Jean-Claude had hired a model to pose nude. It was the first and last time that he fell in love. It was the paintings of Mignon-Marie that won him recognition in the artistic circles of Paris. His first oil on canvas was entitled *Mignon's Eyes*. He never painted a nude of Mignon; her face captivated him, and it was her face that captivated collectors as well. It looked as though it had been sculpted, each feature molded to perfection, and her eyes were the pièce de résistance. Jean-Claude was accepted as an accomplished artist in his own right, and his work became a favorite in many of the galleries, especially the Viaduc des Arts.

Mignon-Marie enjoyed the attention from her husband's paintings of her, but she desired her own success. She always had a flair for interior design and an interest in antiques, so she opened a small antiques boutique on the Left Bank. Her shop was named Le St. Honore des Antiquaires, and overnight she became a sensation. She developed a reputation for a keen eye and maintained an inventory of some of the most sought-after period pieces in France, such as furniture by Gourdin, Blanchard Garnier, and Rousseau that dated back to the seventeen hundreds. After her first year in business she was established in Parisian society as having the premier boutique where only the prominent and titled could afford to shop. Mignon-Marie had created a legacy. Although they had a happy life filled with love and adoration for each other and their son, she would not rest until she had done everything in her power to reunite Jean-Claude with his parents. He was, after all, their only child.

One afternoon she dressed her son in his finest and drove to the château in Marseilles with the intention of a confrontation. As the car approached the château she could not help but be impressed by the beauty as she looked at the lazy waters of the Indre on its way to join the Loire wash against the base of the hill where the castle was built. Driving up the hill again, she was struck by the fortified gates that could be penetrated only by crossing the bridge over the moat.

The beauty of the castle, which stood in the midst of the picturesque rich, green rolling country surrounded by lush fruit trees, was overwhelming. After their arrival, they were led down the wide halls to formal gardens, where they waited for Jean-Claude's parents to join them.

To her surprise, her father-in-law had aged considerably in the four and a half years since she had last seen him. On the other hand, his wife, Jacqueline, seemed as vibrant as ever. Instead of a confrontation, as she had expected, Jacqueline first embraced Mignon, then turned to Pierre-Michel with teary eyes and knelt to embrace her grandson. Pierre's resemblance to Jean-Claude was undeniable. The only difference was that Pierre was a light brown version of his father. The marquess's demeanor softened considerably when Pierre bowed low, as he had been trained, and the St. Honore birthmark on his neck was exposed. No longer able to stand the loneliness from denying contact with his only son, the marquess reconciled his feelings and for the first time allowed himself to truly look upon the lovely woman standing before him. She had the bearing of a queen; he now clearly understood why his son had fallen so deeply in love.

"My dear, forgive an old man his ignorance."

"*Oui, monsieur.*" She took the seat beside him and the two uncertainly began the first step toward bridging the chasm of race and culture that existed between them. Jacqueline in turn took her seat on the other side of her husband, with her grandson planted firmly and lovingly in her lap.

Mignon-Marie could not wait to return to Jean-Claude to tell him the news of the reconciliation. But, again to her amazement, Jacqueline suggested they travel back to Paris together.

"I want to look my son in the eyes and apologize. I want to touch him." Again Jacqueline began to cry.

"Yes, she's right," insisted the marquess. "I have missed my son and I don't want to stand on ceremony. . . . I want to tell him what a fine heir he has given the St. Honore family."

Beaming, Mignon-Marie beckoned to Pierre. "Come along, son; we're going to surprise Papa!"

This joyful reconciliation set in motion an acceptance in circles that neither Mignon-Marie nor Jean-Claude had ever thought to be included in. It seemed as if almost overnight their lives had changed. Instead of receiving acceptance in artistic circles only, they were now invited to dine with other families of noble blood, and the taboo of marriage outside of race and class seemed suddenly to be overlooked. As a result Pierre had been raised as a child of color among the elite of France. He was never exposed to racism; his was a world of privilege, and the uniqueness of his appearance was his signature. With the exception of his color, his features were similar to his father's, but complemented by the full lips and intense eyes of his mother. His hair was fine and straight. By the time he was twenty-four, he was a much-sought-after playboy. Pierre had a wide variety of women to choose from in Paris and had a reputation for dating the latest model of note. Although he was engaged, in an arranged marriage to Philippa de Perusing whose family had lands adjoining St. Honore, this was a marriage of convenience, combining great wealth. Pierre did not love Philippa, and she did not seem to mind. They both understood the conditions and expectations that came as a result of bloodline and heritage. And until recently Pierre had been content with his arrangements, as he thought of them.

That was, until he joined a group of friends at Le Relais Paris to see the much-touted act of *la Foncé Fille*. Sitting at his table, waiting expectantly, Pierre could not even blink when she walked onstage. He sat enthralled as she sang one soul-stirring melody after another. For the next four nights that she appeared he was always in the audience, unable to reconcile his emotions each time he saw her. To his dismay, when he inquired where her next show would be, he found out she had been booked in Frankfurt, Germany. He became frantic, trying to think of a way to see her again. Finally he thought of a way. He persuaded his mother to contact her agent and have her perform at their anniversary party—as a gift. After much prodding, she relented, and now he was being fitted for his tuxedo for the party this weekend.

As he stood enduring his fitting, he could not believe his eyes as Ana strolled in front of the window and stood staring at the mannequin as if she were in a trance. He had to act. Snapping his fingers impatiently, he quickly decided on a plan. Gaining the attention of his tailor, he made his petition and watched as his request was fulfilled.

29

Ana stood at the window of Dior daydreaming, imagining how she would feel in the beautiful hand-beaded chiffon gown. She was completely unaware of the activity inside Dior that surrounded her and the gown in the window. Just as she turned to walk away from Dior's window and the beautiful gown, one of the shop's salesgirls called out after her.

"Pardon, mademoiselle, are you not *la Foncé Fille?*"

"Yes," Ana replied hesitantly, amazed that she would be recognized.

"Please follow me; we have been trying to contact you about your fitting!"

"Oh, I'm afraid there's been some mistake. I am not scheduled for a fitting!" Now Ana was confused. She knew for certain that no appointment had been made with Dior. But the girl was persistent. "Please, if mademoiselle would follow me, I am certain there is no mistake. Madame St. Honore herself scheduled the appointment."

For some reason that name was familiar to Ana but she couldn't think of why it was so familiar. Resolutely she turned back toward the shop with the expectation of clearing up the whole misunderstanding and returning to the apartment on Rue Jacob in enough time to rest before supper that evening. As she stepped into the doorway she was overwhelmed by the attention that was focused on her—especially from the very handsome man who was being fitted for a tuxedo. For a moment Ana felt slightly disoriented, almost like déjà vu. She had seen him before, of that she was sure. She walked mechanically toward the shop manager, following behind the salesgirl in order to explain what was obviously mistaken identity. Standing before the manager, she had to call on all her willpower not to turn and look at the handsome gentleman again. To her surprise, the manager was also insistent that she was to be fitted for the Dior gown of her choice for her performance at the St. Honore anniversary gala Saturday night. Now she knew why that name was familiar; she remembered Sammy telling her how insistent the woman had been about her performing at the gala. Mignon-Marie St. Honore had personally called to request her, and Sammy was beside himself with pleasure.

"You've hit the big time, Black Gal; everyone will be there—so much press they'll read about you back in Houston. I can see it now on the cover of the *Forward Times* newspaper, the headline reading, 'Ana Daniels Wows Paris!' "

Now it seemed as if his prediction had been right, especially if the attendants at Dior were falling over themselves to help her select a gown for the gala event. She decided not to fight it anymore. If they wanted to buy her a gown, who was she to argue? The manager led her to a comfortable cushioned sofa. After she was seated and served a glass of champagne and light hors d'oeuvres, she began inspecting the gowns being modeled for her selection. As Ana watched, she wondered how it would feel to really be able to afford to live like this. *One day,* she thought, *I'll be able to shop here on my own.* Finally she decided upon a beautiful red strapless chiffon gown with a low, heart-shaped neckline that was hand-beaded with seed pearls and crystals. The waist was cinched to show off her small waistline, with a softly cascading skirt that seemed to dance like clouds around her ankles with each step. She knew she had made the right choice when she glanced up at the man in the tuxedo and saw an intensity in his eyes that was unmistakable. Smiling to herself, she noticed she had also garnered the approval of the staff for her impeccable choice. Ana wrote down the address of her apartment, where the gown was to be delivered. As she turned to leave the boutique she looked directly at Pierre with a penetrating stare and surprised herself by asking, "Do I know you, monsieur?"

Startled by her question—and even more by her direct gaze that seemed to pierce his thoughts—he quickly responded, "No, mademoiselle, I'm afraid we have never met."

Ana felt as though a force stronger than any will that she had was pulling her to this man. Without realizing that she was staring, she continued to hold his eyes in hers, as she seemed to hear his response as an echo.

"Then it is my greatest regret." She heard her mouth form the words, but could not believe that she had actually spoken her thoughts aloud. Her face immediately flushed when she saw the look of surprise in his eyes. Turning on her heel, she quickly exited the boutique, and instead of walking hailed a car to take her home.

30

On Saturday morning the gown was delivered to Ana as scheduled, and to her surprise, when she opened the box there was a velvet case in the midst of all of the tissue paper surrounding the gown. Miss Fonteneau, although stern, could not help but be impressed and a little intrigued by the generosity of Madame St. Honore in purchasing a special gown for Ana's performance that evening. After her bath Ana unwrapped the gown and laid the velvet case aside with trembling fingers, and almost missed the note card that was enclosed. Handing the gown to Miss Fonteneau, who immediately began fussing over its beauty and the small fortune that it must have cost, Ana waited patiently as the older woman went in search of the proper hanger for a gown from Dior. Taking a seat on the padded bench by her bed she opened the note and tried to calm the rise of butterflies that filled her stomach. It read simply, *Only the warmth of rubies could rival the warmth in your eyes . . . No regrets, please? Pierre.*

Slowly she reached for the velvet case and opened it, revealing the most exquisite ruby-and-diamond drop earrings with a matching pendant on a chain so thin and fragile that when worn the rubies and diamonds seemed to be suspended in thin air. The combination of the gown and jewelry was stunning, and a matching red velvet cape had been included for the cool evening. Ana felt like a princess as the limousine drove them to the Château St. Honore in Marseilles. As they crossed the bridge over the moat, she surveyed the wooded hillside, trying unsuccessfully to imagine living this type of lifestyle. The car drove around to the main doors and they were escorted through spacious hallways through an annex that led to the theater. She had never seen anything like it before: the stage was larger than any she had performed on, and the room was set with round tables like a very fashionable supper club. The staff was formally dressed and attending to last-minute details. She was greeted by the stage manager, who immediately showed her to her dressing room and escorted Sammy and Miss Fonteneau to their table. Ana was overwhelmed by the beauty of the dressing room and the array of floral arrangements that were artfully placed throughout the large room. As she was checking her makeup the manager knocked at the door again to let her know it was time for her performance. Nervously Ana rose to leave her room and take the stage, smoothing down her gown. Surreptitiously glancing in the mirror, she grabbed her cloak and left the room.

As the curtains opened Ana stood onstage with the red velvet cape completely covering her gown and the hood covering her hair and shrouding any view of her face. The orchestra signaled and the music began to play. Pausing for effect, she slowly raised her head, not enough for her face to be seen in its entirety, but enough for her voice to be heard from the microphone. She began singing softly at first: "No regrets, I have no regrets. I am not a Red Riding Hood afraid of the big, bad wolf!" Her voice slowly climbed as she introduced the song that had made her famous. The audience had immediately been drawn to her haunting opening as they leaned forward, enchanted by this ingenue. Ana threw her head back and swung her arms out, immediately discarding the cloak and unveiling the Dior gown, at the same time singing out, "I'm just a black gal from nowhere . . . hoping that my somewhere is here with you!"

As she continued singing, Ana's eyes panned the audience and she tried to gauge its response. She fed off of the audience reaction. Searching the room, she would look from table to table, finding different faces and singing to them as if her songs, her questions, were just for them. Singing one song after another, she artfully completed her performance to a standing ovation. She accepted the bouquet of roses and waited for the audience to take their seats.

Feeling self-assured, she walked to the edge of the stage and, in perfect French, she thanked her host and hostess and congratulated them on their anniversary. As she had been instructed by the stage manager, she invited the couple onstage to sing a song written by their son in their honor. Ana was surprised when the beautiful Negro woman stood with the assistance of her doting husband—who was a white man. In America this would have never been tolerated, and certainly not celebrated. Quickly gathering herself, Ana waited for the elegant couple to join her onstage. However, Ana could not conceal her surprise when Madame St. Honore turned and beckoned for her son to join them. To her delight the son was the same gentleman she had spoken to in the House of Dior, and who had sent the jewelry that adorned her neck and ears. As the family stood together, the audience saluted them with a standing ovation that Ana considered a blessing; it gave her an opportunity to calm the attack of nerves and butterflies that had assaulted her at the sight of Pierre.

After the audience quieted she began to sing the lyrics of the song Pierre had written in tribute to his parents and their renowned love. But as she sang the lyrics and felt the intensity of his gaze, she closed her eyes and sang as if it had instead been written with her in mind. As she finished the last refrain, she gazed out upon the audience, her eyes filled with unshed tears as they rose to their feet shouting, "Bravo!"

Mignon-Marie, also unable to contain the tears that flowed freely down her face, stepped forward and embraced Ana, kissing her on both cheeks. "My dear, my son was right in having me choose you for such a special night. What special talent and beauty you have. . . . Thank you!"

Jean-Claude also embraced her, thanking her profusely as Ana stood in a daze, watching as they turned to take their seats while the curtain closed with the audience still applauding. For moments Ana could not move, feeling an overwhelming sense of loss and separation as the curtains closed, indicating that her time at the gala had ended. She turned to go to her dressing room and leave with Sammy and Miss Fonteneau, who would both be waiting, excitedly giving her their account of the audience reaction.

But, as if detecting Ana's melancholy reluctance to participate in the camaraderie, the small group was subdued in the cab on their return to the Paris apartment. As they reached the cobblestone street, Sammy was no longer able to contain himself. "This is it, Ana . . . you really did it tonight! We're in the money!"

Even the usually reticent Miss Fonteneau had to agree: "I don't know what happened to you onstage, but tonight you transformed right before our eyes. You sang from your heart . . . and everybody saw it and felt it! I think Sammy's right."

Ana suddenly leaned forward, tightly embracing each of them and kissing them soundly on their cheeks. Surprised and disarmed, Miss Fonteneau became teary-eyed, while Sammy, shocked by any outward display of affection, became extremely interested in the French Gothic architecture they were passing. Clearing his throat, he wondered aloud about the period in which the buildings in the Fifth Arrondissement, also known as the Latin Quarter, had been erected.

"I want you both to know how much I love you, and I couldn't have done this without you cheering me on. I just think that on a night as magical as this one, it needs to be said!"

"I love you too, like the daughter I never had," Miss Fonteneau replied.

"Okay! Okay . . . no more mush! I can't stand it and I'll just have to get out and walk if you two keep it up!" Sammy looked ready to explode.

Shocked, the two women looked at him, perplexed, and then looked at each other. Without a word passing between them they all burst out laughing, enjoying the release and relief it brought.

31

That night Ana fell into a dreamless sleep and slept late into the next day. When she awakened she was surprised to find flowers and a card from Pierre. Tearing open the card, she read, *Can only see your face in my mind, hear your voice in my thoughts. . . . Please meet me at the obelisk between the fountains at the Place de la Concorde at three o'clock.* Looking at the clock in the hallway she noted that it was already well after one o'clock, which didn't give her much time to bathe and search for something suitable to wear. After trying on at least six different outfits, Ana finally settled on a cream-colored linen-and-silk shirt and capri pants with a pinched-waist overskirt, paired with matching silk mules and handbag. Flagging a cab, she anxiously anticipated the meeting that was about to take place. Never before had anyone had such an effect on her as this man.

Pierre was also anxious. He had been standing directly in front of the obelisk, staring at the bronze-tailed mermaids and sea nymphs surrounding the fountains at the Place de la Concorde, since two-thirty, hoping to give himself time to calm his nerves and also analyze why this woman—this girl—had driven him to distraction. It had even been obvious to his mother, who mentioned how affected he seemed to be by this girl. He was sure that was why she hadn't missed the opportunity to call him onstage to thank him. The very private and proper Mignon-Marie would normally never have been so spontaneous. Pierre knew that she was not fond of Philippa, and that she resented his grandfather's participation in arranging a suitable marriage on his behalf. As with his father, he had tied his title and inheritance to Pierre's following through with the marriage. Secretly she harbored the belief that the marquess was repaying her for the loss of Jean-Claude after he chose her. Pierre knew his mother hoped he would not marry for any reason other than love. When Ana had walked onstage last night he had gotten a lump in his throat and couldn't seem to swallow. When she sang about the big, bad wolf, he couldn't help but wonder, *Is that about me?* He became frustrated because it meant so much to him.

After her performance he assumed she'd return to the gala and sit at the table he'd reserved for her agent and chaperon. Instead she left without so much as walking into the ballroom. When he found out she was gone, he was so distracted he could think of nothing else, and several times his mother or Philippa, his fiancée, would call him back to the present. He had secretly thought, even hoped, that if he put Ana in his circle, she would pale against the wealth and division of class, as did even the most successful European models as they tried to fit in. This crowd was notorious for their ability to be condescending and intimidating. But instead Ana had again turned the tables and held them like putty in the palm of her hands from the moment she took the stage until she relinquished it, leaving not a dry eye in the house. Then she left without so much as a backward glance, as if they were not acceptable company for her. Admittedly, even he had felt intimidated by her directness when she had approached him earlier in the week before she left the House of Dior. Now he sat waiting like some lovesick puppy and he had no control over it. Lost in thought, he did not see Ana until he felt her shadow fall on him. Disconcerted, he did not know how long she had been standing there. She didn't reach out to tap him on the shoulder or announce her presence in any other manner. It was as if she had decided she'd just wait it out and see how long it took him to feel her presence. When he looked up and saw her, she surprised him again by reaching out and gently tracing the outline of his face in a light caress.

"You wanted to meet me?" she asked softly.

"Yes . . . I'm pleased you came."

"My name is Ana Carrie Daniels." She could not believe that she had touched this man! For a moment she had to glance at her hand to make sure she had not imagined it.

"Forgive me; I am Pierre-Michel St. Honore. I wanted to introduce myself to you last night but you left so quickly."

"Well, my performance was over . . . so it was time to leave. Although I wanted to thank you for the lovely note and the velvet case."

"It was my pleasure . . . especially to see you wear it." Pierre could not believe that he felt so awkward in the presence of a woman for the first time in his life. He was the one usually so composed and unaffected. Now the tables were turned and he was struggling to right his position. Her touch had an instantaneous physical effect that left him almost shaken. "Would you prefer dining on the Left Bank or Right Bank?"

"I don't mind . . . either side, especially since we're right in the middle."

"Right . . . I had it planned that way. Sometimes it is easier to make a decision when you are right in between, *oui?*"

"*Oui!*"

"Have you lived in Paris long?"

"No. Why do you ask . . . is my French that bad?"

"No! On the contrary, it is quite good . . . although this is the first time I've heard it spoken with a Texas accent," Pierre teased.

"I'm not worried—as long as I'm understood, which clearly you do . . . undertand me, that is." She smiled, relaxing for the first time and enjoying the light flirtation.

"Mademoiselle, I would gladly learn sign language if it was required, just so that I could understand you."

Pierre grabbed both of Ana's hands in his, locking his eyes with hers to make certain she understood the lengths he would go to in order to be with her. Ana blushed from the intensity of his stare and the way his eyes seemed to pull her in. Instead of releasing her hands he held them, slowly raising them to his lips. His eyes held her captive. Without breaking his gaze, he did not kiss her hands, as she expected. Instead he allowed his lips to lightly run across her knuckles, brushing them gently. It was the most erotic sensation she had ever felt, as though electricity were traveling down her spine, sending shivers through her. Her mind raced as she recognized what she had instinctively known from the moment he had walked onstage last night with his parents: this man could easily possess her body and soul. Internal alarms like sirens were going off in her mind, warning her to flee while she still could. But this time her brain was a hairbreadth behind her heart. Her heart told her it was too late . . . possession had already begun. Pierre kept her hand in his, and his voice was husky as he said, "Let's go . . . my car is parked up the street."

He was unable to mask his reaction to the touch of her hand. His heart was hammering in his chest so hard that he almost felt light-headed.

Pierre studied Ana as they took the picturesque drive along the Loire. Neither spoke, both lost in their own thoughts, and each adjusting to the close proximity of the other's presence. Both were unused to anyone having such a stirring effect. Ana, for the first time since her childhood, felt a shyness that overcame her usual self-assuredness. Pierre now understood his mother's insistence that he should marry only the woman he loved. Surely love was the only explanation for the way he felt about this woman who had haunted his thoughts since he first laid eyes on her.

Finally Pierre broke the ice. "So what do you like to do, other than stop my heart each time I see you?" As the words came out he knew he was indeed speaking from his heart.

"I enjoy singing, and since last night I find I prefer songs written by you."

"Ah, not only is she beautiful, but flattering as well—possibly a dangerous combination."

From that point, conversation flowed effortlessly. They decided to dine at Le Grand Vefour. Sitting in a private booth and sipping Taittinger's, they found each other's companionship captivating. Although they had had completely different upbringings, there was still a common ground, and a sense of emotional closeness that had been missing in other relationships. Pierre was intrigued by her quick wit and sound intellect. They spent hours discussing the arts and made plans to spend the following afternoon at the Louvre. Each day Pierre would make plans to introduce Ana to a different part of Paris; each night would be filled with Parisian nightlife.

32

Ana and Pierre were madly in love with each other. Pierre was torn for the first time in his life. Should he fulfill the expectations of his family by going through with the arranged marriage, or turn his back on his birthright, his heritage, for the woman he loved?

For the next year Ana and Pierre were inseparable. Despite her ever-increasing popularity and constant performances, Pierre was always in attendance at the center table. It became obvious to the audience that *la Foncé Fille* had fallen in love. She sang the songs that Pierre wrote about their love, and recorded her first album of her performances live. Within six months she had the number one hit in Europe and a cult following in America. The beatniks had discovered and embraced both Ana and her music. Pierre never wanted credit for the songs he wrote and insisted that she wrote the songs, signing over all publishing rights. He wanted nothing from Ana and everything for her. With the climb of her album and the constant attention from the media, their romance became well publicized. Their affair became the subject of much speculation: would Pierre and Ana become the next Jean-Claude and Mignon-Marie?

Unbeknownst to Ana, Pierre's fiancée, Philippa de Perusing, had been closely following the items about Pierre and *la Foncé Fille* in the society column. In the past she had overlooked his dalliances with the parade of models that hit the Parisian runways. She believed the women to be no threat because they continuously changed. But now Philippa had tolerated all she could from Pierre and was not about to lose him to some performer. She had already become the brunt of cruel jokes among their circle of friends, most of whom were already married. Philippa, unlike her friends who did not love their husbands, was in fact very much in love with Pierre. It was her fondest dream that he would see her for the woman that she was and one day return her love, instead of looking upon her as a responsibility that had to be fulfilled. Panicked by Pierre's apparent lack of concern for appearances, she decided to take matters into her own hands. Making a call to the society editor, she delivered to the paper pictures of her and Pierre taken at the St. Honore anniversary gala. She released the news to the gossip columnist that the wedding date was set and the plans were under way. That would settle this affair once and for all before it got out of hand, and Pierre would probably thank her for helping him out of a difficult situation. With the article scheduled to appear in the next day's edition of the society section, Philippa called the wedding planner to begin working on the big event.

As Ana and Pierre's relationship developed, they spent many evenings and weekends with Pierre's parents. She now felt like she was part of the family. Her mother, Carrie, and soon-to-be stepfather, John had visited several times and had met Pierre and his parents. Remarkably, they all got along, especially Mignon-Marie and Carrie, who seemed to bond immediately. As time passed it had become harder for Pierre to explain his engagement or impending marriage. He instinctively knew that Ana would never understand. He was especially agitated after being confronted by his parents.

"Son, you must tell her before she finds out on her own!" Jean-Claude could hardly suppress his frustration at Pierre over his refusal to tell Ana the truth about his commitment.

"Pierre, your father is only trying to help you. No matter your decision, you must tell Ana the truth. If she hears it anywhere but from you, she will never trust you again, son. I know you cannot bear to hurt her . . . but she must know."

"Leave me be! We are fine . . . she is in love with me and I am in love with her. I will explain to Philippa that we should put off any talk of marriage for a few more years."

"Philippa! You cannot ask her to put off the wedding again! Either tell her it is over or go through with the ceremony as planned. That poor girl has already looked the other way and dealt with the humiliation of your public affair with Ana."

"Your father is right. You know how I feel—we love Ana. Philippa is not my choice for you because she is not the woman you love. I do not believe in a loveless marriage, although it is widely accepted. But it is time to bring this charade to an end."

That evening Pierre left his parents in a foul mood, unable to resolve his fear and indecision. After much soul searching, he finally decided he would tell Ana that weekend when they went away to Versailles.

33

At twenty years old Ana was the toast of France, madly in love with the man of her dreams and four weeks pregnant. She planned to tell Pierre the news this weekend, when they went away to Versailles. Hopefully they would surprise her mother and John with an engagement ring and an announcement of their own when they flew into Houston next week for the long-awaited marriage of John and Carrie. As far as she was concerned it was as though they were already married. The wedding was just a formality, but Ana wouldn't miss it for the world. And she couldn't wait to introduce Pierre to the rest of her family and all of her friends.

"Glad you could manage to finally make it, ladies!" Sam commented as she and Miss Fonteneau arrived.

"Mmm, a little sarcastic . . . bad day?" Ana inquired as she took the proffered seat.

"Not at all . . . as a matter of fact, I've had a glorious day!"

"Good, then, Sam . . . quit complaining and order a good wine—or would you prefer champagne, Ana?" Miss Fonteneau said.

"Neither," Ana replied hesitantly. She had been unsuccessfully fighting bouts of sickness that did not limit themselves to mornings. "I will have seltzer and lime. I still have a show tonight, or did you two forget? But feel free to enjoy!"

Miss Fonteneau watched Ana closely. She had been waiting for her to confide her condition, but obviously now wouldn't be that time. However, she couldn't help but try to draw her out.

"Is anything wrong, Ana? You look a little queasy."

"I'm perfectly fine, Miss F. I am starving, though . . . maybe that's what you see! Pass the gossip column, Sammy—let's see what's cookin'! Miss F., quit worrying. I can see it in your face. Just order us something sinfully rich, okay?"

As Miss Fonteneau studied the menu for something nutritious for her charge, Sammy passed the society section of the newspaper to Ana. Moments later Ana let out a sorrowful moan, startling both Sammy and Miss Fonteneau. Dropping the paper, she seemed to stagger from her seat. "I have to go. I feel sick."

"Wait, we'll go with you," Miss Fonteneau said.

They both rose simultaneously to help her, but Ana, visibly shaken, waved them away. By the time Miss F. reached the sidewalk Ana had already hailed a taxi and left the restaurant without waiting for her friends. Sammy motioned for Miss Fonteneau while he settled the bill. As he placed the francs on the table, he caught sight of the headline and understood why Ana was so upset. Picking up the paper, he saw a picture of Pierre and Philippa with the caption, *St. Honore and Perusing wedding date announced.* The article went on to list the designer of the bride's gown. Sammy felt his blood run hot and then cold. For the first time in his life he felt capable of physical violence. He felt like finding Pierre and beating him to a pulp. Instead he caught up with Marjorie Fonteneau to apprise her of the situation.

"My poor darling . . . no wonder she's so upset. We've got to find her, Sammy. Let's try the apartment first."

"Okay. I just can't believe this—damn!"

Arriving at the apartment, they found it empty, and there was no sign of Ana's return. Sitting down heavily, Sammy realized that they both had been hoping and praying that she had returned to the apartment. Neither Miss Fonteneau nor Sammy had a clue as to where Ana might have gone. Four hours passed and still they had not seen or heard from Ana. Frantic, Sammy put on his coat to walk around the Arrondissement to look for Ana.

As he opened the door to leave, Sammy almost collided with Pierre, who was on his way to pick her up for dinner before he took her to the theater for her performance. Pierre was so preoccupied with anticipating the outcome of their evening that he had not even seen Sammy's approach.

34

Pierre had lain awake most of the previous night thinking about his father's remarks, and decided that it was time to act. This morning he had driven to visit his grandfather and tell him the news first that he was calling off the wedding to Philippa and asking Ana for her hand in marriage. Afterward he went to break the news to Philippa, who took it as the ultimate betrayal—which was exactly what he had anticipated. He felt bad, but better bad for a moment than for a lifetime. What surprised him most of all was Philippa's confession of love, which both saddened and embarrassed him for her. At no point in their relationship had love even been something he considered; he had kissed her publicly only on those occasions where it was deemed appropriate, and even those kisses were chaste.

After unsuccessfully attempting to calm Philippa before leaving, he finally called her mother, who entered the room tight-lipped with her disapproval. Much to his relief she requested that he leave them alone immediately, and he was more than happy to oblige. As soon as he left he went directly to his parents' home to meet with them and tell them of his decision, hoping to receive their blessing. To his delight, his father praised his courage and his mother gave him the St. Honore emerald, a family heirloom and tradition. With the ring safely in a velvet box in his pocket, he planned to put it on Ana's finger at dinner and seal his plan to make her his wife.

When he ran into Sammy, stopping him in his tracks, the man was so angry he was almost shrieking.

"Why did you do this to her, man? Why didn't you tell her?"

"Do what to her? Tell her what?" Pierre demanded with a sinking feeling in the pit of his stomach. He steeled himself for Sammy's response, although he already knew what it would be.

"What's going on out here? Stop all that yelling and come inside before all of Paris knows what is happening in this house!" Miss Fonteneau's nerves were clearly on edge, as were those of the two men faced off in the hallway.

Briskly sidestepping Sammy, Pierre walked into the apartment, feeling a sense of panic overtake him. "Where's Ana? I need to speak to her and find out what he's talking about!" Pierre whirled around, pointing an accusatory finger at Sammy.

"Quiet down, Pierre, and, Sammy, take a seat and try to relax. We're not getting anywhere like this. Pierre, we don't know where she is; she ran off from the café this afternoon in tears and we haven't seen or heard from her since. We were halfheartedly hoping she would contact you and that you would bring her back."

"What do you mean, she ran off? What happened . . . what did she say?"

Disgusted, Sammy threw the society section of the newspaper with the picture of Pierre and Philippa at him. Pierre felt as if the blood had been drained from him. He had been so busy that he had not stopped to read the paper today. No wonder Philippa kept babbling about calling the paper and taking it back. At the time he had no idea what she was talking about; it was just senseless babbling. He had been so anxious to put distance between them, but now it all made sense, her reaction and response when he told her the wedding was off. Now this . . . it came as a startling surprise. Unable to hold back his panic, he looked from Sammy to Miss Fonteneau. "Believe me, it's not what it seems, and it's too complicated to explain. I came to ask her to marry me tonight . . . I was going to give her this," he said, despondently pulling from his pocket the small velvet box that held the family heirloom, an eight-carat emerald ring surrounded by diamond baguettes set in platinum.

"Then find her . . . apologize and ask for her hand," Sammy and Miss Fonteneau urged.

"You're right. I think I know where she might go." But even as he spoke he could not shake the feeling of dread that came over him. Rising heavily to his feet, Pierre set off the way he had come. Getting in his car, he went to the Place de la Concorde and walked to the obelisk, praying that Ana had returned to the spot where they had met over a year ago. Ana was nowhere to be found. Pierre searched everywhere, even going to the theater to see if she had shown up for her performance. It was all to no avail.

Returning to the apartment he ran into a forlorn Sammy and Miss Fonteneau also returning from their own search. To their chagrin she was nowhere to be found.

"She'll have to come home sooner or later. . . . We might as well make ourselves comfortable and wait it out. If we haven't heard from her by morning we will have to let her parents and the officials know."

"I can't even think of that right now. I could not bear it if something happens to Ana."

35

As dawn broke over the city of Paris, it was met by three sets of red-rimmed eyes. Unable to sleep, they each sat watching the door, expectantly waiting for the knob to turn and Ana to walk in. Pierre was not ready to give up, nor did he want to panic her parents. Instead he called the family lawyer and made arrangements for a private investigator to trace her whereabouts.

After four days and no sign of Ana, Pierre was a total wreck. The private investigator had yet to find her. Sammy had begun to cancel her appearances, giving laryngitis as the excuse for the late cancellation. Luckily her schedule was light, due to her plans to return to Houston for Carrie's wedding.

Dreading the inevitable, Miss Fonteneau daily called first Pierre, and then Sammy, with hope against hope that they had heard from her. Unfortunately the answer had remained the same: no sign of her. As soon as Marjorie Fonteneau hung up the phone with Sammy after the fourth day, she picked it up again, giving the long-distance operator the number to Carrie and John's. The last thing she wanted to do was tell them that their daughter was missing just a little over a week away from their wedding, but it seemed she had no other choice.

Carrie picked up the phone on the second ring. "Hello?"

"Carrie . . . it's Marj Fonteneau," she began hesitantly.

"Marj! How are you? Ana told me you were sick with the flu, and that's why you're not with her. I am so disappointed that you and Sammy won't be able to make it to the wedding. But I understand, and thank God he's there to nurse you back to health."

Marjorie's mind raced. *Ana's in Houston . . . thank God, at least she is safe.*

"Carrie may I speak to Ana? I just wanted to let her know I was feeling much better!"

"You just missed her—it's still a madhouse around here and she's out helping run errands. I can let her know you called. Is there any other message?"

"No . . . no other message. Just have her give us a call and let us know when to pick her up."

"Well, that's easy enough . . . but I'm sure her return date and flight haven't changed. She's scheduled to return the day after the wedding. But I will give her the message; she's been irritable and distracted since she's been here."

"It may just be jet lag." Marjorie was so relieved she couldn't think straight.

"You're right, it might be. I really can't be sure. If I didn't know better I'd think she's been avoiding me since she's been here. I think she and Pierre have had an argument—did she mention it to you?"

"No, Carrie, she didn't. Anyway, I don't want to run the telephone bill up. Just tell her I called and give her my love. Oh, and Carrie—congratulations!"

"Thank you, Marj . . . I'll talk to you soon."

As soon as Marjorie hung up the phone she called first Sammy and then Pierre to give them the news of Ana's whereabouts. She ended up spending the better part of an hour trying to convince Pierre not to follow Ana. She also didn't dare tell him her suspicion that Ana might be pregnant. She thought it would be best for him to wait for her to return to France of her own volition; maybe then she would be calm and willing to listen to reason. After much persuasion she was successful in convincing him to remain in Paris, hoping to allow Ana an opportunity to let her anger die down.

36

The announcement of the marriage of Carrie Daniels to John Browning, one of the most respected and sought-after Negro millionaires, was the talk not only of Houston, but of New York, Chicago, Detroit, and, of course, Louisiana as well. *Ebony* magazine interviewed them and played up their story as the chance meeting of childhood sweethearts reunited by fate. Carrie and John knew the truth had been far more torturous than the fairy tale the magazines had created. *The Match Made in Heaven* read the covers of *Jet* magazine and *Sepia*. Carrie could not believe how quickly her life had turned around; for the first time she knew what true happiness was—it was being with John. As the date of the wedding came upon them, they were both anxiously awaiting the day they did not have to pretend and could live together in the same household.

Ana was happy for her mother. To her surprise, Carrie had fallen in love with John soon after they met, on the night of Ana's party four years ago. Ana recalled how she used to secretly fantasize that John was her father; appearance-wise she could easily have been his daughter. She was elated when Carrie had announced their intentions to wed. As the maid of honor, she took it upon herself to surprise her mother and other members of the wedding party with Lalique perfume flasks that she found at a tiny boutique in the Carrousel du Louvre. For Carrie and John's wedding present she had selected antique Baccarat champagne flutes from 1910 at Le St. Honore des Antiquaires. She'd had the presence of mind to call and speak to Mignon-Marie's assistant, Joseph, and he assured her he had already sent them and they had finally arrived yesterday.

Ana was determined to stay so busy she wouldn't have time to think. Constantly volunteering to help things move along, she was lethargic from the need for rest, due to her condition. But she refused to rest, especially since the wedding was just a week away. Ana was looking forward to the wedding day. But she was also in turmoil over the predicament she found herself in: pregnant, and devastated that her relationship with Pierre was over. No matter what she did or how busy she stayed, she thought of him constantly throughout her day. Each night she prayed that he would come after her and explain everything. Then they could get on with their life; she just needed reassurance that he loved only her and that the article in the newspaper had been a cruel mistake.

But in her heart she knew that would not happen; it had already been six days since she had left Paris and there had been no word from Pierre. Miss Fonteneau had called earlier in the week; Ana knew she had called to tell her parents that she was missing, until her mother told her she was already in Houston. Carrie said that Miss Fonteneau wanted her to call and tell her when she was returning, but even Ana didn't know the answer to that question. Sammy called to say he was flying in, after he yelled at her for some time about leaving without a word. Finally she convinced him to stay in Paris, that she needed to be alone with her family and get her thoughts straight. Strangely enough, Sammy had not mentioned a word about Pierre either, and her pride wouldn't let her ask. She was sure that both Sammy and Miss Fonteneau had read or heard about Pierre's engagement by now. Maybe they thought they were sparing her feelings, which meant that it must be true. When the full significance of their silence hit Ana, so did the flood of pain that she had been suppressing, and the tears followed, seeming to flow like a stream that was being fed from a river. No matter how hard she tried to stop the flow of her tears to erase the pain, nothing helped; she had to cry herself out until there was nothing left. She felt both a void of emptiness in her heart and the fullness of life that was forming in her body, both sensations tied to one man, Pierre.

Ana made the decision to tell her parents about the pregnancy and her predicament with Pierre after the wedding. She also intended to tell Sammy and Miss Fonteneau about her condition and the truth of her hasty departure from Paris. She prayed they would all understand and not reject her or the decision she had made. Right now she had to get dressed; Ina and Lena were on their way to pick her up for a day of shopping, followed by a night on the town.

37

Carrie sat at her desk engrossed in the task of reviewing her guest list and the final details of the wedding. She was thankful for Louise's offer to plan and execute the reception. Even at her age, Carrie worked tirelessly on the plans with the caterer to make sure everything was perfect. The wedding was only a week away and she felt overwhelmed by the last-minute tasks. She couldn't wait for her wedding day so she could finally be united with John. Lost in her reverie, she didn't realize she had been daydreaming until she heard the doorbell ring. Startled, she looked at her wristwatch. *Well, at least she's on time.* Getting up from her seat she put her list aside, absent-mindedly checking her appearance in the hall mirror before answering the door. As she opened the door to invite her guest in, she was startled at how much the woman had aged.

Ruth looked around suspiciously as Carrie invited her in and led her to the parlor, offering her a seat. She had no idea why she'd been invited to Carrie's home. Of course, she had read about her impending marriage. Maybe she wanted to gloat: now that Ruth had finally married Logan, she had found out too late that Logan was the booby prize. She greatly regretted that she had spent her life waiting for and wanting him. But she would not grovel or give Carrie the satisfaction of letting her know she had won. As the years passed, Ruth's hate for

Carrie did not dwindle or fade. She held Carrie directly accountable for her own unhappiness.

Carrie offered Ruth a seat and refreshment. She could sense her uneasiness and distrust. But she had not invited her to discuss Logan or their past together; she thought of Logan only as a conduit who assisted her in having her beloved children.

"Would you care for coffee or tea?" Carrie offered.

"No, thank you, I can't stay long," Ruth replied curtly, feeling even more uncomfortable. *I should not have come,* she thought.

Carrie took a seat across from Ruth, she waited a moment before beginning. "Ruth, I invited you here today in hopes of putting our past behind us." Pausing briefly, she looked up to see Megan standing in the archway. Carrie released a sigh of relief; she had hoped Megan would decide to join them. It would be much easier this way. Carrie got up to help Megan as she settled into the deep sofa. Once Megan was settled, she continued: "Ruth, I would like to introduce you to our mother, Megan Devereaux." Carrie paused, allowing her words time to sink in.

Ruth looked at Carrie, trying to make sense of what she had said. She must have misunderstood.

"It is a pleasure to meet you, Mrs. Devereaux," Ruth replied.

This time Carrie clearly stated, "This is your mother, Ruth. She is also my mother."

Ruth had not misunderstood Carrie's introduction. "I don't know what kind of cruel joke you're playing, Carrie Daniels. My mother is a Pruitt, and I'm from Evergreen, Texas!" Ruth replied angrily. "I don't know why you invited me here today; what's worse, I don't know why I accepted. I've never liked you nor you me . . . but why stoop this low and put this old woman—your mother—in our mess?"

Megan had sat quietly as Ruth blew off steam, but she had no intention of listening to her tear Carrie down.

"That's enough, Ruthelen!" Megan interrupted, shocking Ruth into silence. "Your argument is with me—direct your anger at me. What you hated in Carrie all these years is the me you see in her. I am your mama by birthing you—only I didn't want you. I was raped by my daddy—your daddy—he be Robert Devereaux. He was a sick man . . . he wanted the first fruit with every girl who lived on his land." Megan glanced meaningfully at Carrie, who recalled the evening that he had raped her. "You was sent to live with a childless family by the name of

Pruitt in Evergreen, Texas—Christian, God-fearing people who wanted a child." As Megan retold the story of Ruth's conception and birth, Carrie saw Ruth's anger turn to resignation as she realized that for the first time she was finding out the answers to the questions she had tortured her parents with as a teenager.

Ruth looked from Carrie to Megan and back again. She had to get away from these women . . . she felt as if she were suffocating. Standing, her body rigid, she had to gather all the strength she could muster. There was no way she would allow them to see her fall apart. "You made a good choice, old woman." Seeing Megan flinch from her words, she continued: "The Pruitts were good parents." Turning to Carrie she said, "You lose again. Not only Logan—he was always mine from the beginning . . . even when your son died he was with me, taking comfort from me. But you started out losing from birth. Who would want a woman like this for a mother? Someone who could despise a babe at birth and give it away? Poor Carrie, is this the little surprise you had planned for me? Do me a favor . . . next time keep your secrets to yourself!" Ruth rose abruptly, almost knocking over the side table next to her seat, angrily walking to the door and slamming it on her way out.

Carrie rose to try to stop Ruth but felt Megan's hand on her arm.

"Don't try to stop her, and don't fret. She had a right to her anger—I'm glad it's all out. Only the Lord can fix this child. She is a mean, bitter woman, and she did the only thing she knew how—lashed out and caused pain." Megan looked at her daughter, gently stroking her brow. "I'm tired, Carrie, I just want to sit alone for a spell." Carrie could not keep the concern she felt from showing in her eyes. "Don't fret, child, I'm just tired . . . just need time to think and make my own peace with this," she said, hoping it would put Carrie's mind to rest.

"Well, Mama, if there's anything you need—" Before Carrie could finish her sentence she was interrupted again by the ringing of the doorbell. She looked puzzled. Surely Ruth would not return after the scene she had just made, Carrie thought, still trying to wrestle with the anger she harbored against this woman, half sister or not. Swinging the door open she was prepared to confront Ruth woman to woman. To her surprise it was Stella. Carrie was so shocked to see her sister, she forgot to invite her in. Before she knew it, they were holding each other in a tearful embrace.

"I'm sorry to drop in unannounced," Stella began, "but I just heard from John that Megan and Jesse . . . uh . . . I mean Mama and Daddy are here."

Carrie could not believe her ears. She looked at Stella closely, noticing the dark circles under her eyes.

"I'm glad you decided to come," she said earnestly. "I'm right here for you."

Stella leaned heavily on Carrie. "I need you more than ever now, Cara."

They were both nervous. Apparently Stella had decided to mend some fences.

"I told David I wanted to make our marriage work, but I need time to fix some things that are wrong with me. We've decided to give our marriage another try . . . we may even consider adoption, since we will never have a child of our own," Stella finished, clearly letting Carrie know that she had not told David he had a son or confirmed that she was a Negro.

Carrie escorted Stella into the dining room, making her wait until she found Jesse and asked him to join Megan in the parlor. Once Jesse was seated next to Megan, Carrie led Stella into the room. She watched, tears in her eyes, as Megan and Jesse saw their baby girl again for the first time in over twenty years. Stella knelt, placing her head on Megan's lap, openly weeping, asking Megan and Jesse for their forgiveness. After a moment Carrie left the room. They needed time alone to mend and catch up.

38

Hearing a car approach, Carrie looked out the window. *It's about time,* she thought, slightly irritated, as she watched Ana walk to the door. Ana had developed a confidence and sense of character that far surpassed her other children. Black Gal, as everyone still called her, had turned the tables on color and made herself the accepted exception to the rule. She had always wanted to have a career singing and had been singing professionally for a little over four years. With the help of John's attorneys and her agent she had started as a radio personality singing weekly on the Smooth Sammy show. Before they knew it she was signed to an agent, Samuel Martine—the former Smooth Sammy—and had been living in Paris, France, and touring in London, Italy, and Germany. John and Carrie visited her as often as possible and had hired a chaperon to travel with her. Carrie had been determined not to deny Ana her life's dream by being too overprotective, although she couldn't help but worry about her. After the wedding, they intended to go back to Paris with her and honeymoon in Versailles while she finished her tour. Maybe there would even be another wedding, Carrie hoped. They had met Pierre-Michel and his family on their short visits over the past year, and it was obvious to everyone he had eyes only for Ana. And Ana was head over heels for him. Hopefully they would marry and Carrie could relax, knowing her baby was happy and being cared for. Her only concern was that she was certain that Ana was extremely upset about something when she had returned to Houston last week. Carrie assumed they had had a lovers' quarrel. But Ana had been so secretive and evasive she couldn't get her to sit still long enough to talk about anything, let alone her and Pierre. She just couldn't figure out what was wrong, and John insisted that she not pry and allow Ana to tell them when she felt comfortable. For the time being she would go along, but if Ana failed to bring up the subject—and soon—then she certainly would.

Carrie went to the door to meet Ana and tell her that Stella was in the den. Although Ana was twenty and it had been many years since she had witnessed the public humiliation that both Sofia and Stella had suffered as a result of David's betrayal, the subject of David and Sofia was still a sore one for her. Carrie understood that Ana sided with her sister and only niece. David had become the enemy. However, much to Carrie's surprise—for the third time in a day—Ana responded nonchalantly and said she was glad that Stella had decided to work things out. She wished them well. When Ana joined the group in the parlor, there was an emotional exchange between a family that had been broken by color lines for decades.

Carrie observed the group distantly; she focused her attention primarily on her youngest child, Ana. It was amazing to Carrie that Ana had risen above it all, seemingly unscathed by the difference in her complexion versus her siblings'. Unlike Carrie, Ana did not seek a high-yella man. Instead she sought wealth and position and generally was attracted to boys—and now men—who had various complexions. Ana even wore the name Black Gal with aplomb; in France she described herself as *la Foncé Fille,* meaning girl of dark color. This fact was remarkable in itself , especially considering that, in terms of color among Negroes, nothing had changed from the time Carrie had been a young girl. It was still more desirable to be high yella and married to high yella. She thanked God that Ana had not allowed the obstacle of color to impact and ruin her life.

As Carrie joined her family, she wished that this reunion could be in its entirety. It had been too many years since she had seen or even spoken to most of her siblings. She knew she probably would not recognize many of them if they passed on the street. Now her children had turned out to be similar to her siblings. Odele had chosen to pass for white, consequently dissociating herself from Carrie and her siblings. Sofia was pregnant with the first child from her new marriage, and Angel was ecstatic at the thought of being a big sister. Carrie should have been relieved and pleased that Sofia was finally married, especially to a professional man. But she knew Sofia had acted out of spite and was not in love with her husband. She wanted to hurt David, but unfortunately life had not taught her that the best revenge was true happiness.

Eddie continued to live the fast life. He now made his home in Los Angeles, calling frequently to say he was fine and things were going well. During their conversations she never asked what he was doing for a living, and he never offered the information. Praying daily for all of her children, she always asked a special blessing over Eddie for his safety, knowing her son was always in motion, trying to run away from his demons, hoping he'd find the happiness that always eluded him. She knew that until he was willing to confront his demons, his happiness would continue to elude him. It was a lesson that Carrie had lived and understood. She was happier now than she had ever been. Her life had come full circle and she was back with John. Unconsciously, she glanced at her engagement ring, a reminder that this was not all just a dream. Only five more days and she would legally be Mrs. John Browning.

39

To Ana's surprise, the night on the town with Ina and Lena included their current boyfriends and a blind date for her. Irritated beyond words at her two old friends, she was more upset when C.P. walked into the club, taking the empty seat beside her. After a stilted greeting, they made small talk for a while, then turned to watch the show. Ana's mind was racing; she had not spoken to C.P. for almost two years, and so much had happened in her life that it felt awkward to be sitting next to the person with whom she had made so many empty plans and promises.

C.P. also felt self-conscious. He had not seen Ana in so long and was completely unprepared for her sophistication and worldliness. It was not false airs or pretense; she seemed as distant from him as any star in the galaxy. Her life had taken off and she was realizing her dreams, while he had to be satisfied as the assistant coach of the TSU Tigers basketball team. After his knee injury, the doctors told him he could never play competitively again, so he'd settled for second best—coaching. After a seemingly endless awkward silence, he decided to try again to break the ice. This time it worked, and Ana seemed to relax a bit. Before he knew it they were laughing and talking about old times and the years in between. Although Ana didn't seem to have any interest in reestablishing their relationship, he decided he would just give her time and put his best foot forward in the time that she was here. As the evening came to an end, C.P. took a chance: "Are you busy tomorrow night?"

"Not really, you know, just getting ready for Saturday."

"Well, I was thinking since you've never seen me play, maybe you could come and watch me coach."

"Okay . . . that'll be fun. Can I bring Ina and Lena?"

"Sure . . . fine. I'll leave the tickets at will call, and maybe we can get something to eat after the game."

"Sounds like a plan. In Paris we eat dinner late, and so I'm always hungry late in the evening and no one else is. Okay, I'll see you to-morrow, then."

"All right, game starts at seven; I'll be looking out for you!"

"Huh, don't be looking for me—you'd better be looking at your players," she responded jokingly, happy that she had agreed on going out, and not mad at her friends anymore. They knew her better than she remembered. They realized when Pierre had not come to Houston, as she promised he would, something had to be very wrong. And since Pierre had obviously moved on without her, the least she could do for herself was have fun and stay busy.

After that night C.P. and Ana went out constantly, like old chums. He seemed to respect her need for friendship and physical distance, which was just what she needed—platonic male companionship, un-complicated and without expectations. They both discovered that they liked each other's company, and friendship came easily.

40

Carrie could not believe her wedding day had finally arrived. As the dressmaker zipped her into the dress, she smiled at her long-time friend, Louise, whose eyes were filled with tears.

"Carrie, this is your day. I have been anticipating this day as if I were the bride to be. Now it's here, and you are beautiful. God bless you, my friend; you are due this day, and I pray the rest of your life is filled with great joy." Louise embraced Carrie, the two friends fighting back tears. "Okay, that's enough. Before we're both a wreck, I'll go and tell Ana to hurry; the limousine is here and we don't want to be late," Louise finished breathlessly as Carrie smiled.

Louise is more nervous than I am, Carrie thought to herself.

"Let's go!" she heard Louise call.

"Come, Mrs. Browning," beckoned the dressmaker. "Let me help you to the car so you won't ruin this lovely gown."

Carrie accepted her assistance and took her seat in the limousine. Both Louise and Ana were struck by Carrie's unrivaled beauty—this was her day.

The wedding was held in the formal gardens of the home John bought for Carrie, and no expense had been spared with the decorations. Carrie could not calm the butterflies that filled her stomach as she saw John waiting for her at the end of the aisle. There was an audible sigh among the guests when they saw the bride. She was a vision in a strapless bridal gown fitted at the waist and falling to trumpet at the bottom. It was a very pale muted pink that complemented her ring. She did not wear a veil; instead a crown of pale pink rosebuds tightly closed, had been interwoven through a diamond-and-ruby tiara. And instead of a train of fabric, a cape that was attached at the top of the dress cascaded out to a twelve-foot train of newly bloomed imported pale pink roses. Holding the arm of her father and her son, she was glad they were both escorting her to marry her beloved John. As the bridal march played, Carrie moved with the music, putting one foot before the other, marching toward love, toward life, moving . . . moving, feeling all of her cares dropping from her as she was drawn toward his love, his eyes so soulful, so sure, so loving. Then she stood next to John, holding his hand tightly as they were united in holy matrimony, repeating the words over and over in her mind: *Till death do us part.* Although there were over five hundred guests, not including the press, Carrie and John only saw, heard, and felt each other. They had both fantasized and dreamed of this day for years. Nothing could distract or deprive them of the sweetness of this moment. After embracing in a passionate kiss, they turned to greet their guests as husband and wife.

Carrie had not believed she could ever be so happy. John's parents and his sister stood next to him, while Megan, Jesse, Eddie, Sofia, and Ana stood next to her in the receiving line as they greeted the guests. To her surprise, Stella had contacted their brother, William, and sister, Rebecca. Carrie was overjoyed to see them again. As the long line neared the end, Ruth stepped forward to congratulate them. Seeing Ruth, Carrie immediately tensed but was calmed by the slight pressure of John's hand tightening on hers, signaling that all would be well. She accepted Ruth's well wishes uneasily. As Ruth passed John she leaned over and whispered to Carrie, "You lose again."

Before Carrie knew what was happening she heard popping sounds like someone uncorking champagne. Within an instant she felt Megan tug her arm and moan softly. As if in slow motion, Carrie and Jesse both turned in stunned disbelief as Megan slumped and seemed to fold over onto the floor. Carrie screamed as her mother lay limp and lifeless, a pool of blood forming around her body. John pushed Carrie out of the way as he ran toward the direction of the popping sound. Confused and disoriented, Carrie watched the rush of movement as the panicked guests fled the crowded room. Images were blurred in a nightmarish way. Before Carrie could focus on the source, she heard more popping sounds and hysterical screams.

"What's happening? John! John!" Carrie screamed, frantically looking around for her husband. She heard cries and screams of panic and saw another body fall to the floor. *Why isn't someone helping me?* she thought. *Where is John?* She saw her father weeping soundlessly as he held her mother's limp body. She had to find her children. She began to crawl on her hands and knees as she tried unsuccessfully to gain her footing to stand and search for Ana, Eddie, and Sofia. Seeing her loved ones dead, hearing the thunder of screaming filling her ears, and being faced with the sight of blood everywhere she looked, Carrie didn't know which way to turn. Then she saw John, disoriented, seemingly using all of his effort to rise from the floor. He was pale beneath his brown skin. Blood was splattered on his face and saturated his shirt. The realization that she was losing John hit her with the force of a sledgehammer. Carrie began crawling on her hands and knees, trying feverishly to propel herself to her feet. Her gown, which was now soaked with her mother's blood, weighed her down. With pure will and adrenaline, she gained her feet and quickly closed the distance between them. She could not stand to lose him . . . not now. "Please, God, have mercy on me!"

4I

Eight months later

Shivering from a slight chill in the room, Carrie went to place another log on the dying fire and returned to her inspection of the newly framed sepia-tone photographs of her family, lovingly displayed on the Steinway grand piano in their living room. Pausing in front of the portrait of her parents and the baby picture of Sofia, she felt her throat constrict and her eyes fill with tears. She still had not reconciled the loss of her child, although she had tried to make sense of it. She knew that she would never understand the depth of hatred that grew in Ruth, which had caused her to kill their mother, Megan, and Carrie's daughter Sofia, and then turn the gun on herself. The ringing of the telephone startled her; picking up the receiver, she answered tentatively. "Hello?"

"Mom . . . this is C.P. Ana has just been taken into the delivery room. By the time you and John make it the baby will probably be here," he said breathlessly, clearly nervous and stressed.

"Okay, we're on our way; let me get John. How's my daughter doing?"

"She's fine, Mom; you know I'm right here."

"Yes, I do, and she couldn't be luckier than to have you as a husband."

"Thanks." C.P. felt his throat constrict at her comment. He had always thought she disapproved of their marriage. "We're in room two-twelve B."

"We're on our way."

Carrie slowly put the telephone back in its cradle. She realized there was nothing she could do other than be prayerful and accepting. She went to find John. Checking the den first and not finding him, she went to the library. As usual he was seated in his favorite oversize leather chair with his feet propped on the matching ottoman. John was so engrossed in his book that she was almost standing next to him before he realized she had entered the room.

He looked up, smiling. "I heard the phone . . . was it the call we've been waiting for?"

"Yes, we'd better be on our way to the hospital . . . this baby won't wait on us."

Carrie had to restrain herself from offering John assistance in standing; Ruth had missed shooting Ana only because the bullet hit John in the thigh. Although he was doing much better, she could tell it was still painful by the grimace he wore each time he attempted to put his weight on his leg after sitting for prolonged periods. She waited patiently for him to find his keys; then John and Carrie rode in nervous silence to the hospital, each trying to prepare for the worst, but praying for the best. It had almost been a year since she and John had been married. Although it was the happiest time of their life, it also was the saddest. In this time they had buried her parents, her daughter, and her half sister, Ruth. Carrie still had not come to terms with the fact that Ruth had gone crazy and killed Megan. Her daughter Sofia had died trying to save Angel, and then Ruth finally turned the gun on herself. Carrie's father, Jesse, had died in his sleep a week after Megan's death. Eddie, overcome by guilt at not being able to save Sofia, left Texas, and Carrie had not heard from him since the wedding. Instead of the joy she should have felt after marrying John, it had been a time filled with anguish and the depths of despair. Fortunately, John had been by her side through it all, from hell to healing.

Now they were on their way to the hospital so she could be with Ana and Clark for the birth of their first child. After dredging up painful memories that were better left locked away, Carrie had to fight the emotions that she never wanted to feel again. Her baby—her

Ana, the one she had prayed would realize her own greatness and not throw away her dreams—had done just that. To worsen the entire affair, Carrie could not tell her daughter the truth about the man she had gotten pregnant and eloped with. So, overwhelmed and drowning in her own grief in the past eight months, she had not known who her daughter had fallen in love with . . . until it was too late. Now she was filled with uncertainty. She could only pray that God would have mercy on them all. Carrie relaxed in the comfort of John's touch as his large brown hand smoothed her hair and eased her pain all in the same motion. How complicated this all was. She knew that she would not have made it had God not seen fit to give her John.

As the car pulled up to the entrance of Hermann Hospital, Carrie was again reminded of the previous trips she had made to this hospital and how they were all filled with regrettable outcomes. But this time it was different; she was here to be with her daughter, Ana, as she gave birth to her first child. The fact that Clark was Stella's son and Ana's cousin filled her with trepidation regarding the outcome. She willed herself to think positive thoughts. *That's all I'll think about. . . .*

"I'll find out where she is while you park the car," Carrie told John as she got out of the car and headed for the entrance doors. She turned with renewed determination to be a source of strength for her daughter if the birth was unsuccessful or the baby abnormal. Walking to the nurses' station, again she thought back on the night she had brought Edward in to the colored-only emergency ward. Straightening her shoulders she continued to move her legs forward, feeling as if they were wrapped with lead weights. The admitting nurse looked up at Carrie's approach, certain that she was there to see a critical admission. She braced herself for the expected. To her surprise she was asked about a maternity admission. With a ready smile she gave Carrie the information she'd requested: Mrs. Ana Patton had delivered her baby just minutes before Carrie's arrival.

Carrie stood impatiently in the lobby waiting for John; she could not believe it had taken him so long just to park the car. Tapping her foot against the tile floor, she became increasingly irritated at this delay. Just when she had made up her mind to go to Ana's room without him, he entered the doors out of breath as he hurriedly explained he'd had to park a block away. Breathing a sigh of relief, she took his hand walking to the corridor that led to Ana's room.

Standing just outside the door, Carrie knocked softly before entering. As she reached for the knob, the door swung open and C.P. stood beaming proudly. "It's a girl!" he exclaimed. "She looks just like you, Mother Carrie." Gently taking her hand, he led her toward Ana as she lay in the small bed. Looking at her daughter, her namesake, she thought, *Another me, but stronger, surer.* "How's my baby?"

"I'm happy, Mama . . . look at my beauty," Ana replied, her eyes filled with love and pride. Carrie's eyes traveled from Ana's face slowly toward the small bundle she held in her arms. Clark was right: this child looked like Carrie as a baby. Reaching for her granddaughter, she took her in her arms as she felt the stress washing away. Looking at her tiny features, the almond-shaped eyes, wisps of Indian auburn hair, and the beautiful rich tanned complexion, Carrie felt it all come full circle. Her entire life, the pain of being just like this child, was erased, and for the first time she enjoyed the beauty of her brown skin. Smiling broadly as the tears slid unchecked down her face, she looked from Clark to Ana. "What is her name?" she asked.

The couple exchanged a glance as they answered almost in unison, "Mignon."

Carrie looked back at Ana intensely as the enormity of the name passed from daughter to mother.

"That is a beautiful and appropriate name for a beautiful baby." Looking at Mignon, she softly whispered, "You are a new beginning, you are the joy that comes after many sorrows. You will finish what we couldn't." Gazing lovingly at the tiny bundle, Carrie spoke to no one in particular. "Her middle name will be Joy," she continued "Mignon Joy Patton." Tenderly she handed the baby to Clark as he stood beaming broadly, barely able to suppress the tears that filled his eyes, proudly holding his daughter for John to see.

"Come, John," Carrie beckoned. "We have to let Stella and Louise know we have a new baby." Carrie walked over to kiss Ana lightly on the temple. "I will be back tomorrow with Mignon's aunt and godmother."

Carrie kissed Clark on the cheek, smiling to herself when he placed the infant against his shoulder and she spied the oblong birthmark at the nape of her neck. "I would suggest that you use this time to rest; once they get home there won't be much time for rest."

"I know. I asked the nurse for a cot, but she told me to go home. I'll leave shortly."

"We will check on you later—love you all."

As John and Carrie drove back home, she rested her head on his shoulder. Things weren't perfect but they would be all right. She no longer feared what the future would bring. She had lived long enough to understand that whatever it brought, she would be able to endure. All endings simply made room for beginnings. . . .

42

Now, almost fourteen years later, Ana was returning to the city where she had left her heart. It was still unthinkable that she had never seen or spoken to Pierre again. Her daughter, Mignon, was her only link to the one person she had truly loved. It was a pity that he would never know her or see the parts of him in their daughter that were so easily recognizable to her.

Subconsciously Ana recognized that her decision to contact Sammy Martine, now one of the top agents in the industry with homes both in the United States and abroad, would catapult her to the top and back to Paris. She had developed a reputation that was now legendary, and her return was heralded as marking a new era in the return of the jazz soloist. Ana locked arms with Mignon, and the two walked into the terminal, prepared to meet Sammy. Neither was prepared for the warm reception by the Parisian press welcoming *la Foncé Fille* back to Paris. Posing for the press, Ana was aware of the striking effect Mignon would have on a city like Paris. Mother and daughter were a pair to be reckoned with. Some of the reporters were already hinting at Mignon's beauty, speculating that she would be the next great model. Interrupting the press before they could pry too deeply, Sammy artfully whisked the pair away with the help of security that had previously seemed invisible.

Stepping into the limousine, Mignon immediately knew her world had changed in ways her thirteen-year-old mind could not comprehend. She looked at her mother through new eyes. To hear others talk about *la Foncé Fille* when Mignon had been a little girl was no comparison to seeing the reaction of the press when they arrived. Her mother was right: they were treated like royalty. When they arrived at the home Sammy had leased for them in the Eighth Arrondissement on an elegantly appointed street off the Champs Elysées, Mignon was not prepared for its beauty.

Ana was unnaturally quiet as Sammy toured her through the three-story home. When she climbed the familiar stairs to the top floor where the master bedroom was located, she could have walked blindfolded through it and never stumbled into one piece of furniture. It was exactly the same as it had been almost fifteen years ago when Pierre had first brought her to his home. Standing at the French doors that led to the terrace, she slowly opened the leaded-glass-paned door and walked over to the ledge. Gazing at the view of the Arc du Triomphe, she let her eyes follow the link to the obelisk on the Place de la Concorde where they first met. Turning back to Sammy she searched his eyes for answers.

"It was left for you whenever you returned. He wouldn't allow anything to be changed."

Ana sat down heavily; this was too much for her to comprehend.

"Mignon, please feel free to walk through the rest of the house. I'm sure there's a room for you on the second floor."

"All right, Mom. Are you okay? You look funny."

"I'm fine, honey, I need to talk to your uncle Sammy in private for a moment . . . and I'm tired from the trip. Concorde or no Concorde, this flight always takes a lot out of me."

"Okay, I'll look around. Oh, and, Mom?"

"Yes, baby?"

"You were right—I do love Paris. It just feels right." Whistling softly to herself, Mignon turned to leave the room, excited about the opportunity to explore the big house alone. She decided to go back and start again at the beginning. There was something about this house that felt right. Standing on the Italian marble floor in the vestibule, she allowed her eyes to wander around the entrance hall and up the dramatic sweep of the staircase. Taking a step into the entrance hall, she repeated her actions. Standing in one place, she turned slowly on her heel, inspecting each room from the perspective of the hall. Imagining what her life was going to be like, she walked into the great room, which held the largest fireplace she had ever seen. Mignon was five feet, ten inches tall, and the mantel of the fireplace was a few inches above her head. She walked through the room, enjoying the warmth from the glowing fire and the warmth of the choice of colors and artwork. Last year she had had an art-appreciation class and had studied the masters. Walking through this room she saw the name Chagall, with whom she was familiar; he had been her favorite.

Leaving the great room, she followed an annex that led her to a formal library with floor-to-ceiling leather-bound books and large, overstuffed chairs, sofas, and love seats placed in clusters around the room. It also boasted a huge fireplace. Assorted tables that looked like works of art in their own right sat atop a Persian rug placed artfully among the chairs and sofas. Next she walked through another set of French doors that led to a small garden with a fountain in the center. She couldn't resist putting her hand under the cool flow of water.

"Ana? Is that you?"

Startled, Mignon turned toward the sound of the voice; standing in the doorway was a woman who appeared to be in her fifties.

"Ah, no . . . it's not Ana; it's her daughter Mignon. Oh, my God! You look just like your mother . . . but you couldn't be Mignon; you're much too old. Let's see, Mignon would be, um . . . just thirteen now."

"That's right. I'm thirteen. I'm tall for my age."

"And developed too."

"I'm sorry, are you Uncle Sammy's wife?"

Laughing aloud, the older woman shook her head.

"Definitely not. I'm Marjorie Rousseau . . . you may recall your mother speaking of Miss Fonteneau. Well, a lot has happened since your mother was here. I finally married."

"Oh, Miss F—uh, I mean Madame Rousseau—yes, my mom speaks of you all the time. I just thought that she said you no longer live in Paris."

"That's right. My husband and I live in Versailles, but I . . . I mean, we came back when Sammy called and asked us to open the house again."

"Oh, you know the people who own this wonderful home?"

"Yes, my husband worked for him; that's how he and I met. But enough about me. What do you think of Paris so far?"

"Well, I dunno, paparazzi at the airport, whisked away in a limousine and brought to this beautiful home . . . I love it, that's what I think!"

"Well, Mignon, why don't you follow me and I'll show you where the kitchen and the really good snacks are kept. You'd have to be pretty hungry by now. How about some bread and cheese?"

Mignon's face lit up at the mention of food and dropped just as quickly because of the suggestion of bread and cheese.

"Sorry . . . I guess I'll just have some bread. I'm not really a big fan of cheese."

"Oh, that's right, forgive me—it's been so long since I've lived in America that I've forgotten how the taste in food differs. Just follow me; I'll fix you a snack fit for a princess."

Mignon nodded and followed Marjorie Rousseau to the kitchen. To her surprise, bread and cheese were just the beginning of a platter the woman seemed to pull from thin air, filling the tray with exotic fruits, ripe berries, and a variety of cheeses, breads, and an assortment of rolls. Finishing the platter, Madame Rousseau smiled at Mignon.

"Follow me; I'll show you the back way to your suite of rooms." She motioned with her head for Mignon to follow. The older woman led the young girl through rear doors and down a hallway, stopping at a lift that would take them to the second or third floors.

"Push two, dear."

Mignon complied. As the lift reached the second floor and the doors opened, Madame Rousseau turned right down a wide hallway, leading Mignon to her suite of rooms.

"Would you care to sit in the chair in front of the fireplace or would you prefer the terrace?"

"Is this my room?" the girl asked, incredulous. She had seen rooms like this only in the old classic movies she sometimes watched with her mother.

"Why, yes, it is your room. I hope you like it."

"I do! The terrace will be fine. Will you sit with me?"

"Of course. I'd love to catch up . . . I know you only through photographs and your mother's letters."

As Madame Rousseau went about the task of placing the platter on the serving table and setting the small table with linens and plates, Mignon sat on the deep cushions in the wicker chair and surveyed the finely appointed terrace. It was so relaxing to look at the ivy and creeping flowered vines growing along the trellis and trailing along the edges, overhanging like a curtain. Topiaries were placed in each corner, and planters with ficus trees and bowls of lilacs and Dutch tulips were placed on the two tables as centerpieces. She thought, *This would be the ideal spot for me to write my poetry and songs.*

43

After the bread-and-cheese platter, Mignon and Madame Rousseau got to know each other in an amiable conversation. Mignon sat enthralled by the stories about her mother's life when she had first moved to Paris. She could not wait for the opening of her show next month to see a glimpse of the mysterious other side of her mother that she never knew existed. When Madame Rousseau left the room with instructions for her to get some rest, she immediately began exploring the large rooms. Wandering around the main room, she was shocked to find all of the pictures on the mantel above the fireplace were of her mother. Apparently these pictures had been taken before Mignon was born; this was a carefree Ana. Obviously whoever took the photographs knew her mother well. Some poses were sultry or seductive; others were silly or contemplative. *Funny,* Mignon thought, *there are no pictures from any of her performances.* Studying each of the pictures, she realized these had not been recently put here but had occupied this space for a while. When she picked each beautifully framed picture up, there were dust marks indicating they had been there for some time.

Moving to the bookcase, Mignon saw more pictures of Ana, but—again to Mignon's amazement—these were all pictures of Ana with Mignon as a baby and then as a toddler. It occurred to Mignon that all of these pictures appeared to have been shot from a distance. Her father, Clark, was not in any of these photographs. Making a mental note, she decided to ask her mother about the photographs and the photographer. Growing weary from jet lag, she followed Madame Rousseau's instructions and lay down on the chaise longue in front of the fireplace to take a nap before supper.

Ana was completely unnerved by Sammy's renting Pierre's home for her stay in Paris. If she didn't believe him to be well-intentioned she would think it was a cruel joke. After Mignon left the room she spun around to confront Sammy and crumpled into an unexpected flood of tears.

Sammy was shocked; he had been prepared for any number of re- actions except Ana's tears. Never comfortable with outward displays of emotion, he quietly took the seat opposite her, wringing his hands, waiting for the storm to pass.

Once Ana was spent, she looked at him pleadingly. "Why . . ." she started and faltered. "Why . . . did you bring me back here?"

"Because it is where I thought you would be most comfortable."

"Comfortable! What do you mean most comfortable? He didn't want me, Sammy." She moaned miserably. "I still can't believe it af- fects me after all these years. I thought I was over him—and I was until you had to bring me here."

"I had no choice, Ana. Hold on just a minute." Picking up the re- ceiver, he dialed the kitchen, and a few minutes later there was a soft knock on the door, followed by Madame Rousseau carrying a tray with a decanter of cabernet sauvignon and three glasses. Shocked, Ana got up, her eyes glazed over with tears, and embraced her old chaperon and friend.

"What are you doing here? I thought you returned to Devereaux after I didn't return."

"No, I was just like Sammy—I couldn't leave, and then I met Jacques Rousseau."

"You mean . . . Jacques who worked for the St. Honores?"

"Yes. We met, fell in love, and you can guess the rest."

"Oh . . . I see. Now I understand how you got this place. Does Jacques still work for the family?"

"You mean Pierre, dear . . . yes, he does."

"Oh." Ana's emotions felt as if they were whirling out of control. Feelings that had long been suppressed were now sitting on the surface. Unable to sit still, Ana walked through the sitting room, reminiscing as she picked up the photographs that had been taken years before. "I can't believe he's kept these pictures for so many years."

"There's a lot you may not be able to believe, Ana. But one thing you should know is that Pierre did love you very much. That much I know . . . you see, Sammy and I are the ones who literally held him together after you left without a word to anyone."

"Then why didn't he come after me?"

"Because I persuaded him not to. I called and spoke to Carrie the day after you arrived in Houston. She assured me that you were still scheduled to return to Paris after the wedding. I told Pierre and pleaded with him not to travel to Houston. I thought it would be better if you had time to cool off. . . ."

"Go on," Ana implored, although she already knew what happened next.

"We waited . . . he waited. The day your flight was scheduled to arrive Pierre left several hours before your arrival to be on time to meet your flight—but as you know, you were not on it. Unfortunately, we did not hear about the tragedy for almost six months. Pierre took the next flight to Houston when he heard. It took several days for him to find out where you were; then he was told by your neighbor that you had also gotten married and you lived with your husband. He went to the address in Fifth Ward and saw the two of you together standing in your yard. He also saw that you were very pregnant."

"Why didn't you call me . . . warn me . . . ? I could have explained it so that he wouldn't have found out that way."

"Ana, you forgot—after the shootings no one could contact you or Carrie. I tried to send you a telegram, but neither Sammy nor I knew about your marriage . . . until Pierre told us."

"He must hate me as I hated him."

"For a while, yes . . . I believe he did—that is, until Mignon's birth. He had suspicions after he saw you in the yard. He thought that you were far too pregnant for a newlywed. Apparently, after Mignon was born he hired an investigator in Houston. From him he found out Mignon's name and date of birth and blood type. He believes she is his child and therefore his heir. For the past thirteen years he has had photographs sent to him from the same agency he hired after his visit to the States. Ana, you should know that Pierre is certain of his paternity."

"Where is he? Is he here?"

"No . . . neither Sammy nor I would allow him to surprise you that way. I just wanted to let you know that things sometimes are not what they seem. He loved both you and Mignon. He is not here. He is the marquess now and lives in Marseilles at the château with his wife, Philippa, and their daughter, Marie."

Sammy watched Ana in silence, sensing her reaction; he understood that her response to this news was both disappointment and acceptance. Unable to hold his tongue any longer, he interrupted Ana's reflections on misunderstandings made in the past that now had an impact on the present.

Feeling as if the blood had drained from her body, Ana was ice-cold as she continued to listen. Sammy interrupted: "As Marjorie told you, Pierre became suspicious after he saw you and Clark in the yard. He made some inquiries . . . did his math and surmised that the baby had to be his. The investigator was able to confirm that Mignon was not premature, and he was certain when he found out she had been named after his mother. Once he got a copy of her birth certificate it confirmed she had the same blood type as his, and they share the St. Honore birthmark on the nape of her neck. The evidence was too overwhelming to be simple coincidence . . . so he began to plan for this day."

"What do you mean, he planned for this day? Surely he must realize his mistake or he would have contacted me before now. Why would he wait?" Ana realized she was trying desperately to convince herself that they had made the wrong assumption. But she knew by the look on their faces that clearly neither Sammy nor Marjorie agreed with her.

This time Marjorie provided the explanation. "You couldn't be more wrong. He has claimed Mignon as his firstborn child and therefore his legal heir. The entire St. Honore family is aware of Mignon's birth—even Philippa. Their daughter, Marie is much younger than Mignon. Despite what you may believe, Pierre did not rush into Philippa's arms. They married almost three years after you left Paris. She was in love with him and remained by his side, although she knew he grieved for you."

Angered by what she perceived to be unfounded blame, Ana exploded in fury. "I did not leave by choice! I was the one who found out through the society pages that the man I loved—and whose child I carried—was planning to wed another woman. The choices I made were the only choices I had. It may not have been the right thing to do, but I have lived with the choices I made every day. I thought I was giving Mignon a chance. And really, I did . . . it is better to be the legitimate child of divorce than the bastard of some French aristocrat!"

The normally reticent Sammy knelt in front of Ana, imploring her to listen and try to understand. "I know how betrayed you felt . . . we all felt that way. At first I was so upset at Pierre I wanted to beat him to a bloody pulp. I could not believe that he had been so callous or careless as to parade you around town and at the same time plan to get married to Philippa, arranged or not. But we found out that Pierre had no idea that the article was being written. He had intended to ask you to marry him and had even broken off his engagement to Philippa. We know this because it took both of us to console him, especially after he found you. Pierre truly loved you . . . that's why we're here now, in this place. He finally made peace with himself and forgave you. He realized you had been pushed. He felt responsible for putting you in the position where you would be forced to make the choice to marry someone else."

"My dear, Jacques and I have been the caretakers of this home for years, because Pierre always believed you'd return to Paris and he refused to sell,or lease this house. No one is allowed here but Pierre, and after he saw the first picture of his daughter, he assigned ownership of this house legally to Mignon. But don't worry—he will not tell her. He is not trying to destroy your relationship with her; he says that although he does not agree with your decision regarding him, he understands the lies that have been woven about her paternity. He respects your decision and is not trying to make your life more difficult. He just wants to meet her and get to know her."

Again Sammy took up the thread. "Ana, I honestly believe his greatest desire is to introduce Mignon to her paternal grandmother and namesake. His father passed away last year, and Mignon-Marie was devastated."

Stunned by the unexpected revelations and the news of the death of Pierre's father, Ana resigned herself to allow Pierre to meet Mignon. However, she would control the contact he had with their daughter. Although many unfortunate mistakes had been made affecting their lives, she would not allow their misfortune to adversely affect Mignon. "Sammy . . . I'd like you to arrange a meeting between Pierre and me . . . so we can iron out this arrangement. But give me a couple of days to settle in first. I need to get Mignon enrolled in school."

"No problem. I'll call Pierre tonight and give him the . . . er . . . good news." Feeling unusually awkward at being put in the middle, Sammy made a quick excuse about the need to check on the production and left for home. He had had all he could take for one day, and now he had to contact Pierre.

44

After Sammy left, Ana also excused herself. She planned on taking a long, hot, soothing bath and getting some much-needed rest. She had not realized how tired she was until now. As she began unpacking her toiletries, she began to think of how she would introduce Pierre to their daughter—and of the explanation she would have to give to Mignon. For the first time since she had found out she was pregnant, Ana felt an unreasonable fear and sense of loss. Putting aside her unpacking, she went in search of her daughter; she had come too far to lose her now.

As she walked into Mignon's room, the sight of her daughter sleeping peacefully momentarily comforted her. Sitting at her bedside, she gently smoothed her daughter's hair and silently swore that she would not allow anyone to bring her or Mignon any more pain—not even her birth father, Pierre.

Walking slowly back to her suite of rooms, Ana made the decision to act and not to wait on Sammy to contact Pierre. Sitting at the desk, she picked up the phone and called the Château de St. Honore and asked to speak to the father of her child. To her surprise, he answered the phone on the first ring as though he was expecting a call.

"Pierre?"

"Yes?"

"This is Ana . . . "

"I am so glad to hear from you . . . it has been too long!"

Stunned by this unexpected greeting, Ana was momentarily confused as to how to proceed. "I spoke with Sammy and Marjorie this evening. I am in Paris."

"Of course you are, Ana. How can I help you?"

Again Ana was thrown by Pierre's aloofness. He was speaking to her as if she were merely a passing acquaintance. In fact, she thought, that was all she was. He had a wife and a child. Surely he thought of her only because of Mignon. Taking a deep, calming breath, she proceeded, not wanting to give away the strain on her that this conversation was causing.

"I would like to meet you and, ah . . . discuss my daughter Mignon."

"And I would also like to see you again, Ana . . . it has been far too long since we last spoke, and there is much to catch up on. I know a good café, Le Vivarois, near the Place de la Concorde where we can meet. Let's say tomorrow, noon?"

"Noon is fine. I will get the directions from Marjorie."

"Oh, Ana, do you really need directions?" he inquired, his voice deep from an emotion she didn't at first recognize. "It is the same restaurant where you tried and convicted me almost sixteen years ago." Pierre could not disguise the anger he harbored, although he tried unsuccessfully to hold it carefully in check.

"Uh . . . Pierre, I'm sorry. Maybe I should not have called you. It's just that . . . after Sammy left, I thought it was the right thing to do. If you're not comfortable with this meeting, or if it is a bad time, please let me know and we can try to arrange this the next time I'm in Paris."

"No! No! Ana, don't hang up angry. I'm sorry. I'm glad you called; it has just been a very hard day. I hope you forgive me, and I will see you tomorrow at noon. Okay?"

"Okay . . . noon it is." Ana slowly returned the telephone to the receiver, not quite certain of the wave of emotions that had surfaced. She was doubtful of how much she could take; her nerves were already taut with anxiety, and the call to Pierre had not made them any better.

Pierre was furious with himself. It had not been his intention to allow himself to show any emotion toward Ana. His goal was nothing other than to make the necessary arrangements in order to get to know his firstborn daughter, Mignon. Now he was seething. It had been his idea to finance the stage play that would give Ana the opportunity to return to Paris and the stage in the coveted Josephine Baker remake, now starring *la Foncé Fille*. It had been a result of his carefully concocted scheme to send Philippa and Marie away on holiday to Madrid, Spain, so he could arrange this reunion of sorts. And now that it was in the works, he was bitter and angry at all the years that he had lost with his daughter, whom he had never had a chance to know as an infant. He grieved each year that he was not involved in her life, and the lost opportunity for his father to have known his grandchild. By paying private investigators to follow and take photographs throughout the years, he had kept a photo diary of her. He often thought of how he had missed her first days at school and nurturing her as the princess that she was. For that he despised Ana for thoughtlessly making a decision that affected so many. But in the same breath and at the same time, he loved her with an intensity that had not waned over time.

45

Le Vivarois at noon was filled with a bustling, high-energy midday crowd. It was just the place to have a meeting that would not be misconstrued as any intention of creating a sense of intimacy. As Ana stepped from the cab her eyes were drawn to the sidewalk table where she had been seated with Sammy and Marj when she had read about Pierre's engagement fourteen years before. She unsuccessfully tried to swallow past the lump that had formed in her throat, while in her mind she replayed the emotions she had felt that day, coupled with the stinging accusation made by Pierre on the telephone last night. Had she indeed acted as judge and jury? Or had she in fact responded as a young woman devastated by the man whom she considered her Prince Charming?

Either way, it had all come to pass, and here she was many years later to make an attempt to iron out some of the wrinkles in her life that wouldn't shake free. Walking to the entrance of the café, she reminded herself she was not the same ingenue who had fallen for Pierre so many years ago. She was a woman who had made her own decisions when faced with a problem; whether the decision had been right or wrong, she had decided. As she already expected, Pierre had been true to his old schedule; he had arrived early, apparently as anxious as she was. She noticed he was sitting at the bar, and his drink was not his usual wine, but a martini.

Instead of walking right up to him, she gave herself a few moments to study him. Just as she expected, fourteen years had only added to his aristocratic image. Age and a mustache made him appear even more elegant, if that were possible. Pierre was the epitome of Parisian style and grace. Regaining a bit of her waning self-confidence, she took a deep breath to compose herself, put on her best self-assured smile, and strode purposefully to Pierre, touching him lightly on the shoulder.

Seemingly sensing her presence, he turned toward her at the same time she placed her hand upon his shoulder. Stunned by the still-beautiful woman who stood before him, Pierre could not resist the smile that played at the corners of his mouth. There was no denying the fact that he was happy to see her again. Rising to his feet, he held out his arms, and Ana wordlessly entered the warmth of his embrace. Years seemed to be erased and mistakes forgiven in the moments that they held each other. Taking her face in his hands, he stepped back, holding her at arm's length to study the changes that he had missed during the years they had been apart.

It was clear Ana was no longer the young girl whom he had so shamelessly courted. This was a woman of great confidence and self-containment. Instead of her perfectly coifed hairstyle, she now wore her hair au naturel, which perfectly complemented her avant-garde attire. She wore a bright orange–and-hot-pink circular-patterned hip-hugger jumpsuit with matching boots and a handbag that was made of the same fabric as the suit. She was perfectly matched, down to her earrings and eye shadow, and as usual, she was absolutely stunning.

"I thought I would surprise you . . . but you turned too soon."

"I couldn't help it; you had all the men at the bar commenting on the beautiful lady who had entered the restaurant. I didn't want to turn right away, so I waited a minute. Of course I knew that you had arrived . . . who else would make such an entrance?"

"Okay, monsieur . . . flattery will get you almost everywhere," she replied, flirting outrageously.

"Well, if that is true, madame, then I have only just begun," he countered, a willing accomplice. "Are you hungry?" he continued, allowing the double entendre to hang.

"I'm starving . . . it's been fourteen years since I've enjoyed a meal in Paris." Coyly peering from under her lashes, she asked, "Do you know what I miss the most?"

"No, but I'm dying to find out." Again a smile teased the corners of his mouth as he played along with her.

"I miss the foie gras and cold lobster at Aux Crus de Bourgogne . . . it was sumptuous!" She laughed aloud in amusement at the play of expressions that crossed his face.

"Then, madame, why are we wasting precious time here, when we could be there? I'll signal my driver."

Turning, Ana allowed Pierre to guide her hand through the bend in his arm as he gallantly made a big show of escorting her to the car that seemed to miraculously appear at the curb. They rode to the First Arrondissement in companionable silence.

After they were seated in the old-fashioned bistro, complete with bright lights and red-checkered tablecloths, they settled in and Ana waited until Pierre ordered lunch before bringing up the reason for this meeting. She had to get them back on track, because it would be too easy to forget the past for a moment and enjoy the present. Although it was tempting, it was not in either of their best interests; of that she was certain.

"Pierre . . . I just want you to know that I had no intention of hurting you. In fact, the thought never crossed my mind. I was devastated when I read of your engagement. I planned to tell you that evening that I was pregnant—then I read about your impending marriage to Philippa. I remembered her from your parents' anniversary gala and assumed it had to be true. The last thing I wanted was for you to think I was trying to trap you, so I decided never to return to Paris. When I went back home, I still had not decided whether I would keep Mignon or have an abortion." At this Pierre flinched, his body stiffening notably.

But Ana continued, not willing to stop until he heard everything she had held in for so many years. "Anyway, I knew I couldn't go through with an abortion. I decided to go away and have her and face the consequences that lay ahead. After the tragedy at my mother's wedding to John, I was heartsick. Seeing my sister and grandmother killed in cold blood and wondering if the next bullet would strike me or my mother was more than I could bear. I was in such a depressed state that I didn't expect to carry Mignon the duration of the pregnancy. My ex-husband, Clark, and I had begun dating before I left for Europe. Although we had not kept in touch, friends set us up on a blind date after I returned in hopes of rekindling an old affair. He was there for me through the depression and healing. He asked me to marry him, and I knew that I shouldn't. Then I began to think that it would not be fair to the child to have him or her out of wedlock, and that at least it would provide a good start for us all. So I married him and gave my solemn word not to return to the stage. For a while it worked; then we both got tired of living a mutual lie . . . and the rest is bittersweet history." Ana sat silently, allowing Pierre to digest everything she had said. She hoped that he would at least try to understand her reasons, whether or not he thought they were the right ones.

Studying Ana silently, Pierre was overwhelmed by the emotions that flooded him. Reaching across the table, he looked into her eyes, and his filled with tears. "I have spent all these years being angry with you . . . because it was convenient. As long as I blamed it all on you, I didn't have to be accountable for my actions—or inaction. I had broken off my engagement to Philippa that same afternoon. I had no idea that *Le Société* would run an article on us; after all, we had been engaged almost five years. When I found out later from Sammy that you read the article and had fled the restaurant, I was out of my mind with panic. And when we finally heard that you had returned to Houston for the wedding, I allowed Sammy to convince me that you needed time to let your anger die down. Had I only known about the child then, nothing could have kept me from you. By the time I found you, you were married—and so I was prepared to give you up until I saw that you were pregnant. From the pictures given to me by the private investigator I knew that you looked too far into your pregnancy for it to have been by your husband, so I asked for an update after the child was born. When I received those documents and saw that you had named our daughter after my mother, then I was almost certain she was indeed my child. However, when I learned she had the St. Honore birthmark at the nape of her neck . . . well, then I was convinced. After Mignon turned eight, I married Philippa—not for love, but out of a sense of duty and obligation. We have a four-year-old daughter, Marie, whom I love with all my heart." Now it was Pierre's turn to wait in silence and allow his words to digest. Both were full of regrets, some spoken, but most not expressed in words.

"How do you propose to establish a relationship with Mignon? After all, she is a teenager, and she already feels abandoned by her father after he distanced himself from her since our divorce. I was hoping this trip to Paris would preoccupy her and give her a chance to heal."

"I understand, and I am not trying to complicate your life, Ana. As you should be able to tell by now, I would never do anything to hurt you. I want to meet her first and get to know her. I am open to suggestions. I was hoping to be introduced as an old songwriter friend of yours, and perhaps act as your tour guide in Paris. What do you think?"

"Mmmm, I think that is an excellent idea. When do you want to meet her?"

"The sooner, the better . . . how about dinner and the opera tonight?"

"Uh, okay . . . but remember, Pierre, she's an American teenager. I'm not sure you're going to score too many brownie points with opera tickets."

"Okay . . . I get the picture. I'll think of something that a teenager would enjoy. I'll pick the two of you up at seven—how does that sound?"

"Sounds like a date. I guess we should finish here so I can get back and get us ready for tonight."

Signaling the waiter for the check, Pierre settled the bill while Ana waited on the sidewalk for him to join her. As she waited, she could not control the violent attack of butterflies in her stomach at the thought of introducing Pierre to his firstborn child . . . Mignon.

PART THREE

Arrival . . .

46

As Mignon read through this part of the journal, she felt the blood drain from her, and a cold chill seemed to permeate her entire body. Until now she had never known the true identity of her father. Dumbfounded, she didn't think she could read any further. Now the answers to all of the questions that had been unasked and unanswered when she was a teen were right before her in this journal. She had spent the better part of her adolescence and youth yearning for a relationship with Clark, the man she thought was her birth father. Now she found that the man she met in Paris and had her first real crush on was, in fact, her father.

Closing the book, she decided not to read any more; she remembered it all vividly. Again she could feel her father's knowing eyes studying her . . . silently trying to assess the depth of her pain, like a surgeon who watched his patient during observation before slicing him open in order to heal him. She turned to look at the man she now thought of as her father.

Richard continued to wait for the question he knew was coming.

"Have you always known?"

"Yes."

"Then why didn't Mom tell me?" Even as she asked the question, she already knew his answer, so instead of waiting she turned back to the journal and the story that her mother had never told her. At the same time she wondered how much of her story she would be willing to tell her children. How her father had always valued light skin and considered it paramount in all his relationships. How for years he had passed for white, eventually accepting Mignon back into his life when she entered college and he felt it safe to ask her to call him Clark. He never introduced her as his daughter, and when she brought around guys she dated he responded favorably only when they were fair-skinned. His next message to her was, It is just as easy to love a rich man as it is a poor one—easier. On more than one occasion he had advised her that it was the eighties: although she would never be able to pass, with her looks she could always catch a nice white boy. Although Mignon was never able to live up to the latter, she made him extremely happy when she incorporated his goals for her and made them into her reality. Then, as in the past, he melted into the background of her life and she was left to live out the consequences of a poor decision based on poor advice.

The only constant had been her stepfather, Richard, whom she had failed to listen to, but who always came running when things went awry.

47

Ana arrived at the town house to get ready for Mignon to meet her father. It was the best and worst time of Ana's life since she had given birth to Mignon. She entered the house, searching excitedly for Mignon. Finally she found her sitting on the balcony listening to music and reading. Almost bursting with excitement, she exclaimed, "Guess what?"

"What, Mom?"

"I saw my old friend Pierre St. Honore today. Don't you remember me telling you about him when you were younger?"

"Yes . . . you used to sing his songs, right?"

"Right! Well, he's coming by at seven o'clock to take us out on the town. He's even offered to be our tour guide while we're here. Isn't that great?"

"Yeah . . . I guess so." Mignon sensed that something about Ana's excitement was forced. Watching closely, she couldn't understand why her mother seemed so nervous.

Again Ana surprised her that evening with a new outfit, a suede Indian-style warrior skirt with a matching maxi vest with floor-length fringes and moccasin boots. She was so excited by her new outfit that she forgot all about her mother's anxiousness. Rushing to take a shower and get dressed, Mignon was looking forward to the evening. To her surprise, Ana also wore suede, but instead of a skirt she wore suede hip huggers with fringe running down the side and a matching suede jacket with fringe along the sleeves and across the back. She wore suede cowboy boots and a floppy suede hat to complete the outfit. Unlike Ana, Mignon had allowed her hair to grow out and wore it parted down the middle with two long braids. She wore a suede headband with turquoise beads tied across her forehead, and around her head her hair was tied in the back in the traditional Indian style. Together, mother and daughter made a striking combination.

As promised, Pierre arrived promptly at seven o'clock. When he walked into his home and saw Ana and Mignon standing together, he was momentarily speechless. He felt transported back in time. Mignon with very little exception was the spitting image of Ana. Any similarity to him was not immediately recognizable; she was all Ana, and that wasn't at all bad, he thought.

"You must be Monsieur Pierre." Mignon stepped forward, noticing that he seemed to be at a loss for words.

"*Oui,* mademoiselle, I am Pierre—just Pierre, no need to be formal with me."

"Is that okay, Mom?"

"That's fine . . . this time. Only because Pierre is like Sammy and Marj, my closest . . . uh . . . friend."

"Oh, okay. Are you going to show us Paris?" Mignon asked excitedly. After seeing Pierre she understood her mother's nervousness. This was the most handsome man she had ever seen in her life. She couldn't wait to write home to her two best friends and tell them about Pierre and the fun she was already having in Paris.

"Yes . . . your wishes are my command, princess. I will show you both a Paris you never dreamed of."

True to his word, Pierre took them to the finest that Paris had to offer. Each day began with Pierre coming over with fresh croissants before Mignon left for school. The two of them would sit together in the kitchen or the main terrace and plan where the trio would spend the evening. During the day Pierre and Ana spent time becoming reacquainted. On the weekends Pierre would take them on shopping excursions in Monte Carlo or to the various vineyards in Burgundy. For an entire month their lives consisted only of each other; at no time did Pierre or Ana bring up the possibility of a future together. It seemed to be a foregone conclusion that one way or the other they would be. Had fate not interrupted, their bliss would have been endless.

As Pierre was leaving to pick Ana and Mignon up for an evening at Opéra de la Bastille, he received an emergency telegram from Spain. His wife and daughter had been critically injured in a car accident in Madrid. After he hung up the phone with the airlines, the next call he made was to inform Ana and Mignon that he would not be able to make it, and that they should go without him; there had been an emergency and he had to leave town.

As she returned the receiver to the cradle, Ana had a sinking feeling in her stomach. Somehow she knew it was all over; she could not reconcile her feelings for some reason. It had been her intention to tell Pierre she wanted them to explain together that he was Mignon's father. They had already planned to take her to meet her paternal grandmother, Mignon-Marie, over the weekend. Glancing up at Mignon, she saw the disappointment in her eyes and felt her daughter studying her, quietly trying to gauge the seriousness of the call.

"Well, what do you want to do, kiddo? Pierre has some sort of emergency and can't make it. He says he'll try to contact us in a few days. Should we try the opera?" Trying to maintain an air of unconcerned cheerfulness, she knew Mignon nonetheless read straight through her false joviality.

"No, Mom . . . let's just stay in. I'm tired of hanging out."

"Okay . . . what do you want to do?"

"Let's snuggle up, Mom. Is it okay if I sleep with you?" Mignon asked awkwardly, embarrassed by her own request.

"I would love to snuggle up, and honey, you can always climb in your mama's bed . . . you don't need to ask. All right?"

"All right."

So that evening they snuggled up in the oversize bed in Ana's room. Both mother and daughter silently mourned the loss of Pierre's company. Two weeks passed, and neither Ana nor Mignon had heard from Pierre. Mignon had obviously sunk into a depression that surprised Ana, until she realized that Mignon was mourning the loss of her relationship with Clark and now Pierre.

Making a decision, Mignon decided to return home to Los Angeles. That evening she called Sammy to tell him she wanted to postpone her performance in order to return to the States until

Mignon had adjusted to her divorce and the distance from Clark. To her surprise, Sammy breathed a sigh of relief and told her that the production had been postponed indefinitely. When she asked why he had failed to mention it sooner, he confided that it was because Pierre had been the financier from the beginning. Last week he had informed Sammy that when he returned to Paris he would resume the production. Until then he would pay out the contracts in full.

Ana was too stunned for words. Her grief was as strong as the death of a loved one. *How could he play with our emotions this way?* she wondered, angry at him for involving them in his sick scheme. Did he hate her so much that he would try to destroy both Ana and Mignon in one fell swoop? This was too much. She would take Mignon, leave Paris, and never mention Paris or Pierre St. Honore again.

Instead of flying back to the States, Ana decided to make the most of this trip to Europe and took Mignon to Rome, Venice, Frankfurt, and Barcelona. Their final trip was to London, where they enjoyed shopping at Harrods and watching the changing of the guard at Buckingham Palace. For the first time since leaving Paris, Mignon began to relax and enjoy being a tourist. Trying to drag this time out as long as possible for her daughter, Ana booked a cruise to return to the States.

48

The first night aboard the ship, Ana and Mignon were invited to sit at the captain's table. To their surprise, the captain had lived in Paris in the late fifties and remembered Ana as *la Foncé Fille*. After all those years, he had never forgotten how entranced he'd been by the beautiful woman who performed. He also owned copies of the only two albums that Ana had ever released. From that night on they were treated like royalty, and seats were reserved at the captain's table for them for the entire duration of the cruise.

As the captain finished welcoming Ana, he looked up, smiling broadly at a huge black man who was hastily approaching the table. Turning back to Ana and Mignon, he informed them that this was Richard Warner, their seatmate. As the captain turned to greet Richard warmly, it was obvious that they were old friends. This giant of a man enthralled the entire table; his size was matched only by the warmth of his demeanor. Taking his seat as if among old friends and not a table of complete strangers, he engaged everyone in conversation. Soon the conversation at the table was lively and animated. Richard had a way of making everyone feel special and their opinion important. Throughout the conversation, he would make stimulating comments and then sit back and watch the other guests propel the topic along. Ana had never seen anyone like this; her curiosity was completely aroused. Withdrawing from the conversation, she studied him carefully; clearly he knew the effect he had on people. Typically black men who fit his profile scared white people to death, but not this man. He stood at least six feet, five inches tall, with skin like jet and hair and eyes to match. The continuity of his features was classic Negroid: a strong, broad nose and full lips. But his eyes intrigued her the most; large and expressive, they seemed to have been drawn by an artist's brush. His eyelashes could have been almost feminine, had they been given to a lesser man. Richard's eyelashes were as thick as soot, surrounding eyes that stared directly at their object of interest, without apology. His self-confidence exuded from his every pore. It was not pretentious; it was matter-of-fact. The incongruity in his persona was his constant referral to God. *Where is this coming from?* She wondered if he was a minister, but that scenario certainly did not fit. Noticing that he was openly drinking vodka and orange juice quickly put that theory to rest.

As dinner came to an end, Ana regretted having no reason to linger and be in this man's presence. Excusing herself, she motioned to Mignon, who was still enthralled in the conversation at the table, that it was time to retire to their cabin for the remainder of the evening. She had no intention of sitting there like a groupie after a rock star. Ana would never have admitted it to a soul, but she was disconcerted at the lack of direct attention Richard had paid to her. She was used to men—especially black men—being captivated by her. His nonchalance toward her was unsettling; throughout the evening he had treated her with no more singular interest than any of the other guests seated at the table. Rising to leave, she turned to say her goodnights to the guests seated at the table. Taking Mignon's hand she turned to thank the captain; as she did Richard spoke to her in flawless French. Stopping her conversation in midsentence, she turned and looked at him in fascinated surprise.

"Pardon me," she replied hesitantly. She had already dismissed Richard as probably being interested only in white women, in order to assuage her bruised ego.

Now as she stood to leave he asked her if she would deny him the chance to hear her sing "Black Gal in Paris."

Caught off guard, she stared at him intently, prepared to deny his request, when Captain Parks chimed in along with the other guests at the table that she must perform, at least that song. Releasing her daughter's hand, she allowed the captain to lead her to the stage, where the bandleader, familiar with the song, played piano as she sang.

Mignon watched her mother perform a song she had listened to all of her life, but this was the first time she had seen her perform like this. When Mignon was a child, Ana had always become melancholy when she sang, but tonight it was as if the request made in French had infused new life into her. For the first time since Richard had arrived at the table he sat completely still, his eyes never once leaving Ana's.

Ana could not believe she was standing onstage singing this song to a man whom, moments before, she had decided to dislike. Now as she sang, she could feel the ghosts of the past—of Clark and Pierre—peeling away from her, as if she had shed dead skin. Her eyes were locked onto Richard's and she could feel her heart beating wildly in her chest, and for the first time in almost fifteen years she ended "Black Gal in Paris" with a verse of "That's All I Want from You." As she sang the last note the audience burst into applause, their ovation taking minutes to die down. Ana bowed low and thanked them for their kindness. When she turned back to her table, Richard had gone. For some reason she felt a keen, unexplained sense of disappointment. Turning to find Mignon, she signaled for her to meet her by the doors.

Again walking hand in hand with her mother, Mignon was in awe. As they walked through the doors she looked at Ana. "Mom, I never knew you could sing like that. You were incredible."

"Yes, she is, isn't she?" Turning in unison, the women were surprised to be standing beside Richard.

"I used to see your mother in Paris and Germany—I'm sure before you were born, Mignon—and it is an experience I will never forget."

"You knew my mom when she was in Paris?"

"Unfortunately, no. But my friends and I were regulars at all of her shows. I guess you could say we were her biggest groupies!" Richard continued in mock regret.

"Oh, so it was your group doing all the rowdy catcalls, huh?" Ana joined in playfully.

"Guilty as charged, kind lady, and thank you again for the beautiful reminder of days long past. Good night, young ladies, and God bless you."

Never having been exposed to anyone like this, both Ana and Mignon were taken aback. Again Ana's face showed some confusion as she and Mignon exchanged curious glances.

"Good night," they both said in unison, walking in silence back to their cabin.

The next evening, when Richard Warner again joined the guests at the captain's table for dinner, changed the whole cruise for Ana. His presence filled the room. As he approached the table, his face seemed to light up in a smile that welcomed everyone equally. As he was introduced around the table, he greeted each female guest by saying, "God bless you, pretty lady."

As the evening progressed the conversation eventually shifted back to him, and they learned that he in fact was a very successful banker and retired officer in the marines, taking a leisurely trip back to his home, also in Los Angeles, after a month-long business trip in Great Britain. As dinner progressed Richard engaged Ana in conversation. She learned that he was a widower; his wife had died of cancer five years before. She told him she was divorced and working at resurrecting her career. The flow of the conversation soon shifted to politics, and they were engrossed, each trying to persuade the other of their political savvy and knowledge on local versus world politics. To Ana's surprise she learned Richard was a Republican. She made the assumption that he was also an Uncle Tom, trying to pigeonhole him. He countered by posing the question, "What would you do without the spook sitting at the door?"

Stunned, she burst out in unexpected laughter. "I really can't say. . . . I guess if he hadn't been sitting by the door, we would have never known when Massa intended to move about."

"My point exactly, pretty lady."

When dinner came to an end, instead of making an excuse to retire to her cabin, Ana continued conversing with Richard. He was extremely well-read and, as she was to find out, down for the cause.

Waiting for an opening, Mignon leaned over to her mother, telling her she was tired and wanted to return to their cabin. To her surprise Ana told her to go on and she would see her shortly; she wanted to stay for a while.

After Mignon left the table, Richard invited Ana to join him at the cabaret to see jazz great Lionel Hampton. Accepting his invitation, they walked to the cabaret in companionable silence. Surreptitiously eyeing Richard, Ana felt as if there was something oddly familiar about him, as if they had known each other before this evening. If Ana could read minds, she would have been both shocked and pleased to learn that Richard was also thinking the same thing about her. When they arrived at the door to the cabaret, the maître d' greeted the couple with a welcoming smile.

"I'm so glad to see you found each other," he offered with a knowing expression.

"Uh, I think you've made a mistake . . . we just met a short while ago," Richard corrected him in good-natured manner, winking at Ana to suggest that a mistake had been made.

"No mistake, sir. I meant that anyone can see you should have found each other, and you did! But please, pardon my boldness . . . sometimes my biggest problem is learning not to speak my mind."

"God bless . . . there's no harm done. I couldn't agree more." Turning and looking directly into Ana's eyes, Richard continued, "I couldn't be more pleased than to have found her."

Ana could not believe that she was actually blushing. *Who is this man?* she thought. His confidence was a rarity among the men she'd known. As the maître d' led them to the table reserved stageside, Richard walked behind Ana, with his hand acting as a gentle guide on her waist. It was so natural, as if they just fit. For the remainder of the evening they were entertained by the legendary jazz great. Both were enthralled by the performance, applauding enthusiastically at the end of his set.

After the show ended, they remained in their seats and delighted in each other's company. Conversation was effortless and seemed to flow as easily as water running downhill. They exchanged stories about their backgrounds and upbringing. The uniqueness of this exchange was not in the retelling of life-shaping experiences or the honest baring of their souls. It was joyous, like the ritual of harvest. They had both sown good and bad seeds in their lives, but for the first time recounting the events did not feel tragic. In contrast, it felt empowering, as though two energy sources had met and melded, so they allowed their stories and that night to begin the formation of a portrait of the landscape of a life spent together.

After that night Richard and Ana were inseparable. Each day as the

ship made progress across the Atlantic, so their relationship progressed. Richard had been the perfect gentleman, always considering
both Ana and Mignon in planning activities, whether on board, or
when the ship docked at the ports along the way.

As a tour guide he was knowledgeable and patient. But despite his
best efforts, Mignon constantly compared him to Pierre and the
whirlwind tour that he had shown her while in Paris. The more Ana
tried to discuss Richard and his attributes, hoping to win Mignon
over, the more she refused to approve of him, although she had to
admit he was extremely likable. Subconsciously, she was protecting
herself and maintaining a position to protect her mother. Life had already taught her that it was just a matter of time before the other shoe
dropped.

On the final day of the cruise, when the ship reached port, Richard
surprised both Ana and Mignon by asking Mignon's permission to
contact Ana and take her out once they returned home to Los
Angeles. Stumped by this unexpected request, Mignon nodded her
approval and excused herself. She was clearly embarrassed and at a
complete loss for words. She went to say her farewell to friends she
had met on board and to promise to stay in touch. Returning to her
mother's side, Mignon recoiled slightly when he lightly kissed her on
the top of her head. Holding both of her hands in his, he placed a
small velvet box in her palm.

"God bless you, Mignon, and thank you for allowing me to spend
the cruise with you and your mother."

Mignon opened the small box, revealing a small gold charm that
was a likeness of the ship they had sailed on, with the ship's name and
the date inscribed on it. Beaming, Mignon held out her arm and
asked Ana to put the charm on the charm bracelet that had been a
gift from Pierre when they had met.

"Thank you, Mr. Warner . . . I really like it."

"You're very welcome. I admired your bracelet when we met and I
thought you might enjoy a reminder of your first cruise. Well, anyway,
have a safe flight home and I will speak to you soon."

"Okay . . . good-bye, Mr. Warner. Mom, I'm going to wait by the
plank." Mignon waved and began to walk toward the plank to look for
the car waiting to take them to LaGuardia Airport.

Turning back to Ana, Richard stared into her eyes meaningfully.
"You know this is the beginning of forever, right?"

"Yes . . . I do."

"Good, because 'I do' is the right answer. I have to stay over for a meeting in the morning, but I'll call you tonight."

This time Richard held her in a tight embrace; stepping back, he smiled and walked with her to get Mignon. Helping them find their car, he waved as they got in. Watching the car drive away, he knew he would not rest until he was with Ana again.

49

Mignon could not believe they had been back in Los Angeles a year. So much had changed in their lives. She had finished middle school and was getting ready for her first year at Hamilton High School. The biggest change, however, was the one she was making today: Ana and Richard were getting married in a small ceremony in the backyard of their View Park home. There would just be close friends and some family. Although Mignon could never see herself married, she was thankful that her mother was remarrying. *After all,* she thought, *she's the marrying kind.*

Mignon had even grown accustomed to Richard. In her own way she loved him; she was just afraid to trust that he would be there for her. She knew it would still take a while for her to accept his uniqueness in not being self-conscious of his love for God. Ana adored it, on the other hand. Whenever he would profess his love for God in some way, Mignon would cringe. He would proclaim, "God bless you," or greet friend or stranger by saying, "The Lord is my shepherd, I shall not want." That was the way he responded whenever anyone asked how he was doing.

All in all this was a start, Mignon thought as she walked down the rose-covered path as her mother's maid of honor; family and friends surrounded her. Her Meemaw, Carrie, and Papa John sat in the front row, nodding their heads toward her in encouragement. She would be spending this summer with her grandparents, as she had done in summers past. Glancing around, she noticed many familiar and unfamiliar faces. Fifty sounded a lot smaller than it really was, but each time she glanced around she was met with a smile. She didn't know why she was so nervous; after all, it was not her getting married. As she took the final few steps to the gazebo, she glanced up at Richard's face and was met with a proud smile and a sense of calm. She felt a sort of peace, as if she could relax and step off the tightrope. Catching her eyes with his, she knew he was bursting with pride. It was odd; she could not yet refer to him as her father, but he already referred to her as his daughter—the daughter that God had in store for him, as he told her when he had asked her permission for her mother's hand in marriage.

As the bridal march played, she watched her mother make her entrance on the arm of her brother, Eddie. As he escorted his sister, walking barefoot down the path that was covered in fresh rose petals, she appeared to float in her dress of light blue organza. She had discarded the Afro and wore her hair in a Peter Pan cut uniquely designed to bring out her features. In her ears she wore sapphires and diamonds, a gift from Richard to match her sapphire-and-diamond engagement ring and wedding band. This day was for Ana and Richard. Their eyes held each other; they could have been on an island alone. After the vows were exchanged, before the minister pronounced them man and wife, he announced that at the groom's request, Richard would pledge his own vows.

Surprising everyone, Richard held Ana's hand, and they both extended their hand to Mignon as Richard recited a vow.

"Dear heavenly Father, as I cleave to this woman and take her as my wife, I also take the responsibility and give thanks to you, oh Lord, for the daughter that you have given to us to raise. I vow to love, honor, and support my daughter as her earthly father, leaning on you, dear heavenly Father, for guidance. Amen."

Releasing Mignon's hand, Ana turned her back toward Richard to allow him to release the clasp from a small sapphire-and-diamond heart-shaped pendant she wore around her neck. Unclasping the delicate chain from around Ana's neck, he placed it around Mignon's neck and secured the clasp. Taking his wife's and daughter's hands, Richard turned back to the minister.

"By the authority vested in me by the state of California, I now pronounce you man, wife, and family."

The three held each other in a tearful embrace, and then, as if on cue, Ana and Richard released Mignon's hand and sealed their vows with a kiss.

As Mignon turned to walk to her grandparents, she overheard Carrie say, "My baby has finally found her peace. Thank you, Jesus."

Leaning toward her grandmother's ear, Mignon whispered, "Amen."

PART FOUR

Learning . . .

EPILOGUE

Closing the journal of Carrie's and Ana's lives, Mignon contemplated her future, wondering where it would take her, thinking back on where she had been.

She never could have imagined that at thirty-five years old she would be starting over again with three small children. A statistic? No, just ending a chapter in the journal of her life. Her time to tell her story for her children had come.

She glanced at the journal one more time, determined to start listing her objectives as her father suggested. Mignon sat for minutes staring at the worn leather cover, not knowing exactly how to begin or where to start. Richard always told her that in times of confusion the Holy Spirit would be her guide. She picked up her pen and began to respond to a still, small voice urging her along. *It's time to tell your story, the truth for your children's sake. Don't worry about order; it'll take care of itself.* Reaching forward, she picked up the journal. It was her turn now.

What am I supposed to say? she wondered. *Self-searching? Soul searching? I know! I'll explain about my broken marriage, the pain, frustration, humiliation, anger, depression, hope . . . freedom.*

Mignon had so much to say; she had lived so many stories. *Where to begin?* she thought. *Begin right here,* the Spirit told her. *Don't tell his story—that's not important. Don't tell a love story—it didn't last. Tell the story; it lives in you.*

So her fingers begin to write of their own accord, a sweet release. *Is it cathartic? No, it's sweeter. Is it hopeful? No,* hope *is too soft a word. Is it faith?* Everything was faith . . . trusting, loving, giving, growing, leaving, learning, ending . . . to begin again.

"Why, oh Lord, hast thou forsaken me?"
Has never been my cry!

I knelt many times on bended knee.
Though loved ones suffered and died near me
I knew You were standing next to me.

To suffer is not your way.

For me to live, Your son was killed
But rose again on the third day.

You said walk by faith, not by sight.
I did again and again, knowing You were right.
—Mignon